THE SHADOWMAKER

BOOK THREE THE SOULWEAVER SERIES

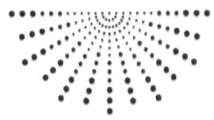

HEIDI CATHERINE

SEQUEL HOUSE

Copyright © 2020 by Heidi Catherine

Artwork by Stefanie Saw (seventhstarart.com)

All rights reserved.

No part of this book may be reproduced in any form or by any electronic or mechanical means, including information storage and retrieval systems, without written permission from the author, except for the use of brief quotations in a book review.

For Ashley.
My sun.

PART I
VALENTINA

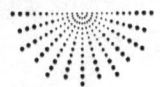

CHAPTER ONE

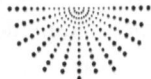

*H*alf of Valentina's genetics might be shared with her brother, but it seemed to her that the other half was far more dominant. She often wondered if his pod had been switched when he was an embryo.

Being born on the same day to the same biological parents technically made them twins, but in reality, they couldn't be more different.

She liked to surround herself with friends, whereas Buzz was a loner. She liked to dream, whereas Buzz liked to analyze. And Buzz was tall and muscular with eyes the color of night, whereas she was short and petite with eyes like the summer sky.

Their parents' feelings toward them were a similar contrast. Their father loved Valentina as if his soul was on fire, making his love for Buzz seem a warm flicker in comparison. And the sight of baby Buzz in his pod had made their mother smile, yet the sight of Valentina had sent her running so far across the planet that she'd never made her way back.

Sometimes Valentina wondered if their mother would have left them like that had she carried them in her womb. Buzz said she was being ridiculous. It had been hundreds of years since a human had lived inside another. He thought babies were far better off developing inside pods filled with amniotic fluid, lined up in neat rows until they were ready to hatch. Perhaps he was right. She didn't want to think about how babies in ancient times had made their entrance into the world. The idea made her cringe.

Her father had been the one to press her hatching button, which made him the first person she ever saw. She was sure that's why they had such a close bond. He was her best friend, as well as her father.

Buzz had been hatched by their mother. Their father had told them the story about how she'd held Buzz lovingly in her arms, before swapping with their father to hold Valentina. It was straight after this that she'd left, never to be seen again. It was hard not to take this story personally, even though their father hadn't intended it like that. What kind of a baby had that effect on their mother?

Once, Buzz had asked Valentina if she thought it possible that the story they'd been told wasn't true. Buzz was like that. He talked a lot of nonsense and she told him so. If their father said that was the way it had happened, then as far as she was concerned, that was it.

She secretly feared it was her fault their mother had run. It was because of her blue eyes. Over the past thousand years, almost all recessive genes had been bred into extinction. Just when scientists believed that blond hair or blue eyes had disappeared from life on Earth, an anomaly like Valentina would be born. She was a freak.

At least her hair was black and trailed past her shoulders and down her back. And her dark skin matched that of her father and brother, who'd begun to look so similar lately that she sometimes had to blink when one of them walked in the room to distinguish who it was.

As a child, Buzz had reminded her of a puppy, with hands and feet that seemed far too large for his needs. He was growing into them though, already possessing the body of a man. His athletic frame stood him almost as tall as their father and she'd noticed bristles of hair had begun to sprout on his upper lip and chin.

He was becoming annoyingly good looking. Her friends would find pathetic excuses to visit, in the hope of catching a glimpse of him. Valentina played a private game where she timed how long it would take them to casually enquire whether Buzz was home. It didn't usually take more than a minute.

Unlike Buzz, Valentina was tiny. She was short and slim, with a chest so flat it made a pancake look curved. But she was sort of pretty, she supposed. Well, she wasn't ugly. She couldn't really complain, except for the color of her eyes.

Whether or not their mother's departure was due to her blue eyes, as far as she was concerned, they didn't need her. They had the best father in the world and that was enough.

It was no surprise Buzz disagreed. He yearned for their mother. He loved their father, but not with the same intensity that she did. Often their small family felt more like a twosome, with a third person on the sidelines. It never felt like three.

Buzz may have inherited their father's good looks, but she knew she was the one who'd won his heart. He favored her over Buzz, trying his best not to let it show, but it always did. His face lit up whenever she entered the room, like a spark had been ignited from a place deep inside him. Was it possible for your father to be your soulmate? It certainly felt like that.

She wondered, now, if that inequality in her father's feelings for his children was what had caused Buzz to enter the space program as soon as he reached the eligible age of fourteen. Perhaps his decision had more to do with wanting to impress their father by following in his former footsteps, than having a legitimate interest in the field. Valentina also suspected it might have something to do with Buzz being a loner. The idea of living in a small colony on a faraway planet held an appeal for him that she found impossible to understand.

Whatever the reason, her father had been looking at Buzz with a whole new respect in the six months since he'd joined. Valentina wasn't sure how she felt about this.

"What are you working on?" he asked Buzz, throwing his brown raincoat over the back of a chair and taking a seat. She'd always hated that coat, telling her father he looked a hundred years old when he wore it.

Buzz launched into an account of how he and his classmates had been asked to come up with ways to divert a hypothetical asteroid set on a path that would see it crash into Earth with devastating consequences. Valentina listened with far less passion than Buzz spoke.

"I don't understand," their father said, crumpling his brow. "That's too easy. You could just intercept it before it reaches our atmosphere."

"Not this one, Dad. It's too big. It's bigger than anything we've ever seen before." Buzz plugged into his school portal to more clearly demonstrate his assignment.

Valentina watched the two men in her life, sitting side-by-side with their eyes glued to the virtual word that appeared before them. The room fell into darkness as stars and moons hovered in the air. Lines of data streaked across the virtual sky and Buzz pointed to different figures and explained what he'd learned. It all sounded very complicated.

She yawned, glad she'd resisted her father's pleas to join Buzz in the space program. The science of the stars just wasn't her thing. She far preferred the science of the soul.

This was a fascination that began when she'd first dreamed of her mother— a dream so vivid it had taken days to shake it off. In this dream, her mother had been a good person, her kindness radiating from the smile in her eyes. She couldn't have been kind though. A kind mother wouldn't leave her children.

Other times she dreamed she was lying on a dirt floor and staring up at a roof so yellow it seemed to have been made from sunshine. In these dreams her father would appear, only he didn't look like her father. He had hair the color of fire and would reach out his hand as if trying to rescue her.

But lately she'd been plagued with dreams of walking into the ocean, naked and alone, her dark skin glistening in the moonlight.

It wasn't her belief that dreams could predict the future. Rather, she thought it was possible that dreams could tell you about the past, long before you were born into this lifetime, when your soul lived as another person.

Reincarnation wasn't a theory widely accepted and it was her goal to find some evidence to prove her unusual beliefs. If she could put a scientific spin on it, then maybe people would start to listen. It was an ambitious goal, but her father had raised her to believe she could do anything, and she intended to do it all.

Buzz interrupted her thoughts by disconnecting from his school portal, causing the room to fill with light that bounced off the curve of the walls. Their house was made from a plastic polymer, manufactured from household waste. It was strong and cheap, and its invention had solved the world's waste crisis. Almost every home on the planet was made from this stuff now. Garbage had never been so sought after.

"It's just a project, Dad," Buzz said.

She looked across at their father, whose face was pale, his head shaking and his mouth flapping as if he wanted to say something. He was never normally lost for words.

Valentina's stomach tightened at what that might mean. "Dad, Buzz said it's just a project."

"It's not just a project," her father said, finding his words. "It's real. We've known about this asteroid for centuries, but nobody ever saw it as a threat. The chance of it hitting Earth was considered so minor that nobody gave it too much thought."

Buzz looked confused. "Why would they give us a real project and tell us it's hypothetical?"

"They told you it wasn't real, so you wouldn't panic. And the reason they gave it to you was because they have no idea how to solve it themselves. They're getting desperate."

Valentina sat up straight in her chair, suddenly interested in their conversation.

"But we're not even trained yet," said Buzz. "It doesn't make sense. Wouldn't they have the experts working on it, not a bunch of students?"

"The experts will be working on it." Their father stood and paced the room. "But clearly they're not getting anywhere. They must be hoping one of you will be able to come up with something they haven't thought of yet. There's an old expression about thinking outside the square. That's what they're trusting one of you will be able to do."

"But we haven't come up with anything," said Buzz. "What does that mean?"

"It means we're in serious trouble."

Valentina got up and went to her father, placing her hands on his arms to stop him pacing.

"I'm sure it's nothing to worry about," she said, wondering why he was getting so worked up. Everything would be okay. It always was.

He didn't reply. He just pulled her to his chest like he used to do when she was a child. She didn't complain. There was something serious about the way he held her. Something that made her wish she was still a little girl whose father could protect her from the world.

With all the warning systems that'd been implemented across the planet, Valentina wondered why one hadn't yet been invented for events that were going to change the course of your life. Because she'd had no idea when Buzz explained what he'd been learning at the space program, that her life would never be the same again.

Life had been happy before then. Why did he have to ruin it? Or more to the point, why did her father have to ruin it? Why did he have to try so hard to be a hero? All she wanted was a normal dad.

No, that wasn't quite right. She wanted the dad she had—she just wanted him to be more normal.

Besides, what he was saying wasn't true. Nobody believed it, least of all Valentina. He was making it up. If only he hadn't broadcast his view to the world, then things could go on as normal.

It was the year 2880 and it was about time he started acting like it. These days people didn't talk about giant asteroids flattening the Earth and extinguishing all life upon it. They'd just press a button and blow it out of the sky. The planet was indestructible.

"Hello? Earth to Valentina," said Buzz.

"What?"

"You're thinking about it again, aren't you?"

He ruffled her hair. She hated it when he did that.

"Of course, I am," she said. "How can I think about anything else?"

"Is it the asteroid that's worrying you, or is it Dad?"

His question seemed serious. Surely he must know the asteroid posed no threat.

"Doesn't his behavior bother you?" she asked.

"He means well." He shrugged as if their father's strange behavior was the most normal thing in the world.

"Go and talk to Dad if he's bothering you so much," said Buzz.

"He's working."

"He's never too busy to talk to you." She could detect no malice in this comment. He'd always seemed to accept their closeness. Buzz was a free spirit, not needing to tie himself to others in order to feel whole.

"What do you think he's doing in there?" she asked. "He's been making a lot of noise."

"I don't know. Dad always makes a lot of noise."

That was true. She'd grown up with the sound of hammers and welding, being drowned out only by the classical music he piped through the house. The music was good for them, he said. It would feed their souls with creativity. It certainly seemed to feed his soul. The beauty of various pieces of music regularly reduced him to tears. It wasn't uncommon to find him standing in the center of his workshop with his eyes closed and his arms outstretched as he drank in the music. Sometimes his fingers moved as if he was playing the piano himself. He would've made a wonderful musician himself if only his attention hadn't been captured by other pursuits.

Another loud bang sounded from the workshop and they heard their father cheer. She wished she could see what all the fuss was about, but they'd been banned from entering the workshop at around the same time their father had broadcast his warning to the world. It annoyed her. He'd never had secrets from her before. She liked hanging out with him and watching him tinker with new inventions. What was he doing in there that was so secret he couldn't even tell her?

It was like he'd become a different person. Or was this the person he'd always been, and she'd failed to see?

Her father had been an astronaut before his mandatory retirement at the age of forty, a year before Valentina and Buzz's birth. He'd have worked until the day he died if only the government hadn't insisted he step aside and give a younger worker the same opportunity he'd had. He fought against it but was told it was the law. No exceptions could be made.

He'd loved his work. There wasn't anything he didn't know about stars or comets or the far corners of outer space. He'd named Valentina after the first woman to fly in space back in ancient times—a Russian cosmonaut. Buzz had been named after the second man to walk on the moon. This seemed odd. They'd asked their dad why not the first and he'd said he liked Buzz Aldrin's style. Apparently he was a spiritual man who'd stood on the surface of the moon and asked the world to pause and give thanks. Their father believed it was important to demonstrate gratitude in life.

This was a logical explanation and Buzz had seemed pleased. Besides, he said he didn't think much of the name Neil.

In the height of his career, their father had travelled extensively across the solar system. He'd been a regular visitor to outposts on Mars, Venus and Mercury, as well as the moons of Jupiter and Saturn, but he insisted that Earth was where his heart lay. This was the planet where humans could live freely without relying on artificial sources of oxygen or water. Earlier in the century there'd been a disaster on Mercury where the cables powering the oxygen generator had blown, wiping out the backup system, and the entire colony had suffocated. The world had come to a standstill as people tried to come to terms with how such a disaster could occur.

Perhaps that was why people refused to believe her father's warning. Accepting the loss of a colony had been difficult but accepting the impending loss of their entire planet was the talk of a man who'd lost his mind.

Their father had offered his services to the space agency, but they'd refused, denying any such threat was real. He walked away feeling ridiculed, although this did little to dampen his determination. Instead it ignited a new fire within him, and he uploaded a video to the cosmonet warning the world to prepare themselves for the end.

His message had soon been projected to millions of people across the globe and they'd uploaded their own responses, imitating and belittling him.

There's no asteroid, they said. No such thing could happen. The world has never been safer.

Buzz was expelled from the space program for revealing what they claimed was confidential data. He appealed the decision, asking how hypothetical data could possibly be confidential. They didn't have an answer for that.

Valentina also left school. She wasn't expelled, she just didn't bother to log into her classroom in the morning and her father didn't care. He said there was no point in going to school when the world was about to end. She didn't have the heart to tell him that wasn't the reason for her withdrawal. She was being bullied to the extent she felt she had no choice but to cut herself off from everyone until all this blew over.

She'd even put up with her friends drooling over her brother if it meant she could see them again. But not even having a good-looking brother was enough compensation to excuse the fact your father was insane.

Her dreams of becoming an expert in the science of the soul ebbed away. Her father's actions had ruined her life. Some days she wished the asteroid threat was real and it would hurry up and end her misery.

She missed more than just her friends. She missed her schoolwork and her teachers. Most of all she missed her father. He was distracted. Obsessed. Distraught.

She'd had enough.

"You're right," she said to Buzz. "I'm going in there."

"There's no need," said her father.

She hadn't heard him enter the room.

He stood before them, smiling. Relief was woven through every line of his face. "I've done it."

"Done what?" she asked. "Given up this ridiculous quest to scare the world half to death?"

"Not half to death," he said. "This asteroid is certain death."

"You've worked out how to divert it, haven't you?" asked Buzz.

He shook his head. "It's impossible."

"Then why do you look so pleased?" Buzz's brows were knitted together in such a way it made Valentina's heart race, almost as if his fear was contagious.

"Because I'm going to get you out of here," their father said. "We'll leave this planet far behind."

"I don't want to go." Valentina's voice rose to a shriek. She had no desire to step foot outside their front door, let alone off the entire planet.

"Mars or Venus?" asked Buzz, excitement brimming behind his eyes.

"That won't work," their father said. "Once the Earth's been wiped out, our colonies won't be able to survive."

"Of course. The control centers here will be gone," said Buzz. "They won't be able to regulate their oxygen levels or their temperature zones."

"Exactly."

"You mean they're all going to die, too?" asked Valentina.

"I'm afraid so," said her father.

"Then where are *you* going?" asked Valentina, determined not to accompany him on this suicide mission into space. If she was going to die, then she preferred to do it right here on Earth.

"W*e* are going to another solar system. A safe one. It's our only chance."

"Dad, please. This is ridiculous. I can't believe you're saying this. What if you're wrong? What if there's no asteroid and I'm left here looking at the sky, wondering where my father and brother ended up?"

"You're coming with us, Valentina." His voice was stern. He meant it. She knew he'd never leave without her.

"I think we should do it," said Buzz.

"Good man."

Valentina held her head in her hands and fought back tears. Growing up in a house as the only female had taught her that tears were useless. She had a better chance of winning her father over with her words than her ploys for sympathy.

"Trust me," said her father, placing a hand on her back and patting her gently.

This small sign of affection was too much. Tears spilled down her cheeks.

"No, Dad. I don't trust you. I'm not going. I'm staying here."

"You have to go," said Buzz. "You know he won't go without you. Do you want us all to die?"

"Nothing's stopping you," she hissed. "If you're so keen, why don't you go on your own?"

She hated that he'd taken her father's side so readily. Their family unit still felt like two against one, only for the first time she was the one.

"Valentina," said Buzz, bending to level his eyes with her own. "We're a family. Families stick together."

"Yeah? Then where's our mother?"

"That's enough," her father snapped.

"I'm sorry," she said, knowing she'd pushed too far. He'd never liked her speaking about their mother. It seemed to make him feel he'd failed as their father, when the truth was anything but. She was just bitter and felt ganged up on. He was asking her to give up everything, most likely including her life, all because of a hunch.

"It's coming," said her father. "I've shown you the evidence. You're the one always talking about how important evidence is. Why won't you believe me?"

"I do believe you," she said, realizing it was true.

She'd always believed him. The moment he first mentioned the asteroid, she'd known in her gut it was real. It was just easier to pretend she didn't believe it. Far less scary to choose to believe what he was saying was a lie, than accept the death not only of her planet but all the people she'd ever known. *All* of them, from her best friends at school to every person she'd ever walked past on the street. Her neighbors, her teachers, her mother—if she was still alive. Every single one of them would soon be dead.

Nobody could believe that. That was why she hadn't been able to accept the asteroid as real. The reality of it was too frightening. She could understand why the rest of the population had chosen to laugh at her father instead of taking his words seriously.

"If you believe me, then why won't you come?" he asked.

"I want to die on the earth, not in the sky. It's where I belong." She kept her voice calm, doing her best to accept her imminent death.

"You don't have to die," he said. "I've found somewhere safe. It'll all be fine."

"Where?" asked Buzz.

"Far away from here. I'll have plenty of time to explain it to you on the way. Right now, we need to think about leaving."

"When are you going?" Valentina asked, still determined to stay behind.

"Now. We leave now."

"Why now?"

"Have you been listening to a word I've been saying over these past months? It's coming. It's on its way. We don't have any time to waste. Have you heard the news today? What have you been doing out here?"

Valentina huffed. They hadn't been allowed to know what he was up to in his workshop, yet he wanted to know what they'd been doing.

"What happened on the news?" asked Buzz, ignoring her.

Their father pressed a button and a hologram of a news report appeared before them. It was the first time Valentina had wished television would revert back to the way their ancestors had watched it—on screens. Seeing images of people running down streets, screaming in terror, almost as if they were in the same room, was frightening.

A news reporter stood at the front of the crowd explaining that the government had confirmed recent rumors that had been circulating about an asteroid destroying the planet.

"It's nice how they mention your name when they don't believe you," said Valentina. "But as soon as your information is confirmed, they claim it to be their own."

"I'm glad," her father said. "We don't need attention drawn to us right now."

Buzz hushed them, straining to hear the report.

The reporter continued on, explaining that they had days, possibly only hours before life on Earth would come to an end.

Valentina became distracted by the reporter. Why she was standing before the camera in her suit, doing her job, just like any other ordinary day? What was the point? How did her career matter now? Surely she had a family to spend her final moments with.

Perhaps her job was the only thing that mattered in her life. Maybe she thought what she was doing was making some kind of difference.

Valentina sighed. It didn't make sense, although she wasn't sure why she expected it to. None of this did. It was no wonder pandemonium was breaking out.

The reporter was shoved to the side by a man shouting, his voice high-pitched and frantic.

"Xander Forrester," he said.

Valentina stiffened at the mention of her father's name.

"Are you out there, Xander?" the man continued. "You need to help us. If anyone knows where Xander Forrester lives, it's your community service to make that information public. He's the only one who can help us. Xander, come forward and help us. Please."

Her father pressed a button and the hologram disappeared.

"We don't have much time," he said, sweat beading on his forehead. "Hurry. Come with me." He walked quickly from the room, indicating for them to follow.

Valentina turned to Buzz, only to find him on their father's heels. Why was he so keen to walk toward his death?

"Valentina!' her father called in a voice she knew better than to ignore.

She went to the workshop to see what his grand plan entailed. How would he transport them to another solar system? How did he think he could achieve what the world's greatest engineers had failed to? No spacecraft had been able to withstand travelling such a distance at speeds sufficient enough to deliver them to their destination before they died from old age.

Whatever she expected, it wasn't what she saw.

Her father had constructed what looked like a giant incubating pod—the kind they'd grown in as embryos. The surface was dark gray with a rough appearance like sandpaper and it sat on a stand made from a shiny metal. She wondered what the pod was made from. How had her father managed to construct it on his own in such a short space of time? Had he poured the shell from some kind of liquid?

Whether it flew or not, it was a work of art. She was impressed.

Classical music poured from tiny but powerful speakers on the workshop ceiling, filling the room with the sad sounds of a violin concerto. It was almost as if the violin was mourning them. She wished she could turn it off.

A hatch was open at the top of the pod with a ladder leaning up against it. Her father's head was poking out.

"Come on," he said, his eyes brimming with excitement and fear. "Buzz is already inside."

She hesitated. He could lock the hatch the moment she was inside, and she'd be trapped. He'd said he wanted to leave immediately.

"I will, Dad. Just give me a moment." She needed to buy some time to absorb what was happening.

Her father's head disappeared inside the pod.

She looked at the ladder. Would she be able to take these steps that would change the course of her life? She didn't want to leave. This was her home. She felt tied to this planet in a way she couldn't explain.

She'd once had a dream of having lived a life on another planet. It was a strange life where she'd breathed underwater using a set of gills on her chest. In the small snippets she'd seen, it'd been a happy life, until it was torn apart by grief when a bolt of lightning had killed the boy she'd loved, and she'd frozen to death deep under the ocean. The dream had disturbed her greatly. Living on another planet hadn't felt right. This was the planet she belonged on. Leaving it would be certain to spell disaster once more.

But how could she contemplate a life without her father, even if that life was to last only a few short days? Or minutes.

Neither decision was the right one. If she stayed, she'd be miserable. If she went, she'd be miserable. It seemed life had no happiness left for her. She was doomed no matter which way she turned.

She heard a loud knock on the front door that quickly became a desperate banging. The kind that demanded an answer.

She instinctively turned toward it.

"Valentina, don't answer that." Her father's head appeared at the hatch again. "Hurry up and get inside." There was desperation in his eyes. It was a look that gave his game away. Her hunch had been right. He was going to leave the moment she climbed aboard.

There was another loud noise at the front door. It sounded like an explosion. She went to the window only to find her father had blacked it out. What was going on out there?

"No, Valentina!' her father called. "Quickly, get in here. We don't have much time."

The pod hummed, softly at first, then increasing to a load roar, drowning out the violin concerto as the engine gathered momentum. It was getting ready to launch.

A sharp noise caught her attention and a rock whizzed past, skimming her nose. The window had been broken.

She brought her hand to her face.

"Valentina!' her father called over the noise of the engine. "Now!'

She looked across at the window just in time to see a large hand holding a stone smashing the glass from the window frame. At the same time, she heard footsteps in the hallway. Someone had managed to break down their front door.

She froze, terror gluing her feet to the floor. She wanted to run to her father. She wanted his protection, but she couldn't bring herself to go to him. Her fear of what would happen to her once inside the pod far outweighed her fear of staying.

A man crawled through the window. He was tall and muscular, not the sort of person she wished to pick a fight with. His hair was wild, his eyes filled with terror.

"He's in here," he called out the window, and more faces appeared as people began climbing into the workshop.

A crowd appeared at the door and soon the room held dozens of angry people banging at the sides of the pod. More people were pouring in the window.

They were panicking. Finally, they'd come to realize the truth in what her father had been telling them. After ridiculing him without mercy, they now sought his assistance.

"Take us with you," the wild-looking man called to her father as he put his hands on the ladder and began to climb.

"Stop!' her father said. "There's no room." He glanced

across at Valentina, who'd been pushed backward, away from the ladder toward the rear of the pod.

His eyes pleaded with her, but it was too late. She'd never be able to get past the crowd of people all hoping to get aboard the strange pod her father had built.

How ironic that the one person he wanted to climb aboard was the one person who'd refused.

She motioned at her father to leave without her. He looked back at her with an expression she'd never seen before. It was as if his soul was breaking apart. His spirit was dying a thousand deaths and she knew he'd never be the same.

For a few precious seconds, the room seemed to freeze. The violin concerto fought its way to her ears over the sound of the engine and her father's pained expression filled her heart.

"Do it now. Go!' she called, as the intruder got close to the top of the ladder.

Her father glanced inside the pod, said something to Buzz that she couldn't hear, then hauled himself out, closing the hatch behind him.

He slid down the side of the pod, landing awkwardly at Valentina's feet.

"What are you doing?" she said, crouching beside him, as the noise from the pod grew louder.

A hot blast of air shot from its base, sending the crowd of people backward as they scrambled to get away.

The man who'd climbed the ladder was beating on the hatch that refused to open. He was thrown to the ground as the pod shook violently. Tremors rocked the house and for a moment it felt as if the walls were alive. Her father sheltered her from the blast of heat and falling debris as the ceiling crumbled. Large shards of plastic broke away and fell to the ground like knives.

A burst of light brighter than a thousand suns lit the room as the pod disappeared into the sky.

Her brother had gone, and her father had sacrificed his life to stay with her.

She'd forced the person she loved most in the world to make a decision nobody should ever have to make. She'd made him choose between his children.

He'd chosen her.

She wished he'd chosen Buzz.

If the asteroid didn't kill her, then her guilt was certain to.

CHAPTER TWO

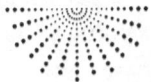

*I*t took Valentina several minutes to work out that her father was dead.

She crawled out from underneath his weight and rolled him onto his back. He had a large cut on his head from a heavy beam that had fallen from the ceiling. She pressed her hand to the wound. Blood seeped through her fingers as the life flowed out of him. The warm liquid felt like all she had left of her beloved father. All that was there to remind her that this body that lay before her had once lived.

"Dad," she sobbed.

It felt like the blast from the pod had burnt her retinas. Clouds of smoke billowed around the room. It was hard to see. She rubbed her eyes, trying to bring them into focus. Her ears were humming from the eerie silence that surrounded her. There was no violin concerto now. No cries of desperation. Everyone who'd been present when the pod had exploded into the sky was now either dead or in shock.

Slowly, the atmosphere around her came to life once more. People groaned as they stirred. Some emerged from the rubble and tried to climb over it, causing more of it to crash to the ground as it shifted under their weight.

People were inching toward her, tugging at her father's clothes, begging him to help them.

"Get away from him," she hissed. "He can't help you now."

He couldn't. Not them and not her. Not even Buzz.

Poor Buzz. He must be petrified, whizzing through the air not knowing if he was going to live or die.

Not that she felt that was any different to what she was experiencing now.

"Get away," she said again as a man put his hand on her father's arm. "He's dead. What more do you want from him?"

She removed her jacket and placed it over her father's face. He deserved more dignity than this. If only she could give it to him.

People retreated, almost as if death was contagious.

Why hadn't her father gone with Buzz? She hadn't asked him to stay with her. Hadn't wanted him to stay. She could've withstood any death the universe had planned for her if only she knew he was safe. How would she face what was to come now, knowing she'd killed her father and sent her brother to certain death? Buzz wouldn't be able to survive in the pod without their father by his side to guide him. He was as doomed as she was, and it was all her fault.

As the smoke cleared, she saw the workshop had fallen to the ground. The house had shattered into pieces of plastic that lay scattered like matchsticks. She could see several bodies pinned to the ground. None of them concerned her. In normal circumstances she would've gone to them to see if there was anything she could do to help. There seemed no point in doing that now. They were all going to die soon anyway.

Besides, she hadn't invited them in. If they hadn't broken into her house they'd be outside alive and well—for a few more minutes anyway. Or days. Who really knew how long they had.

Perhaps her father would be alive too if they hadn't interfered. She would've climbed on board if only they hadn't interrupted and made her panic.

She rubbed at her eyes again, knowing that wasn't true. The truth was she hadn't wanted to leave. She wanted to stay on planet Earth, and she wasn't sure why. All she knew was that it had something to do with her dream of the sadness she'd felt when she lived on the faraway planet. That dream had ended with her begging the Creator to send her back to Earth. She'd told him it was her home. Somehow it had seemed important to fight for the right to stay here, knowing how hard she'd fought for that same right in the past.

None of that seemed to matter now that she saw the result of her fight to remain behind. Her father was dead. She knew she should've climbed aboard the pod. It was too late now. She'd been foolish.

As the dust settled further she looked up to see what remained of her house. It had been reduced to a pile of rubble even higher than that in the garage. Pieces of metal and plastic had folded together, compressing what had once been the home of her childhood.

She saw her father's brown raincoat hanging from a beam.

The sight of that ugly thing hanging there, never again to adorn his body made her feel incredibly sad. She'd do anything to see him wear it again.

Her father hadn't planned for her to see any of this. She was supposed to be safely by his side in the pod with Buzz.

The smell of gas filled the air and a sickness built in her stomach. She leaned aside and retched, her vomit pooling on the ground with her father's blood.

If only it were a time machine her father had built,

instead of a spacecraft, she'd go back to this morning and never leave his side. Then he'd still be alive.

Her dreams hadn't told her this would happen, further evidence that the future was unable to be predicted. The pain of her grief gripped her by the spine.

"I'm sorry," she whispered, lifting her jacket and kissing him gently on the cheek. He felt different now that his soul had left his body. He no longer felt like her father. His body was his shell, not the essence of who he was.

She replaced her jacket over his face and made her way across the rubble, turning only briefly to see the wreckage of her house. So great was the loss of her father, she didn't care. The house meant nothing to her. Nothing would ever mean anything to her again.

Her father's raincoat fell from the beam above.

She scrambled toward it, desperate to get hold of it.

Her footing slipped, and she almost descended into the pile of rubble, catching herself on an upturned table.

She hauled herself to her feet to see a boy she recognized from the neighborhood get to the raincoat before her. He picked it up and draped it over his arm.

"That's mine," she shouted, tugging it from his arms. She put it on, the raincoat so large it almost reached the hem of the white dress she wore.

"Oh, sorry," the boy said, letting her take it.

She looked at him, all the fury of recent events pouring from her soul to his.

He grabbed her firmly by the shoulders and she flinched certain he was about to hit her. Instead he planted a kiss upon her lips.

She squirmed, trying to turn her head.

He broke away, smiling in triumph.

"I've always wanted to do that," he said.

She wiped her mouth with the back of her hand. The end

of the world didn't give anyone the right to touch her like that.

He leaned toward her and she took off before he could touch her again. She didn't want to leave her father's body, but felt she had no choice. She had to get away from here. As far away as possible, even if that meant leaving him lying in the rubble. It never occurred to her that he might be right by her side no matter where she was.

The streets were chaotic. People were swarming as they shouted and cried, running in circles, not knowing where to go next. They were all going to die. Their last words would soon be spoken, their last actions would soon be done. They had apologies to offer, love to make and fights to pick. There was no time to waste.

She pushed her way through the crowd, heading in the direction of the beach, still wearing the raincoat that smelled like her father.

It took over an hour before she felt sand beneath her feet. Night was falling, and the sky hung above her like a black curtain.

She made her way to the shoreline, spread out the raincoat on the sand and walked to the water. It was cool, lapping at her ankles and soaking into the fabric of her dress.

Returning to the raincoat, she sat down on it and stretched out her legs.

There was nobody else here. They were too busy panicking in the streets to think about leaving quietly.

Was that what this was? Was she leaving Earth? Was this the end?

She looked to the sky and saw one star burning brighter than the others. Was that her father's soul? Or was it Buzz— either in his spaceship or not? Was he still alive?

It soon became clear it wasn't Buzz. Or her father.

It was the asteroid.

She lay back and dug her hands into the sand.

"Take me," she said to the sky. "I'm ready."

She was. There was nothing left for her here. No people left to love, no possessions left to hold. It was just her, the beach and her father's raincoat.

She closed her eyes and tried to bring back all the dreams she'd had of her past lives, but her mind remained firmly rooted to the present. There was too much happening now for her to be reminiscing about the past. She had to take comfort in the fact that if she'd lived before, then it made sense that she'd go on to live again.

Who would she be born as next time? Was it even possible to be born again given that there'd be no Planet Earth? Maybe she'd be sent to wherever it was Buzz was heading. If that happened, she was certain she'd find him.

She imagined her father's soul being sent there, too. One day it was possible they could be together again.

The asteroid was looming larger by the second. It was huge. And it was moving quickly.

She flinched, feeling more alone than ever before. It was hard to be brave in death, even when that was what she wanted. Humans were wired for survival.

She realized she hadn't asked her father how she would die. Would she burn? Would she drown? Would she choke for air?

It didn't matter. She just hoped it was quick.

Adrenaline flooded her body, preparing her for the end and one of her dreams came back to her. It was her dream of walking naked into the ocean. How strange that she'd found herself here on the beach in her final moments.

Perhaps it wasn't strange at all. It was as it was meant to be. Her dream had been warning her, preparing her for how her life would end. She'd been wrong about the future being impossible to predict.

Being right here, right now, was her destiny. There was nothing she could've done to change that. She was never meant to go aboard the pod. If she had, then she wouldn't be here now.

This thought brought her peace. She hadn't killed her father. There was a power greater than herself working here. No matter what she did, somehow she was always going to end up here on the beach alone.

She got to her feet and pulled her dress over her head, throwing it on top of her father's raincoat. She slipped out of her underwear and walked naked into the water. It hardly mattered who saw her now. She wanted to be one with the Earth, feel the warm night air in her hair and the cool caress of the ocean on her skin.

She hadn't put in her colored contact lenses before leaving the house. She would never have been able to find them in that pile of rubble even if she'd wanted to. It felt good to be in the outdoors without them, her blue irises flashing at the sky.

It'd taken an event like this for her to embrace her differences. She didn't look like everyone else because she was unique. This was something to be celebrated, not hidden away in shame.

As the waves lapped at her waist, she threw her hands into the air.

"I love you," she called out, not sure who she was talking to. The universe? Her father? Buzz? Perhaps she was talking to herself.

It was important her last words were words of love, for that best summed up the girl she was. A girl who knew how to love with all her heart. A girl who'd asked the world for everything and had instead been given nothing.

Valentina wasn't certain what it was that took her life, only that it'd been taken.

Her fear had evaporated. Her guilt ceased. Her sadness shifted. As her soul had flown toward the sky, she was at peace—with herself and the world.

She was in a tunnel of warmth and light. It cocooned her, comforted her, soothed her. She was safe.

"Valentina," she heard a voice call.

It was the voice of a thousand angels. She followed it, gliding down the tunnel, not pausing to wonder what she'd find.

A bright light beckoned. It shone and swirled as it continued calling her name.

She stepped into it and waves of love washed over her. Tears of light spilled from her eyes as joy captured her every cell. She was at one with the light.

A purple mist circled at her feet and spun upward in front of her as a man appeared.

He was breathtaking. Black hair fell in waves upon his head, framing his flawless, pale skin. He wore a cloak of purple light and kindness in his dark eyes. Despite his youthful appearance, wisdom shone from his soul. This was what made him so breathtaking. Not his physical appearance, but his aura. Goodness and light poured from him, making her want to reach out and touch him and envelope herself in his light.

She remained still, resisting the urge, worried she might break some kind of spell and find herself falling back to Earth.

"I'm Shen," he said. "I'm the Soulweaver. You may call me Father."

"Where am I, Father?"

"You're in the Loom. You're safe with me."

She'd known she was safe before he'd said these words.

Wherever he was, she'd be safe. A soul as pure as his would never hurt her.

"It's time for the knowing," he said.

She nodded. She had so many questions to ask. Questions she knew the Soulweaver would answer. She'd done this before.

He reached out his arms and wrapped her in his cloak. No spell was broken, and she didn't fall back to Earth. Instead, joy filled her to the core and together they flew upward. She felt the wind in her hair and peace in her heart.

As they flew, she saw images of her past lives. Some lives were clearer than others.

She saw herself in ancient times as the queen of a desert. Then she saw herself in the sky with her own cloak of light, only her cloak was spun from gold. She had blonde hair, fair skin and the same blue eyes she'd possessed in her life as Valentina. She was welcoming souls into the Loom, just as she'd been welcomed herself and she instinctively under-stood she'd once been a Soulweaver like Father—in a time when souls had called her Mother.

Her cloak faded as the light seeped out of it and she saw the image of herself covered in shadows, her face twisted in agony. Someone more powerful was dragging her away from her life as a Soulweaver, far away to the distant planet she'd dreamed of.

As always in this dream, she was swimming underwater. More than that... she was breathing underwater, sucking oxygen into a set of gills on her chest, as her blonde hair trailed behind her. She was with a boy so beautiful he made her soul ache. She'd loved him. He'd been the first soul to weave himself into the fabric of her being and he remained there still. It was the boy who'd been struck by lightning. The boy who'd been reborn many lifetimes later as her father.

Then she saw that life ebb away and she was begging to

be sent back to Earth. The being who held her life in his hands was the Author of the universe and he was looking at her with the same expression as a parent faced with a disobedient child—there was both love and sadness pouring from his eyes. He was disappointed in her yet was still choosing to believe in her. She was his child and he was refusing to give up on her.

He disappeared, and she saw herself falling to the Earth once more. In that life she'd looked almost exactly as she had as Valentina, only with the dark eyes she'd longed for. Her eyes didn't bring her happiness though. Her life was a difficult one, filled with hunger and struggle. Despair was etched on her face and love held her soul together like some kind of binding. This was the life she'd dreamed of where she'd stood by a man with hair made from fire and a soul she recognized once more as her father's.

She saw Buzz in this lifetime, too. He was her protector —a man who lacked words, but whose heart overflowed with kindness. A man who chose to stand alone in his youth, just as he had in his lifetime as Buzz. He'd married her sister and been her brother then, just as he was her brother now. She looked at him standing on a pile of rubbish with an old wheelbarrow and her heart filled with love.

There were many lifetimes after this one and, in each, her soul had been intertwined with the soul who made her feel whole—the man whose hand she'd held deep under the water, then soared to the greatest heights of joy. He wasn't always her lover, although often he was. He'd also been her son, her brother, her teacher and friend. In her most recent lifetime he was her father. Her beloved father who'd given up his life in order that they not be torn apart.

It was no wonder he'd favored her over Buzz, no matter how hard he'd tried not to. He loved her with a force so great it'd baffled him. It was a love he felt in the depths of his soul and she loved him in return.

Everything made sense. The sum of all her lives had woven her soul into what it was today. She'd worked hard, and she'd loved harder still. She'd made people smile and she'd caused them pain. She'd begged for forgiveness and she'd forgiven others in return.

This process of wronging and being wronged, loving and being loved, had taught her the true meaning of her life. It was so simple. She just needed to be the best person she could possibly be, to get up when she fell, cherish those she loved and look forward—never back. She couldn't change the past, and the future was uncertain, but if she took each moment as it came to her and lived it to its fullest, then her soul would continue to evolve.

Her journey back in time came to an end and she found herself floating, still wrapped in the Soulweaver's arms.

"You're a special soul, Valentina," he said.

"We're all special," she replied.

He smiled. "Are you ready for your reflection now?"

A lake appeared before them. The water was almost impossible to see under the billions of brilliant lights that bobbed on its surface. It was a lake filled with all the souls of the world.

"The lake has never looked like this before," said Father. "I've never had so many souls in my care at the one time."

She couldn't help but notice the grief in his eyes, despite the serene expression he held to his face. What would happen to these souls now that returning to the Earth was no longer an option? And how would one Soulweaver be able to give due attention to each of the souls awaiting their fate?

"These are not your concerns," he said, reading her thoughts as if she'd spoken them aloud. "You forget that time ceases to exist here in the Loom. There's time enough for the right care to be taken with each of these souls. Do not be afraid."

She nodded, trusting him.

"Where will you send me?" she asked. "I want to stay on the Earth, but I know that's not possible now. Will you send me to my father?"

"He's still here in the Loom. But yes, you'll be together again. Except when you find him next time, he won't be your father."

"And what about my brother? Where's Buzz?"

"He's not here. He's the only one of Earth's souls not in my care."

"Will I see him again one day, too? Will you send me to wherever he is?"

The Soulweaver nodded. "You'll find your brother again."

"Except he won't be my brother, will he?"

"No. He'll still be Buzz, but your time as Valentina is over now."

She realized that wherever she and her father were to be sent to live their next lives, it had to be to whatever strange planet the pod had taken Buzz. Staying behind on Earth hadn't prevented her from being sent there, too. It had simply delayed it.

"The Author needed you to stay behind," said the Soulweaver. "He needed you to join Buzz in a different lifetime, not as Valentina. You did the right thing."

This confirmed the belief she'd held as she'd walked naked into the ocean. Her path had been paved long before she walked it.

"You're an important part of the Author's plan," said the Soulweaver. "He wanted you to save the Earth as its Mother, but it wasn't possible. As you see, I too, failed at this task. Yet the Author still has faith in you. There's another planet that needs you. It's in serious trouble, only its inhabitants don't know it yet. You lived on this planet many lifetimes ago and you must return there now. And this time you'll save it, not as Mother, but as a mother."

"What do I have to do?" she asked.

"First you'll need to listen to your heart. Then you'll need to follow it."

"How will I hear it?"

"Don't worry." He laughed. "It will be impossible not to hear. You've done this before."

"I don't understand," she said.

"You don't need to."

She smiled, trusting him. He was right. She didn't need to know anything right now, other than she would soon be with her father again. And Buzz, on the troubled planet that he was headed for.

"It's time to reflect," the Soulweaver said.

"Thank you, Father."

She waded into the water just as she'd done in the last moments of her life. The sea of lights parted, welcoming her in, sheltering her from any fear.

She faded into light and became one more piece of the giant puzzle of life.

She knew in lives gone by she'd been able to use this lake to return to Earth and make peace with the souls she'd left behind.

Not this time. This time, all the souls were here in the Loom. Apart from one and she had no peace to make with Buzz. Her heart swelled with love for her twin.

Besides, there was only one soul she was interested in finding. Where was he?

Her light drifted across the surface of the lake, pulling her gently to the other side.

She was getting closer. She was being drawn to him. Could he feel her, too?

One light shone brighter than the others and she knew it was him. He'd been waiting for her.

She heard the unmistakable sound of a piano as if someone was tinkering lightly with its keys. Not playing a piece of music as such but talking to her through the quavering notes. It grew louder the closer she drew to the light. The notes soon became a melody of love that could never be broken, of two lights that were impossible to separate.

She reached the light at last, closing the space between them.

They were together again, as they'd been since they first found each other a thousand years before.

As their lights merged, sparks shot in an arch across the lake and glorious music filled the Loom. It was an orchestra of a hundred instruments, sending ripples across the water in gentle waves. As all the souls of the world rose and fell in time to the rhythm, they woke as if from a deep sleep and began searching the lake for the other half to their own souls.

Soon the lake was lit by the joy of reunion and instead of lights bobbing on the water, they were dancing, sending sparks flying across the surface in waves of color.

Valentina had found her father. Instead of shining as two separate lights, they now shone as one.

Not even they knew just how brightly they were still destined to shine. The future of a million souls depended on it.

PART II
BUZZ

CHAPTER THREE

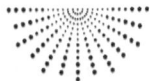

The only thing traveling faster than the strange pod that held Buzz's body, was his mind.

When he'd climbed aboard, he never expected to have to pilot this thing alone. Although, had he known, he'd still have gotten in.

Remaining on the Earth was certain death. At least now he had a chance, however small that chance might be.

He pressed his face to the shell of the pod. Despite its rough, gray surface on the outside, it was completely transparent when seen from the inside. He hadn't had time to ask his father what strange substance it was made from. It didn't matter now. Whatever it was, it held the power over his life. If it were to disintegrate now, then he was finished.

His breathing was coming in short gasps and sweat poured from his brow, not because it was hot—the pod seemed to be regulating the temperature reasonably well—but because of what he'd just seen.

The end of the world.

Nobody could have survived that collision. It'd been catastrophic. He'd seen fire that turned the Earth from blue to crimson to gray. The planet had become so shrouded in dust that he could no longer see it. It'd been extinguished, along with all the life upon it.

"Dad!' he'd cried out. "Valentina!'

He'd continued calling their names until his voice was hoarse, despite knowing they were dead. They had to be. Yet from this great distance, it was hard to believe. He still felt as if they were with him.

Why hadn't they come with him? He wished they were here now. Alive. Safe.

Was he safe?

He wasn't sure, although, he was safer than they were. His father's efforts had kept him alive longer than if he'd stayed on the Earth, but how much longer would the pod sustain him? Would it really be able to take him to a destination where survival was a possibility? It seemed so unlikely.

He reminded himself that he trusted his father. He was the smartest man he knew. Or rather the smartest man he'd *known*. He wasn't ready to think about him in the past tense yet, despite knowing he should.

As the Earth had disappeared from view, his attention was drawn to the vastness and beauty of outer space. He'd been on virtual tours before, but nothing could prepare him for seeing it in reality. The universe was beyond spectacular. Tears stung his eyes as he took in its magnificence.

Bright stars shone from the black canvas of the sky. Planets and moons sat in silent beauty watching him streak by. What must he look like to them? He felt like a speck of sand in the dunes of the Sahara.

He saw pinks and yellows, oranges and greens. The universe was majestic— a seductress, reeling him in, stealing his senses, leaving him unable to breathe.

He tore his eyes from the sky. He was alone now. The last man left on Earth. Well, the last man left *not* on Earth—apart from those living on colonies in space. But soon they'd perish, and it would only be him. What a strange thought that was. He'd never imagined he'd outlive all humans.

As the first man, Adam had seen the world in, and now he was seeing it out, only without Eve. Without anyone for that matter. Not that he believed Adam had ever existed. It was a nice story though and he liked the idea of someone else experiencing what he was going through now, even if Adam had had his feet on the ground, while Buzz was whizzing through the air at who knew what speed.

Perhaps it was better he was on his own. He'd never minded being alone, often wondering if that was a result of his mother abandoning him. If even she didn't want to be near him, then why should anyone else?

His father had also abandoned him in the last moments of life.

"It's up to you now, Buzz," he'd said, as he climbed out of the pod. "I love you. Make me proud."

Buzz had been shocked—stunned—to realize his father was leaving him. He'd tried to open the hatch to go after him, but it was locked, designed so that once you'd made your decision to take off, there was no chance of changing your mind.

He'd shrunk back into his chair and fastened his harness, his heart pounding so hard he could barely hear the roar of the engine. He'd seen the swarm of people banging on the side of the pod, desperate to get inside.

Valentina had been pushed away from the ladder, a frightened expression stuck to her face as their father had landed at her feet. Buzz had pressed his hands to the surface of the pod trying to let them know he loved them.

Why hadn't his father stayed long enough for Buzz to tell him that he loved him, too? If only those people hadn't broken into the workshop, his departure wouldn't have been so rushed. Perhaps they'd have had time to convince Valentina to come aboard.

There was no sense in lamenting this now. The people had come in through the window. He had left without Valentina and his father. The past couldn't be changed. People wasted far too much time wishing it could.

He wasn't surprised by his father's choice to stay with Valentina. He'd almost expected to be cast aside one day.

No, he couldn't think like that. His father had his reasons for leaving him, just as his mother must have. Whoever she was, she was dead now, too. He'd never even seen a photo of her.

He wondered if she looked like Valentina. She was a pretty girl. If only she wasn't so self-conscious about her eyes then more of the world would see just how pretty.

Not anymore, he reminded himself. The world would never see his sister again. She was gone. He hoped it wasn't painful. He loved her, despite the obvious differences between them. He'd just never known how to show it.

His father hadn't had any trouble showing his love for Valentina. He'd doted on her.

At least they'd gone together. It was what his father would've wanted. Buzz was sure he'd be holding tight to Valentina's soul even now.

He looked to the sky once more and sent them love, wherever they might be. They were the only family he'd known. The only family he'd ever know.

Now wasn't the time to mourn them too deeply. He couldn't let their loss into the center of his heart right now. He had enough to worry about already. Besides, the best way to honor their memory would be to somehow survive this catastrophe himself.

He calmed his breathing and turned his gaze to the control panel. Its simplicity troubled him. His father hadn't installed anything but the most basic functions. There were no communication devices, no radars, no warning lights, no indicators to tell him his speed, direction or oxygen levels.

He was at the mercy of this pod to deliver him to wherever his father had programmed it to go. He should have plenty of oxygen and food given it had been designed for three people.

This thought punched pain into his gut as he looked at the two empty seats beside him.

He'd never see another living soul. At least he could never again be abandoned. His heart would never be broken, assuming it had ever been in one piece.

Not knowing whether he had seconds, minutes or decades of life remaining, he leaned back in his seat and drew in a deep breath. He'd often wished everyone would just disappear. Now that he'd gotten his wish, he longed to have them back.

The pod was larger than he'd thought when he first saw it, perhaps two body lengths in each direction if he were to stretch his arms above his head. Two of his body lengths, he thought, not Valentina's. She was so short, it would take three of her to reach from one side to the other.

Supply cabinets lined the ceiling and lower part of the pod, leaving a wide transparent band in the middle to see out of. He wondered what was in the cabinets. They were no doubt filled with whatever his father had determined would be necessary for survival.

He reached up to touch the transparent panel. It seemed to be broken in two, with a thin, silver strip circling the girth of the pod. Was that how his father had joined the pieces together or did it have some kind of purpose? He ran his finger down the band. It was smooth and warm under his skin.

The pod had a strange smell to it. He tried to think of the

word it reminded him of. *Sterile* was all he could come up with. It could be worse.

He opened the cabinet closest to him and saw it was filled with tools and stationery. Hopefully, he wouldn't need any of the tools. He wouldn't have a clue what he was supposed to do with them.

He took out a black marker and without giving it a lot of thought, drew a large smiling face on the door of one of the supply cabinets directly in front of him. He instantly felt less lonely.

"Where are we off to, Neil?" he asked the face, naming it after the first man to walk on the moon. That had been a successful mission despite it being a first for mankind. Maybe this one would be, too. It made him smile to think of Buzz and Neil once again flying into space and the unknown.

"Yes, yes, I know it's a little too early in the journey for me to lose my mind," he said to Neil. "But if you don't tell anyone, then neither will I."

He noticed a button inside the door of the supply cabinet and wondered if he should press it. He knew it was never a good idea to press buttons unless you were sure what they did, especially in a situation like the one he found himself in, but he decided it could do no harm. If the button was dangerous then his father would hardly have located it so innocently inside a cabinet. Surely it would have one of those glass domes covering it to prevent it being accidentally pressed.

"What do you reckon, Neil?" he asked.

The face continued to smile at him in response.

"Excellent. I couldn't agree more."

He pressed the button, wincing as he waited to see what would happen.

Classical music filled the pod, drowning out the silence.

Buzz shook his head and laughed. Of course. There was

no way his father could plan a journey like this without thinking about his music. That would've been as important to him as the food supplies.

He was glad. Music would be a good distraction. He just hoped he'd be able to turn it off when he wanted to.

He picked up the black marker again and drew a line on Neil's face.

"Day one," he said.

Buzz continued to draw one line each day on Neil's chin until it began to look like a beard, slowly growing in thickness and creeping up the sides of his face toward his ears.

Buzz was growing his own beard to match. It wasn't nearly as bushy as Neil's. It was quite patchy, but impressive nonetheless for a boy his age. He wondered if he'd live long enough for it to take proper shape. Or if he'd ever have the chance to shave it off?

His hair had grown, too, reaching his shoulders. He caught his reflection occasionally in the side of the pod and laughed, thinking he looked like Valentina with a beard.

What would Valentina's friends think of him now? Would they blush a deep shade of pink when they spoke to him or lose all interest they'd had? He wasn't sure. He'd never quite understood their attention anyway. It made him feel uncomfortable, despite his father's insistence that one day he'd be pleased with all the fuss.

He may not be missing Valentina's friends, but he was missing her peculiar way of looking at the world and her insistence that her dreams held so much meaning. She never seemed to be able to accept they were just dreams and nothing more. Did it help her to think that she'd lived other lives before this one? Perhaps it had brought her some comfort in her death to think that one day she'd live again. If that were the case, then all those crazy dreams were worth it, even the one about her being queen of the desert.

"What's she doing now, Neil?" he asked his friend on the wall.

"Not much," came the imagined reply.

"I don't know about that," he said. "I reckon she's got all the souls in heaven wrapped around her little finger by now. Maybe she's learned to play the harp."

This thought never failed to amuse him. It also never failed to make him cry.

It seemed like this journey in the pod had opened up a part of himself he'd kept hidden all his life.

He'd been so determined to protect himself from getting hurt that he'd never noticed all he was managing to do was hide his pain in a place deep inside. This pain had built up over the years and was now exploding out of his chest in waves.

It scared him. He was losing sense of who he was. He was strong, independent, brave. Not this sniffling mess whose tears floated around the pod like raindrops.

He hoped he'd reach his destination soon, no longer caring if it was another planet or death itself. Sometimes limbo could be more painful than the depths of hell.

He sang himself happy birthday when he turned fifteen and blew kisses to the sky for Valentina. It felt strange to have a birthday without her.

He consumed three sachets of food in celebration and drew a party hat on Neil.

"Best party ever," he said to his friend on the wall, his eyes filling with sadness.

He decided to skip the usual series of exercises he put himself through each day and instead took an extra-long nap. It was difficult being trapped inside such a small space for so long. He longed to take a walk, breathe fresh air, or even just stretch out and sleep in a bed.

It felt like only minutes later that he was woken by the sound of a siren and sat up in a daze. It had been so long since he'd heard a sound other than his own voice or his father's music that it took him several minutes to figure out what was happening.

Looking out the window, he saw he was headed for a planet that looked strangely like Earth. It was blue and green with clouds of white circling above it.

Had the pod been designed to travel around the universe only to return to Mother Earth when it was safe? It wasn't possible. The Earth had been blown to pieces. It didn't exist anymore.

Then again, anything was possible.

He studied the planet as best he could, trying to pick out the familiar shapes of the continents. This was where the difference lay. The landmasses upon this planet were unfamiliar. Was there another planet out there just like Planet Earth? Maybe it contained human life? His heart leaped at the possibility.

He'd known his father was smart, but he must have been a genius to have figured out this planet existed.

As he got closer, he noticed a dark gray plume of smoke billowing toward the sky. Was this planet on fire, too? It didn't look like fire, though. Just a constant stream of some kind of thick fog pouring from a brown patch of land.

The siren in his pod grew louder and he turned to the control panel to work out what he was supposed to do. It would be devastating to get this far only to crash.

"Help me out, Neil. It's time to land this thing."

Neil smiled in reply, as he always did.

"It's no time for jokes," Buzz said. "By the way, you look silly in that hat."

He strapped himself into his harness. This was the moment he'd been waiting for. The next chapter of his life was about to begin. Or was his life about to end? It was just as well he had no time to be scared.

The pod rattled violently as it entered the strange planet's atmosphere and he clutched his harness and closed his eyes. He wasn't sure if he believed in God or a Creator, yet he found himself begging the universe for his life to be spared. He wasn't ready to die.

A light flashed on the panel in front of him. It was a green button, blinking, as if asking him to push it. Why else would it be flashing like that?

He reached out his finger, trying to steady himself from the jolting of the pod, frightened he might press the wrong button.

He suspected the flashing green light must release the halo that ringed the center of the pod. It would be impossible to land without a parachute. This was the only possible place one could be hidden.

His finger steadied on the button and he pushed down.

The ring on the pod broke apart and voluminous amounts of silver fabric billowed out, dragging behind to form a giant parachute.

He stared at it in wonder. How had so much fabric been hidden in such a small panel? Light bounced off it, making it sparkle. It almost seemed to be made from diamonds. Valentina would have loved to have seen that. If only she were here.

"Woo hoo!' he hollered. "You did it, Dad. You're a bloody genius!'

The pod passed through the rays of the sun and he saw a shadow roll across the surface of the planet. He'd shrouded it in darkness, turning day into night. This silenced him.

There'd be no creeping up on this planet. If life did indeed exist upon it, he was certain they'd be very aware of his arrival. He just hoped they were friendly.

His gut clenched and the smell of burning plastic filled the pod. Was it on fire, or had it gotten so hot it'd started to melt? He couldn't see any flames.

The pod floated toward the ground and the violent shaking stopped. He reached for the button that would fill the pod with his father's music. It seemed right to have it playing at a time like this. It's what his father would've done. And if he couldn't have his father with him, this was the next best thing.

For a few precious seconds, he felt like an eagle floating gracefully to the ground. This planet he was about to land on was beautiful. It was covered in trees, just like the Earth had been once. They coated the surface like a soft blanket, their branches swaying in the wind as if waving to him, welcoming him to his new home. There was no sign of the gray smoke now. Had he imagined that? All he could see was mother nature in her most spectacular form. He was going to be happy here. He could feel it.

The pod landed with a thud that shook every one of his bones, silencing the music and waking him from his thoughts of the planet's beauty as he dropped straight back into the reality of his situation.

He was a fifteen-year-old boy, all alone, the last surviving member of the human race and he'd just landed on a strange planet with no idea about his chances of survival.

He drew in a deep breath, feeling slightly dizzy at having come to a stop and no longer moving through the sky.

Where was he? Would he be able to breathe if he opened the hatch? He wasn't even sure how to open it. Steam was hissing from the outside of the pod as it attempted to adjust to its surroundings.

He undid his harness and looked around. He'd landed in a

field. The pod was cushioned by lush green grass and he could see a forest surrounding him.

The trees were tall with dark green leaves dancing in the breeze. Their welcome for him was even more beautiful on the ground than it'd been in the sky. His pod suddenly felt tiny next to these ancient giants of the forest. Trees were a good sign. They produced oxygen. There was hope for his survival.

He spotted a few bright specks of color amongst the leaves, not certain if they were flowers or birds. His eyes ached with the joy of taking everything in.

It looked so much like planet Earth before humans had destroyed the forests. Had he dreamed the whole journey? Had his father tricked him? Maybe the pod had never left the workshop and his father had been streaming him videos designed to fool him into seeing different surroundings.

No, his father would never do that. This was real.

"How do we get out, Neil?" he said, longing to stretch his legs and stand on the ground. Sharp cramps shot through his body at the thought of his muscles being used once more, like a mouth that waters the moment a delicious meal appears.

He blinked, certain that Neil's expression had changed. Was he frowning? No, that wasn't possible. Spending so much time alone in that small space had clearly messed with his mind. Neil might feel like a friend, but he was a drawing —and drawings didn't change their expressions.

Slowly, the hatch opened on its own. The steam dissipated, and fresh air flooded the pod. He drew it in, taking deep gasping breaths, not realizing how much he'd missed the taste of fresh air. It felt so clean in his lungs.

The forest beckoned him to come and stand beneath its canopy.

He breathed in the scent of the forest. It was earthy and

damp and he was certain he could smell the bark on the trees. There was nothing artificial or sterile about this smell. This was the smell of nature in its purest form.

"I guess this is it," he said, reaching out to touch Neil's face. "No, I can't take you with me. Sorry."

He found the black marker and drew one last line upon Neil's beard.

Before he could change his mind, he stood and hoisted himself out of the hatch.

As often as he'd imagined this moment, it was nothing like the reality. In his mind, he'd seen his feet land firmly on the ground, his fists pumping the air in triumph.

So, when his legs buckled under his weight and he fell to the ground, unable to stand, it came as a shock.

Did this planet have some kind of super-gravity? He felt like he was being pinned down by a giant sitting on his belly.

He lay down and resisted the urge to fight against it. His hands ran across the grass. It was moist, small dewdrops clinging to each blade.

Lifting his hand, he waved it in the air in front of his face.

It wasn't super-gravity. It was regular gravity and he was out of practice living within its rules.

He sat up and slowly pulled himself into a kneeling position. Laughing, he realized he looked like he was praying. Perhaps he was. He was certainly happy to be alive. That in itself was a prayer.

It was amazing. Here he was, millions, if not billions, of miles from Earth about to take his first steps.

He remembered his namesake and how he'd paused on the surface of the moon to give thanks.

"Thank you," he said, wishing he knew the exact words Buzz Aldrin had used, so he could repeat them now.

Bringing himself slowly to his feet, his knees trembled under the weight of his body.

"You did it, Dad," he called out to the sky, his gratitude bringing tears to his eyes. "You actually did it."

He thought of all the work his father had done to build this pod that took him to safety. But more than that, he thought of all his father had done to raise him to be the person he was. He may not have had a mother and although he'd missed her presence greatly, he'd been given all he'd needed and more.

His life had been a happy one and he'd lived it in constant awe of his surroundings. That was why he'd wanted to be an astronaut. The universe had created such an impossibly beautiful planet in Earth that it made him crave to see what other wonders it had to offer.

He looked around, soaking in the quiet magnificence of the planet he now found himself on. He was alive when others were dead. He had a chance when others had none.

He promised himself he wouldn't waste this opportunity. His father's work wouldn't be for nothing. He'd make him proud. He'd make his sister proud. Most importantly, he'd make himself proud.

He walked toward the trees.

"I'm coming," he called.

CHAPTER FOUR

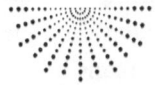

*B*uzz walked into the dense forest. His legs were a little wobbly at first, but before long he settled into a rhythm.

He would normally have thought of the forest as quiet, but to his ears it was deafening. After spending so long in the pod, the wind rustling the leaves in the trees sounded like a hurricane, the small twigs that broke under his footsteps were like thunderbolts and the birds in the trees screeched like sirens. He felt so alive and free.

The trees stretched into the sky, asserting their magnificence like soldiers on a battlefield. Earthlings should've tried harder to preserve the forests their ancestors had enjoyed. It was a crime to have wiped them out so ruthlessly, using their timber to make furniture that was disposed the moment it had a scratch on it and pillaging all the nutrients from the ground as crops were grown and cattle grazed.

As the Earth's population had boomed, cities crept outward until they joined with other cities, the borders between them impossible to find. Trees took up valuable space and governments were far too busy figuring out ways to feed hungry citizens to give any thought to preserving the forests—or the animals who'd called them home.

Not on this planet, though. Here, there were animals everywhere. Big ones, small ones, ones that he could eat for his dinner and others that could eat him.

He knew animals like these had once existed on Earth, but many had become extinct long before he was born. Cows and chickens had been plentiful. Pigs, too. They were useful to humans. It was ironic, really—the fact that the survival of these animals was entirely due to the fact that they were bred to die.

Not that it mattered now, he supposed. None of it existed anymore. The Earth was gone. It was hard to remember that.

He soon became lost amongst the trees. Why hadn't he thought to take food and water? He'd been so excited to get out of the pod, he hadn't stopped to make any kind of sensible plan. He'd just walked into the forest with a big smile on his face. His father would be disappointed with him. What a stupid thing to do.

Needing to find his way back to the pod, he turned and looked at his surroundings. Everything was the same. It was useless. This forest was vast, and he'd already been walking for hours. Trying to find his way back would only result in him walking in circles, exhausting himself in the process. It'd been a long time since his legs had walked so far.

He'd be better off using his energy to search for a water source. The animals had to be drinking something.

He soon realized that finding water would be as hard as trying to find his pod. He had no idea what he was doing. How did anything survive out here?

A branch broke in the shadows and he jumped. Was someone following him? He thought he glimpsed a tail and some powerful hind legs in the distance. Some kind of large cat perhaps. If they were anything like the ones that had once roamed the Earth, they could be dangerous. He poked around on the forest floor looking for a stick he could use to defend himself.

Picking one up, he held it in front of him, shaking his head at the flimsiness of his plan. This stick wouldn't save him from a wild beast. Still, he tucked it into the waistband of his trousers. It wasn't like he had a better plan.

Thirst gripped him and soon water was all he could think about, the idea of cool liquid sliding down his throat a torturous fantasy. He was dehydrating quickly, and his feet and legs ached.

As night fell, he decided to take shelter in a small hollow under a shelf of rocks. The dirt was smooth, almost like someone had made it for him. Rabbits hopped past, tilting their heads at him in curiosity. He made a few feeble attempts to catch them, deciding he'd be more effective in the morning.

He curled up and fell almost instantly asleep, although this didn't last long as he woke with a sharp pain in his arm. He sat up and looked around in the darkness. The full moon cast eerie shadows across the forest.

Perhaps it was a cramp, he thought, rubbing his arm. His body wasn't used to moving around so much. He lay back down, only to feel the pain once more. Had someone thrown something at him?

"Who's there?" he called out.

This time he saw the rock flying through the air. It hit him in the stomach.

He jumped to his feet and braced himself, ready for a fight. He was under attack.

Adrenaline surged through his veins, pumped by the rapid beating of his heart. He could defend himself. He hadn't travelled this far to die only hours after his arrival.

He raised his fists in front of his chest, shaking so

violently that he was unlikely to succeed at scaring away a rabbit, let alone whatever was throwing rocks at him.

"Show yourself." He knew these aliens wouldn't speak English, but he had to say something.

A dark figure stepped out of the shadows. It was tall, looming over him, making him feel half his size.

He squinted. It wasn't human. Why had he expected it to be human? Everyone knew aliens had green skin and large eyes like saucers, but this creature was nothing like that. It was covered in black hair, like a dog. It reminded him of a stuffed toy he'd had as a baby. A teddy bear, his father had called it.

He remembered a picture he'd seen once of an animal that had long ago ceased to walk the earth. It was a grizzly bear and they certainly weren't a creature you'd want to cuddle up to at night. What a strange toy to give to a baby.

He reached for his stick, gripping it tightly in front of him. Sweat beaded on his forehead and rolled down his face as the bear stepped forward. It was going to kill him and there was nothing he could do about it. He must have been sleeping in its den. No wonder the ground had felt so smooth with a weight like that lying on it every night.

The bear opened its mouth, revealing a set of teeth sharp enough to slice a man in two, and made a noise so loud the leaves on the trees shook.

He froze, as much as a person who is shaking all over is able to. His feet glued themselves to the forest floor and he remembered Valentina adopting a similar pose when their father was calling her to join him in the pod. The fear of death can do that to you. And he was certain this was it. He was going to die.

A high-pitched sound escaped his lips, his futile protest at his imminent fate. He tried to stop the sound but couldn't.

Another rock came flying through the air, only this time it hit the bear.

Startled, the bear turned, taking a step toward a dense thatch of trees.

Buzz saw his chance and took it.

His feet unglued themselves and his body sprang into action.

He ran.

He ran so far and so fast, not knowing where he was heading. He could run into a whole group of bears for all he knew.

The further he ran, the more he felt himself calm. His heart rate slowed, his breathing deepened, the shaking of his hands and legs stilled. It was quite the opposite effect to when he normally ran, although there was nothing normal about this situation.

When he was sure the bear wasn't following, he stopped to catch his breath, certain he'd been running in circles. He bent over with his hands on his knees, his eyes darting around for any sign of movement in the scrub.

A rock hit him on the leg, the sharp sting of it jolting him back into panic and he took off again, running from the source of the attack and dropping his bear-poking-stick.

The rocks continued to pelt him and each time he turned and ran from them.

He wasn't sure how it happened, but eventually he stumbled into the field. The familiar shape of the pod sat in the distance. He couldn't get there fast enough, climbing aboard and slamming the hatch, wishing it would lock behind him.

It was a relief to be back in familiar surroundings. He heaved for air as sweat poured down his forehead.

The seat in the pod was blissfully cool and he leaned back, pulling up his legs and burying his face in his knees.

When he'd left the pod, he hadn't expected to ever return.

In those blissful moments of ignorance, he hadn't known what was out there. This planet may look like Earth from the sky, but it he was quickly finding out there were a few important differences. Very tall, very furry differences. Differences that had very sharp teeth and no longer existed where he'd come from.

"I'm back," he said to Neil, reaching for the tube that connected him to his water supply and taking long gulps.

It was dangerous out there. More dangerous than he'd anticipated. He wasn't sure what was more frightening—the bear or whatever creature it was that had been throwing stones at him.

He peered out into the night, wondering if whoever, or whatever, it was had followed him. He grabbed hold of the rim of the hatch and tried to force it into a locked position. It was no use. He'd just have to hope whatever it was didn't have the intelligence to figure out how to get in.

The night remained still. It was quiet. The perfect conditions for sleep, yet his dreams took a long time to claim him.

The next morning brought with it a sense of calm.

He'd survived his first night. Whatever had thrown the rocks at him had decided not to kill him in his sleep. When he thought about it logically, whatever it was had actually saved his life by leading him back to the pod. Then why hadn't they shown themselves? Were they as scared of him as he was of them?

He knew it should be a comfort to know that life existed on this planet. Yet the reality of it filled him with fear.

When he was flying here, he'd been longing for the day he could leave the pod and stretch his legs. Now that day had come, all he wanted was to lock himself back inside.

"Looks like it's you and me," he said to Neil, realizing he'd missed him. How sad to miss what he logically knew was a drawing in the same way he missed his father and Valentina. Neil had become like family to him. He knew this made no sense, but he couldn't deny this was how he felt.

It was a sunny day outside and green grass of the field began to tempt him.

He climbed out into the quiet. He'd be all right if he took it slowly and got used to his surroundings little by little. No more ambitious ideas about taking off into the forest again. It was time to make plans for his survival right here in the field.

He was wearing a pair of black pants and a blue tee shirt he'd found aboard the pod. His father had packed several changes of clothes for each of them and he was grateful. It would've been awful to spend all that time wearing the same clothes he'd left in. He hadn't touched Valentina's clothes, or his father's. It didn't seem right.

He had shelter and enough food and water to last at least a few months, but what would he do after that? A few months didn't seem like very long to live. He needed to work out a way to collect water, assuming it rained on this planet. He looked at the parachute, still trailing behind the pod. It was perfect. If he dug a hole in the ground, he could line it with the silver fabric. It looked like it was watertight. He might even be able to make himself a bathtub. This beard of his was getting itchy. He longed to soak in some water and feel clean once more. Sponging himself inside the pod had never felt completely adequate.

Once he was able to figure out how to collect water, he could worry about food. Surely rabbits wouldn't be too difficult to catch if he put his mind to it. He'd also need fire. He'd once seen someone rub two sticks together to create flames.

No doubt that was harder than it looked, but he'd give it a go. One step at a time. First the water.

He didn't have a shovel to dig with, so decided instead he'd look for a flat rock or a heavy tree branch to do the job. Or both. He could tie a rock to the end of a branch and scoop out the earth that way.

He took a small knife he had in the supply cabinet and cut one of the ropes from the parachute. Now all he needed was a branch and the right type of stone. It was a shame he'd dropped his stick last night. That would've been perfect.

He wandered into the edge of the trees, eyes darting around the forest floor, not game to venture too far. Losing his pod again would be certain death. He found a branch that seemed strong enough and used it to fossick amongst the fallen leaves, looking for a stone.

This was more difficult. Whoever had been throwing stones at him the night before hadn't seemed to have trouble finding a constant supply, yet he couldn't find a single one.

His shoulders slumped as his optimism dampened. This wasn't going to be so easy.

Perhaps there was something he could use inside the pod instead. If he could take off the door to one of the supply cabinets, that might work as a shovel. It'd probably even be better.

It seemed wrong to start dismantling the pod his father had so painstakingly built, but it wasn't like it would ever fly again. Parts of the outside had melted during the landing and it wasn't anywhere near the perfect specimen he'd first climbed aboard. If it could help him survive out here, then he was sure his father would be happy with whatever he did with it.

He slid himself back into the pod and took a sip of water, drinking less than he wanted. It was time to start rationing.

He looked across at Neil and blinked. He must be imagining it. This couldn't be real. He rubbed his eyes. What was going on?

Neil wasn't alone.

Drawn next to him was the face of a girl.

The drawing was incredibly detailed, making Neil looked like he'd been sketched by a young child.

It wasn't the face of an alien or a bear. The face was undeniably human. The girl in the picture smiled at him, her large eyes glinting with playfulness. Her hair was cropped so short her gender should have been hard to determine in a drawing, yet the prettiness of her features gave her away. She wore a party hat, identical to the one he'd drawn on Neil.

She was beautiful. Her eyes reminded him of Valentina's.

Who was she? And more to the point, who'd drawn her?

He reached out and touched the drawing, making sure it was real and not just a figment of his confused mind.

"What's going on?" he asked Neil, looking around the pod for signs of the intrusion. Someone had been in here. They must have. Had they taken his food?

He opened the supply cabinet, his heart thumping. If his food was gone then the intruder may as well have taken his knife and killed him then and there.

But his food was still there. Nothing had been touched. If it weren't for the drawing, he never would've known anyone had been in there at all.

Had he lost his mind? Perhaps he'd drawn it in his sleep last night.

No. There was no way he could draw like that. This picture had been sketched by someone who had a talent he didn't possess. Poor Neil looked like he'd been drawn by a toddler in comparison.

He climbed out of the pod, deciding to hide amongst the trees and see if his new artist friend would return. If he got lucky, they'd climb aboard to draw a new picture and he could block their exit.

He found a comfortable spot behind some scrub where if he lay down on his stomach he could see the hatch of the pod. He waited.

And waited.

Nobody came.

He shifted his weight from elbow to elbow. It was getting uncomfortable. He'd make a terrible spy.

"Ouch," he cried, as something fell from the tree above, landing directly on his back.

He looked up, squinting into the sun.

There was something in the tree. Or someone. A monkey perhaps. He liked the idea of befriending a monkey, having never seen one before.

He saw a flash of pale skin disappear behind a branch. It wasn't a monkey. It had looked human. How was that even possible?

"Who's there?" he called, picking up the rock and throwing it into the tree. It hit the branch below the one that hid his attacker. Perhaps that was a bad idea. He was at a disadvantage, not just due to where he was standing. He was certain this person—if that's what it was—knew a lot more about him than he knew about them.

"Come down," he called, holding out the palms of his hands to show he meant no harm.

He saw a movement and very slowly a face peeked out at him from behind the branch.

It was the girl from the drawing, only this time she wasn't smiling at him. She looked afraid. She looked younger than her drawing—maybe only twelve years old and her features were fairer than she'd been able to represent with a black marker. Her eyes were a pale shade of blue, and her hair was so white he doubted it contained any pigment at all. She looked almost like an elf.

"I won't hurt you," he said.

He just hoped she wouldn't hurt him. Looks couldn't always be relied upon and given her age she may not even be alone.

She looked at him, blinking slowly, reminding him of a younger, fairer version of Valentina.

With several quick movements, she came sliding down the tree, landing at his feet. His heart lurched as he remembered how his father had landed in a similar way as he'd leaped from the pod to remain by Valentina's side. Only his father hadn't managed to land on his feet.

The girl stood as tall as she was able, barely reaching his chest. She wore a black suit made from some kind of stretchy material. It had been cut jaggedly so that her arms and legs stuck out. Her skin was pale, smeared with dirt and she'd painted lines across her face with mud. It was no wonder she'd been difficult to spot amongst the foliage.

He continued to hold up his palms, showing he held no weapons.

She studied his empty hands with a look of fascination. It was like she'd never seen hands before, despite hers dangling by her side.

Then, glancing at his face, she brought up her hands and held them in front of her. He was surprised to see that she had webbing between her fingers. Perhaps she wasn't as human as he'd first thought. That was why she'd been so interested in his hands. Everybody here must have hands like hers.

The skin on her right hand was scarred with angry red lines trailing across the surface in raised bumps. That didn't look like something she'd been born with. She'd been injured in her past and he couldn't help but wonder how.

He looked down at her bare feet and saw that her toes were webbed, too.

She pressed her palms to his.

"Peace," he said.

"Peace," she replied, only it sounded more like "peashh."

He realized she had no idea what she'd just said. It was amazing enough that she looked human, having her speak English would have been a miracle beyond comprehension.

She locked her gaze on his face and giggled.

Sometimes language was unnecessary.

He bent forward, trying to put them at eye level and she tentatively reached out her hand, stopping just short of his cheek. Her eyebrows rose as if asking him for permission to put her hands on him.

He nodded.

She touched his face, cautiously at first like he might give her an electric shock, then when she saw it was safe she got more adventurous, poking and prodding him.

"Okay, that's enough," he said when she stuck a finger in his eye.

She withdrew her hands and pointed to herself.

"Nahlah," she said.

"Na-la," he repeated.

She shook her head. "Naaah-lah."

"Nahlah," he tried again.

She nodded, looking satisfied this time and pointed at him.

"Buzz," he said.

"Buzzzzz." She laughed.

He wasn't sure why, but he laughed with her. It felt so good to be in the presence of another human. Was she human, though? Could he call her that even though she came from another planet? Her skin might be fair, and her hair looked like it'd been spun from fairy dust, but she certainly seemed human to him. How strange to find human life so far away from home.

A raindrop landed on his cheek and he looked to the sky in surprise. If only he'd had time to dig his well, he could be collecting water right now.

Nahlah's eyes widened and she took off in the direction of the pod. He saw her scamper inside.

He followed, climbing in behind her and closing the hatch to keep out the rain.

She was curled up on the seat, scowling at the field around them.

"You don't like the rain?" he asked.

She didn't reply. She hadn't understood what he'd said.

"Are there others?" he asked.

She looked at him blankly.

He pointed to Neil, realizing she thought he'd drawn a picture of himself, most likely why she'd sketched herself next to him.

"Buzz," he said, playing along. Then he pointed at her drawing. "Nahlah."

Picking up the marker he drew stick figures next to them.

"Others," he said, shrugging his shoulders. "Are there others?"

Her eyes lit up as she understood his question.

She took the marker from his hand and drew lines around the crowd of stick figures. She held the marker firmly, tilting it at an angle as it rested on the soft folds of skin between her fingers.

He looked at it in puzzlement as her drawing took shape. She was drawing water. The people were under the water. Had they all drowned?

Then she added more stick figures of people swimming, eating at tables, sleeping in beds, and playing in parks.

The drawing took some time for her to complete, but

soon he understood there were many others here on this strange planet, only they seemed to live underwater. That explained the webbing between her fingers, but however did they breathe?

Next to her drawing of the water, she sketched a forest. On the edge of it in a barren clearing was some kind of square building with a large pipe protruding from its roof. Smoke was billowing out of it and dirtying the sky. This was what Buzz had seen when he was landing, and he wondered how far away they were from it now. The air smelt so clean here.

He pointed to the underwater world. "Nahlah. Do you live there, Nahlah?"

She started to nod, then shook her head.

Had she run away? She certainly looked like she had. Surely she was too young to look after herself.

Now she was pointing at Neil.

"Others?" she said, wanting to know if there were others like him.

He shook his head. "Just me. No others." Then, taking the marker he drew planet Earth with stars around it. He traced an arrow from one of the stars to the Earth, then drew fire all around it. He added his pod, drawing another arrow to show how he'd travelled. Then he drew the planet he'd landed on.

Nahlah took the marker and added a parachute to his pod.

He nodded, realizing she'd seen him land.

"Earth," he said, pointing at his planet.

"Neron," she said, pointing at hers.

"Neron," he repeated. He'd better get used to that word, for now it was his planet, too. His home, whether he liked it or not.

She shuffled to the other side of the pod to draw on another clean cabinet door. It wasn't stick figures like the

66

drawings they'd just shared. This one was a masterpiece, much like the one she'd drawn of herself earlier in the day.

He sat back and watched, marveling at her talent. Could the others who lived under the water draw like this? He doubted it.

She was drawing the forest. In a tree sat a girl. It was Nahlah. Below it was a boy with a scruffy beard running in terror. Behind him was a bear. She drew a rock flying from the girl to the bear.

He'd already figured out it was Nahlah who'd rescued him from the bear and had continued to throw rocks, steering him in the right direction back to his pod, but he let her draw in peace.

She put the finishing touches on her drawing, then smiled at him, stifling a laugh.

"Boolah," she said.

He had no idea what that meant but was fairly sure it wasn't a compliment.

"Boolah," he repeated.

She giggled, and he fought a sudden urge to reach out to her.

"Thank you." He put his hand on his heart. She was an unlikely hero, but he owed her his life. He didn't take that lightly. She could call him any name she liked.

Over the following weeks she called him many names. She called him *Ardorna* as she slept in the crook of his arm at night. She called him *Beedar* when he finished building their drinking well. And the day he'd come home with a rabbit he'd snared, she called him *Raddick*.

It was strange to live in such close quarters with a person with no language to connect them. He had so many questions he wanted to ask. How long was she planning to stay with him? Did she miss her family and weren't they worried about her? Would she take him to the water one day or would she be the only other person he saw for the rest of his life?

This thought didn't bother him. He liked Nahlah and they soon discovered they made a formidable team. Where he was strong, she was smart. Where he was courageous, she was cunning. Where he was quiet, she filled the air with chatter.

She talked constantly, whether to him or herself. He couldn't understand what she said, but soon began to recognize words. They spent hours pointing at different objects and teaching each other the names for them in their own language. In this way, they gathered words that Buzz hoped would one day be strung into sentences.

Once she pointed at her heart and said the word *Ardorna*. He blushed, remembering this was the name she called him when she was at her most tender. Was she telling him she loved him? They were too young for romance. She was more like a little sister to him. Perhaps that's what she meant? After all, Valentina was his sister and he'd loved her.

Nahlah even talked in her sleep, either crying out for her mother or screaming out her word for *stop*. He'd hold her close and tell her she was safe, and after a while her breathing would calm, and she'd fall into her troubled dreams once more.

The only time she was silent was the first time she saw his bare chest. He was aware of her eyes upon him, as he'd stood by the pod in his underwear, scrubbing himself with a sponge.

"What are you looking at?" he asked, feeling embarrassed.

She approached him, reaching out her hand, placing her fingers on his chest. Her eyes were wide. She was fascinated with him.

"What's wrong?" he asked.

She began to lift up the top section to the suit she wore.

"Stop," he said, turning his face away.

"Buzz, look Nahlah," she said.

He spun around at her use of English and gasped when he saw her. She had two sets of slits in her skin on either side of the lower part of her chest.

"Gills," he said, unable to stop himself from running his fingers across them. They stirred in response to his touch.

So that was how this planet's inhabitants managed to live underwater. They not only had webbing between their fingers and toes, but they had gills. He could never have imagined that. They weren't human at all. They were mermaids and mermen. Mer-people? It was astonishing.

Then Nahlah did what she always did when she was uncertain about something. She laughed.

She had a beautiful laugh. It had a way of winding itself around his insides and making him laugh, too.

He almost forgot about Neil, barely looking at his picture anymore when inside the pod. A drawing was no competition for a living, breathing companion—however she breathed. He couldn't remember hearing of an animal that could choose to breathe through either their lungs or their gills. Not even the extinct animals from ancient times. It was fascinating. His father would have loved it.

The thought of his father made him sad. He should be here with him now. If only Valentina hadn't resisted his pleas.

"Water?" he asked Nahlah every day, begging her to take him to the others.

She'd shake her head and point to his chest. She was right. There was little sense in going there. He wouldn't be able to join her under the water. And what if they went and her parents found her and took her home with them? He'd never be able to follow. Then he'd be alone again. That wasn't a thought that filled him with joy.

He knew he'd never be able to find the water on his own, so eventually he stopped asking.

This was his life now, however strange it was, just the two of them living in a field surrounded by a forest. Life could be worse.

They soon grew tired of living in the pod. It was impossible to stand up in and Buzz craved the idea of living in a house once more.

Nobody was going to build him a house out here, so he made plans to build one himself. Nahlah watched with interest as he sketched his plans in the dirt with a stick. She soon realized what he was drawing and made suggestions, pointing out when his plans got too outlandish or he needed more thought with the construction process. It was fun to dream of building a ten-room mansion, but better to start with one room and go from there.

Together, they gathered strong branches, stripping them of their leaves and standing them upright, tethering them with rope from the parachute. But in the slightest breeze they fell over, tipping slowly at first, then coming crashing to the ground in a rush.

Each time they'd begin again, adding more support beams and tethering using different knots and loops. With each attempt, the house would get a little stronger.

This process went on for weeks. Building a house during the day, only to have it fall on their heads at night, leaving them scuttling to the pod for shelter. Thankfully the climate wasn't as cruel on Neron as it was on Earth. The nights were cold, but never freezing. Still, Buzz was determined to build a house that would last.

What he didn't realize he was also building, was a lasting bond with Nahlah. As they negotiated their plans, they learned to listen to each other. As they pushed down their disappointment at their failures, they learnt to console each other. And as they discovered new ways to do things, they learnt to respect each other. In this way, as the branches of their home were tied together, so were their hearts.

When the first room of their house was sturdy and complete, they didn't need to ask each other if they'd continue to make it bigger. They knew they would, and they worked to add a second room, deciding that one would be for sleeping and the other would be a living room and kitchen. The pod was used as a type of storeroom or workshop. It was where they'd sit when they drew up plans or when their roof leaked.

They constructed a small shack several yards from the house to be used as a toilet, digging a hole as deep as they could manage with their crude tools. They decided if the stench got too bad, they'd fill in the hole and move the shack elsewhere.

Their final construction was to add walls around the bathtub that Buzz had dug out near the well. They saw no need for a laundry, instead washing their clothes when they washed themselves. It saved both water and time.

Once the house was complete, they put their energy into making furniture to fill it with.

Nahlah wove them mattresses from long plant fronds and Buzz carved branches into chairs, tables and benches. The work became both their obsession and their savior. It kept them busy and stopped Buzz's mind from wandering back to planet Earth. He assumed it also kept Nahlah's mind from returning under the ocean.

Life wasn't easy, but it was satisfying, and Buzz realized that despite still feeling the pain of losing his father and sister, he'd never been happier. All his possessions and pastimes from back home that he'd thought made him happy, were so meaningless now. He didn't need a computer or a phone or television. He had more important things to do now. And so many of them.

He and Nahlah would rise with the sun and work hard until the daylight dipped below the horizon, falling into their beds with exhaustion. They had berries to collect in baskets woven by Nahlah, rabbits and birds to catch using slingshots she'd crafted from tree branches, and fires to light by rubbing sticks together. It took many failed attempts until they got that technique right. It also proved to be a good way to teach each other some of the more colorful words in their languages when their initial attempts failed to make as much as a wisp of smoke. They persisted though, knowing their survival depended on it. There could be no greater motivator than that.

Their house also required daily maintenance, as did their water catchment. Then there was their dwindling food supply from the pod. They knew it would run out eventually, so were careful to ration the food, confident that with each new day in the forest they would find more options to eat. They discovered roots and leaves from plants that tasted bitter at first, until their palates adjusted. There were fat grubs that lived beneath the soil and if they closed their eyes and swallowed them whole they could fill their stomachs without their brains realizing what they were doing. Then there were precious dandelions growing on the forest floor that could be eaten whole. They even found a clump of cacti with flesh that tasted like little pieces of heaven.

There were a few disasters that went along with discovering new foods and many times they went to bed with their stomachs groaning, but they used caution along with curiosity and eventually established a list of foods they knew were safe.

Life wasn't all work, though. They tried hard to leave at least a little bit of time in the day for fun so they could draw pictures in the dirt, climb trees, shoot targets with their slingshots or lie on their backs and make pictures out of the clouds.

It was the most satisfying existence Buzz could imagine. He was responsible for every aspect of his survival.

Each day presented new challenges, not all of them good. There was the time a bear wandered into their house looking for food, or another time when the rain came down as mud, ruining their water supply. A few times the wind changed direction to blow at them from across the forest and the air went hazy, filling their lungs with smog that they had to cough up for hours afterward. Then there was the time it rained so much they couldn't get their fire to light and had to go to bed hungry, or the time Buzz scraped his knee and it became infected. Buzz had almost convinced Nahlah to take him to the water for help when she remembered that her grandmother used the leaves from the bronak tree to draw out infection. She'd gone into the forest to look for some leaves, her lengthy absence leaving him sweating, both from the infection and the fear that he'd lost her to the ocean. Perhaps the memory of her grandmother had been too much and she'd decided to return. But she'd come back to him, as she always did.

He chose not to dwell on these hardships, preferring to remember the happy times—the way Nahlah danced around the fire at night, the way she laughed no matter how dire the situation and the way her eyes filled with love when she looked at him.

He longed to know the story behind how her hand had become scarred, but each time he tried to ask, she'd pretend she didn't understand, even though it was obvious she had. Eventually, he gave up asking. He also noticed she had a small patch of hair missing at the back of her head. She went to such great efforts to hide it that he never had the heart to let her know he'd seen it. So, he never asked her about that either. Nahlah was far more complicated than she let on, but then again so were most people.

As the weeks rolled into years, he could barely remember his life back on Earth. He loved his life on Neron.

Most of all he loved Nahlah.

She'd grown into a beautiful young woman. He was certain it happened overnight. One minute she'd been an elfin girl scaling to the tops of trees and the next she'd grown curves that made him blush and ache with desire. She'd let her hair grow long, keeping it tied in braids that trailed down her back. He almost forgot about the patch of hair that he knew was missing.

Having long ago outgrown the clothing she'd arrived in, Nahlah now wore the clothes his father had packed aboard the pod for Valentina. This had unsettled him at first, but he'd had to think of these as Nahlah's clothes. She needed them more than Valentina did.

He began to spend more time alone, embarrassed at the feelings she was awakening inside him. He loved her like a brother. It didn't feel right to love her as anything more. So why did he? He couldn't help it. It wasn't just that she was the only woman around—there could be a sea of women before him and still she'd be the one shining bright. There was something about her that drew him in.

He'd taken to sleeping in the living quarters of their small house. Lying by her side while she slept was becoming impossible. As a child, she'd slept tucked under his arm. He'd made her feel safe and he'd enjoyed the affection after so long alone in the pod. As she'd grown into a teenager she'd pulled away, perhaps sensing she was making him uncomfortable.

He woke one night to find her sitting beside him in the

living room. She was staring at him, the moonlight glinting off her fair hair. She was so beautiful.

"You scared me," he said, using her language. "I thought you were a bear."

She didn't laugh. She didn't even smile. Something was terribly wrong.

"I'm going home," she said.

"Home?" He was half asleep and confused. "You are home."

"No. Home. I'm going back to the water."

"That's fantastic." He sat up. "I've been asking you to take me there for years."

"No, Buzz. I'm going alone. You're not coming." Her arms were crossed. Her face devoid of expression.

"What's happened?" His held his breath. This was something he'd always feared. That he wouldn't be enough for her and she'd go back to her people, looking for more. She'd told him about her mother and sisters, her eyes stinging with pain as she said their names. He'd asked about a father or any brothers and her eyes had filled with a different kind of pain as she shook her head. He sensed there was more to this story, but just like her missing hair or scars on her hand, he'd never pressed her to tell him more. She'd tell him when she was ready.

"I thought you'd be happy to see me go," she said.

"Happy? I don't understand. You're my whole world, Nahlah. I don't want to live without you. I don't even know if I can live without you."

"You'll be fine. You don't need me here. You've made that obvious."

So that was it. She thought the distance he'd placed between them meant he didn't care, when it was in fact the opposite. He cared too much.

"I'm coming with you," he said. "If you don't take me, I'll follow you."

"You'll never find your way. You'll get lost and end up getting eaten by a bear."

She stood.

"I thought you said you belonged here in the forest," he said, getting desperate.

"I thought I did, too. And maybe I do. But I miss my family. I need to be someplace where people want me."

He couldn't believe it. She was really going.

"Don't leave me, Nahlah. Please. *I* want you. I … I love you." He got to his feet and found her hands in the dim light. He drew them upward so their palms were touching. The webbing between her fingers was no longer strange. It was part of Nahlah, and her hands would seem odd without these soft webs of skin.

She pressed her palms against him, and his stomach clenched into knots at the close contact. It was time to tell her how he felt.

"Do you remember when we first met?" he asked.

"Of course, I remember."

"You saved my life."

"We saved each other's lives."

"You held my hands like this. Then you touched me like this."

He put his fingers lightly on her face and stroked the soft contours of her cheeks. He drew in the scent of her. They had no perfumes or soaps to use out here, yet she smelt like a flower freshly picked from the forest. He'd always thought it was the innocence of her soul he could smell.

"You were just a child when we met," he said. "I came to think of you as my sister, but lately I don't know what's happened. You've…grown. And you're beautiful. It scares me. You mean everything to me. *Everything*. I pulled away from you because I was scared if you knew how I felt, you'd run away."

"How do you feel, Buzz?" She was still tense. He didn't have her forgiveness.

He hesitated. If he told her how he felt, surely she would run away. But wasn't that what she was doing anyway?

"I love you," he said. "More than that. I'm in love with you."

She stepped forward, closing the gap. Her hands slid to his shoulders and she urged him toward her. Their lips met, and he tasted the softness of her mouth. Desire lit his every cell as he deepened the kiss.

She responded with a hungry urgency and soon they dropped to the floor, desperate to feel the deepest connection of their souls.

They didn't need a ceremony to seal their commitment to each other. Their actions were their vows. Their kisses were their promise. They knew they'd be together forever.

Once more, Buzz felt like Adam—the first man to draw breath.

Only now he had his Eve.

PART III
NAHLAH

CHAPTER FIVE

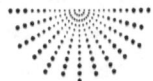

*N*ahlah wasn't sure when she first felt life stirring within her belly. The realization came to her slowly, seeping through her consciousness in waves until it broke through with such force it woke her from her dreams.

She sat up, goose bumps tingling down her arms.

"What's the matter?" asked Buzz, placing a hand on her. The coolness of his skin made her feel like she was on fire.

"I have life," she said.

"What do you mean?" His voice was croaky, as it always was when he woke. Normally she found this endearing, but not today.

"Life. I have life."

"I don't understand. What does that mean? You're alive?"

She sighed.

The language barrier had been hard to break through, but most of the time they managed to understand each other. It was like they had their own special language—a combination of both of theirs, although Buzz insisted on mainly speaking hers. He said he was in her world now. He needed to know how to speak her language more than she needed to speak his. At times like this, she got frustrated. Clearly, his language used another expression for having life.

"A baby," she said, pointing to her stomach, wondering what else she had to do to make him understand.

"You're pregnant?" He sat up next to her, his hands flying to her belly.

"Pregnant," she repeated, as was their habit whenever one of them used a word they'd never heard.

"How do you know?" he asked between deep breaths. Was he taking this as good news? She realized she was happy. She wanted him to be happy, too.

"I just know," she said.

"I'm so sorry." He took his hands from her and buried his face in them. His deep breaths weren't from joy. He was upset.

"You're sorry?"

"How did this happen?"

"You know how it happened." She was astonished. In the many times she'd imagined having Buzz's baby, she'd never thought he'd react like this. She'd been sure he'd be as thrilled as she was. Raising a family in the forest would be difficult, but they could do it. They could do anything when they put their minds to it. Nobody would've bet on their survival out here, but they'd not only survived, they'd thrived. They'd built a wonderful life. Why not share it with children? It was a natural progression.

He started rocking back and forth, causing their woven mattress to crackle under his weight. She hadn't seen him this upset since...had she ever seen him this upset?

"You must've realized this would happen eventually." She drew her knees to her chest and wrapped her arms around them.

"No, I didn't realize. How would I?"

He'd lost his mind. Either that or he had no idea about

reproduction. She knew he'd grown up without his mother, but surely his father had explained to him how these things worked.

"Buzz...that thing we've been doing...we made life." She was struggling to find the right words. Was it really up to her to tell him how a baby was made?

"But people haven't made life like that for hundreds of years," he said. "I didn't even think it was possible anymore."

"What do you mean? How else do you make life?" She knew things had been done differently on his planet, but she'd always assumed this was a universal concept.

"The doctors make the life. They take a girl's eggs from her when she's a baby. Then when she's grown up and ready, they take a sample from her mate and make the baby."

"And they implant it in her womb?"

"No, she doesn't have a womb. They take that when they take the eggs. They grow the baby in a pod."

"That's horrible." She was disgusted. How impersonal was that? For a baby to grow without the comfort of its mother's voice. Without a voice to be heard. Babies weren't vegetables to be grown in farms. They were human beings.

"It's not horrible. It's just the way it is. Carrying a child inside you is dangerous."

"Buzz, it's not the way it is. It's the way your people made it. *This* is the way it is." She reached for his hand and placed it on her belly. "This is your child inside me. A child that's part you and part me. *We* made it. Not a doctor. Just us."

His hand softened in her grasp and he stroked her belly. Gentle, slow movements—the kind that were responsible for getting her in this state in the first place.

He was so handsome. She'd loved him the moment she'd first seen him wandering through the forest, oblivious to the danger he was in. Maybe she'd even loved him before that. He'd taken her breath away despite the fact she'd only been a child. She'd fallen instantly in love with him and his strange fingers that dangled from his hand without any webbing to hold them together. She was amazed they didn't fall off. Then there were all his other differences. His skin and hair were dark. Nobody on Neron had features like that.

He'd been tall back then, but had grown even taller, his body lined with a fine layer of muscle that made him look like some kind of strong, lean giant.

But that wasn't what had hypnotized her into falling in love with him. It was his eyes. They were like black pools of liquid and she'd feel herself sinking into their depths whenever she looked directly into them.

She'd had no chance really, although when she first met him it was probably more of a crush than actual romantic love—she'd been too young for that—but it'd taken her by such force that she'd known instantly she'd never leave his side. He was hers and she longed for him to make her belong to him.

It'd taken him a lot longer to catch up to the way she felt, but he'd gotten there eventually. As she'd grown into a woman, rather than drawing closer to her like she'd hoped he would, he'd pulled away. He didn't seem to want her there, sleeping in the living room and avoiding looking at her when she spoke to him. She knew her body had changed and thought he was repulsed by her new curves. It was obvious now that repulsion was the opposite to the way he was feeling, but without a friend to ask for an opinion or a mother from whom to seek advice, she'd had to draw her own conclusions.

She'd been so offended, she considered going home to the ocean. She missed her mother and living with Buzz behaving as if she were a stranger was too much to bear. But there were other things under the ocean that were even harder to bear. She hadn't been ready to face them. Nor had she been ready to leave the forest.

Or Buzz.

So, she'd threatening him with leaving, when in reality she wasn't going anywhere. Not then and not ever. Sometimes she felt guilty for lying to him like that but telling him she was leaving was what had prompted the change in their relationship. She'd forced him to open up to her and as a result they'd grown closer than she'd ever thought possible.

His hand stroking her belly like this felt so good. She'd made the right decision—in both making an empty threat and deciding to stay.

"How will the baby come out?" he asked, his face still heavy with shock.

"The same way it got in." She laughed, trying to break him out of his mood. "Buzz, are you happy about this, or not?"

"I'm scared, I suppose."

She noticed his shoulders relax. He was loosening up.

"The baby will be fine, I promise."

"It's not the baby I'm scared for. It's you. It just doesn't seem natural."

"There's nothing more natural."

"You know, Valentina used to wonder if our mother had carried us in her womb like that, if she'd have stuck around, but I always said she was being ridiculous."

Nahlah nodded. "If your mother wanted to leave, she would've left, whether she carried you or not."

"True."

"So, I'm going to ask you one more time. Are you happy about this baby?" She closed her eyes and prayed to hear the answer she needed.

"I'm happy," he whispered. "Scared, but happy."

"Please don't be scared. For if you are, then I have to be, too. And I can't do this if I'm scared."

"I'm happy," he said again.

She knew his words weren't true but hoped with all her heart that one day they would be. Surely he'd love his child. He loved her. She felt that with every cell of her body. They were meant to be together.

When the shadow from Buzz's pod had crossed the watery sky of her underwater world she'd been making one of her many secret trips to the forest. She broke through the surface of the water to see Buzz's pod in the sky with the silver parachute trailing behind, catching the light and shining so brightly she had to shield her eyes. It was the most beautiful thing she'd ever seen.

She wasn't the only one to see it. Some workers had turned their heads to see what had turned day into night.

But Nahlah was the only one who followed it into the forest. It seemed to only be calling her name.

As a young girl, she'd heard stories about how people had once lived on the land. It was said that if you went to the surface you could still see the homes they lived in. None of her friends seemed to know if this was true or not as nobody had ever gone to look. She'd suggested it once and they'd laughed at her, not realizing she was serious.

So, she'd snuck away from school and taken the decompression tunnel to the surface alone. There were others in the tunnel, workers responsible for maintaining critical systems like the air vents that pumped oxygen into shops and homes. She'd had to hide, crouching down in her seat in case someone thought to ask why a girl of no more than six years of age was traveling unaccompanied to the surface. Her mother would never let her out of the house again if she found out.

She remained hidden in her seat until the workers cleared the tunnel. From there she swam quickly to the shoreline, gasping at the feeling of dry sand under her feet as she emerged from the water.

The first thing she noticed about life on the surface was the noise. When she was underwater, the only sound she could hear was the water passing through her gills and sometimes the beating of her heart. Even when she was inside her home, using her lungs to breathe, there was a silence that hung in the air as the water insulated their life from their surroundings.

But not here. Here, the trees made a noise as the wind moved through their leaves. It was like they were whispering to her, beckoning her to step beneath their canopy into the forest that loomed before her. She listened more closely and heard a sound. Not just one sound. Many sounds. Whistling and chirping that filled her soul with peace. The forest was singing to her and this was how she knew it was her friend. She felt safe here, belonging in a way she'd never felt she belonged to any place before.

She didn't dare venture far into the forest that first day. She was too afraid she'd become lost. There were secrets in there. Secrets she was determined to unlock, but she knew if she tried to solve them all at once she'd fail.

So, she became a regular visitor to the forest, skipping school as often as she could without drawing too much attention to herself. Sometimes months would pass between her visits. At other times, only days. With each visit she ventured further, learning more about not just the forest, but the other creatures that called it home.

The whistling in the trees came from birds, every size and color imaginable. There were tiny insects with shells the color of the sun and large beasts covered in fur the color of night. There were trees wonderful for climbing and resting in their branches and others that left red marks upon her skin. She watched which berries the animals ate and which they left alone, just as she learned which animals were a threat and which posed her no harm.

Sometimes, she'd sit in the forest with a sketchpad and draw the things she saw, feeling strangely like she'd done this before.

The forest became part of her. She longed to tell her two sisters about it but knew this would be a mistake. They wouldn't understand. They never understood anything when it came to Nahlah, looking at her as if she'd come from another planet. She'd often wondered if perhaps she had.

It was for this reason that when she'd seen Buzz's pod soaring through the sky, something had lit inside her, reminding her of the day she'd first seen the forest. It was almost as if she'd been awaiting his arrival.

As she'd left the ocean to follow the pod into the forest, she knew she'd never return. *This* was how humans were meant to live. She felt it in the deepest part of her soul. *This* was her home and if there was life contained within the pod *that* was her family.

She knew now this was simplistic thinking. Or wishful thinking perhaps, because there were times that she missed her mother so much her heart physically ached. Although, she supposed that in many ways she'd been right. The forest had become her home and Buzz most certainly had become her family. And now their family was growing. Soon, two would become three.

She still found his dark skin a constant source of fascination. His deep brown eyes drew her in just as they had the moment she'd first seen them. He hadn't seemed to change too much over the years. He'd just stretched taller, his hands had grown broader, and his feet were so big she wondered how he didn't trip over them. She'd come to envy the strange way his digits sat separate without any webbing. It was certainly more practical for life upon the land. His hair fell to his shoulders in messy waves that he insisted she cut for him. His beard had become far too difficult to shave, so instead he trimmed it as short as he could without using a razor.

He looked so different to anyone she'd seen before. It had been such a long time since her people had lived underneath the sun. They'd become so pale that blue lines could be seen underneath their skin as blood pumped in their veins. And their hair was kept short, a necessity for life underwater. How she'd loved growing her hair long as she'd embraced her new life in the forest. It was like a badge of honor that she wore with pride. It also covered one of her darkest secrets. She was glad Buzz had never noticed her missing clump of hair because that wasn't a story she wanted to tell. Stories like that didn't belong in the forest.

She wondered what their baby would look like. Dark or fair? Like Buzz or like her?

He shifted his weight in the bed and sighed.

"Go back to sleep, Ardorna," she said, using the name she'd given him long ago. The word didn't translate easily into Buzz's language, but it was the word used to describe the feeling when you recognize someone from a life gone by —not with your eyes, but with your heart.

"I can't sleep," he said. "I don't think I'll ever sleep again."

She laughed.

"You'll sleep again." She lay on her side and traced gentle circles on his temples. This never failed to send him to sleep and soon he was breathing deeply once more.

She looked at him in the dim light. Her Ardorna. Had she really known him in a past life? Did past lives even exist? Buzz had said his sister had thought so. It did make a lot of sense. It certainly explained why she felt like she did about him, despite him being such a boolah when she'd first laid eyes upon him. Who would choose to sleep in the den of a grizzly bear?

Buzz would. He could be as naïve as he could be brilliant. He fascinated her now, just as he'd fascinated her then. To think he could've traveled from the other side of the universe only to be eaten by a bear within hours of his arrival. It was comical. It was also one of the reasons she loved him so much.

He needed her just as much as she needed him. Nobody back home in her life under the ocean had needed her. Her sisters certainly hadn't. They'd ignored her most of the time. Her brother hadn't needed her, either. She shuddered at the thought of him, quickly pushing him from her mind as she turned her mind to her mother, who was always so busy working it didn't feel like she'd had much use for Nahlah. Her father died before she was born (or to be more precise, he died *while* she was being born), so that ruled him out, too. She doubted anyone had even noticed she was missing yet.

She often told herself this, despite knowing it wasn't true. How would she feel if her baby grew up and disappeared without so much as a word of goodbye? In truth, she hadn't even grown up when she disappeared. She'd still been a girl, so young that the first night she'd arrived she'd slept in the crook of Buzz's arm so she could pretend he was her mother.

Still, she hadn't had much choice. Walking into the forest that day had been her destiny. She'd felt it then, just as she felt it now.

She rubbed her stomach, wondering about the life that had begun to grow inside her. Did she deserve to be a mother after the way she'd cast her own mother aside? Perhaps this baby would run away to live under the ocean, inflicting upon her what Buzz had described as "karma".

With any luck, the baby would be born like him, without gills, unable to ever leave her side.

This wasn't a fair wish for her baby. It should have the choice in where it wanted to live, just as she'd had herself.

"Do you think it's a boy or a girl?" asked Buzz, drowsily.

"I thought you were asleep."

"Not yet. So, boy or girl?"

"A boy, I think. A boy, just like you."

"Then I think it's a girl, just like you."

"Sleep now." She took her hands from her belly and returned them to his forehead.

It didn't really matter what either of them thought the baby was. The universe had already decided. She had no choice but to trust it, just as she always had. Whatever was meant to be, would be.

Giving life was painful. More painful than Nahlah had imagined was possible. By the time she realized the pain was going to be too much for her, it was too late to seek help under the ocean.

She yearned for her mother like never before. Had giving life to her hurt as much as this? If only she were here now to stroke her forehead and tell her everything would be all right.

Instead, she had Buzz, hovering around, looking as if he was the one having his insides torn apart.

She should've known he'd be like this from the way he'd behaved in the months leading up to this day. The more her belly had protruded, the more he'd retreated. Having never seen a woman with life before, he seemed more frightened than fascinated, more perplexed than he was pleased.

This attitude had hurt, and his actions planted a seed that grew inside her like a vine, its roots twisting around her innards and piercing tiny holes in her heart.

She'd asked him about it, and he said he was worried about losing her.

"You're jealous," she shouted. "You want to keep me to yourself."

"I'm not," he protested.

"You are. Just because your father loved your sister more than you, doesn't mean—"

The expression on his face made her stop mid-sentence. She'd hit a nerve. He'd told her many times about Valentina's close relationship with their father, claiming it never bothered him, although it was obvious it did. Pretending he didn't care was his way of dealing with it. She could understand that. Clearly right now he was worried about their little family of two becoming three, no doubt picturing himself standing on the sidelines once more.

She wanted to tell him his worries were false and he had nothing to be concerned about, but it wasn't true. She still loved him of course, but already she loved this baby more than him. It was part of her, being fed oxygen from her lungs, its heart beating inside her like a drum.

When she'd met Buzz, she'd thought he was her destiny. Perhaps the path she thought was leading her to him was actually leading her to this child that now grew in her belly.

She'd ceased crying in pain hours earlier. It took too much energy. Instead she concentrated on her breathing, counted each bead of sweat that dropped from her forehead and clawed at her thighs with every contraction. Maybe Buzz had been right. There had to be better ways to bring babies into the world.

"I don't know what to do." Buzz clutched his own belly as if in pain. "I don't know how to help you."

He touched her forehead, his shaking hands irritating her. She pushed him away, even though what she wanted to do was draw him close.

"Promise me you'll look after the baby if I …" Her words fell into a whisper. There was no point finishing the sentence. He knew what she was going to say. It didn't seem right to speak of death in a moment that was supposed to be about life. It was her baby's birthday. The day this child would celebrate in years to come in memory of the first breath they drew. Would it also be the day this child would mourn the loss of their mother, just as she'd had to mourn her father each year she turned a new age?

"You're not going to die," said Buzz, determination plastered to his face.

He went to the end of the bed and gasped.

"I can see the head. I can see our baby's head."

He sounded shocked. Amazed. What else was he expecting to see?

She summoned all her remaining energy and with one almighty push, felt the baby slide from her, straight into its father's hands. It was both the most agonizing and exhilarating feeling she'd experienced.

"It's a girl," he said, tears streaming down his face as he looked into his daughter's eyes. "She's perfect."

"Let me see her."

He took a knife from his belt, cut the umbilical cord in just the way she'd told him he'd need to, then placed the baby on her chest. For a moment she didn't think he was going to hand her over, so close seemed their bond.

The baby cried out, the pitch and volume startling Nahlah. How could someone so small make such a loud noise?

"My sweet baby girl," she said, running her hands over the baby's chest, realizing her wish had come true. This perfect child was exactly the way she'd hoped. She had no gills, which meant she was unable to leave her in the same way she'd left her own mother.

She held out her finger and her daughter clutched it tightly, her cries coming in short angry gasps.

"You're a noisy little thing," said Nahlah, fighting back tears of her own as she prized her daughter's tiny fingers apart and saw they had no webbing. She was a miniature, female version of Buzz. Her skin was a lighter shade of brown than his, but still far darker than any other human to be born on Neron. She was more beautiful than Nahlah could have ever imagined.

"She looks just like you," said Nahlah, wondering if her own genes had made any kind of impact on this child.

"But she sounds like you," said Buzz, laughing.

Nahlah smiled, regretting how harsh she'd been on him. He'd only been scared for her. Now that she'd experienced the pain of giving life, she knew his fears had been for good reason.

"Thank you, Ardorna," she said. "I'm sorry I've been..."

"No! Please don't. It's me who's sorry. Really I am. But now that I see our baby, I know that this was right." He pressed his lips first to Nahlah's brow then his daughter's.

The baby silenced at his touch, blinking at him with her unfocussed eyes.

"Can we call her Valentina?" asked Buzz, his pupils wide with hope.

Nahlah tensed. How could she tell Buzz that she'd named this baby as soon as she'd known it existed, hoping it was a girl? There was only one name she wanted to give this child. She had her father's skin and gill-less chest, surely she could at least have the name Nahlah had chosen for her? Her own mother's name. It was the best way she could think of to keep her mother close.

"I was hoping to name her Eevangela," she said. "We can call her Eevie."

Buzz nodded, unable to hide his disappointment. "Of course. Your mother would like that."

A sharp pain stabbed at her abdomen that went beyond the guilt for not wanting to give this baby Buzz's sister's name. Something wasn't right.

"Take her," she said, gesturing to Eevie, without the strength to hold her in the air.

"Are you okay?" He took Eevie in his arms.

"I'm fine," she said. "Please, just leave me for a moment. Take care of our baby."

She wasn't fine, but so besotted was Buzz with his daughter that he listened to her words instead of looking into her eyes. He carried their daughter into the living room.

The pain came again, this time worse than before. She fought the urge to push, worried about what might happen if she did.

Then she realized.

This birth wasn't done yet. There was another baby. Just like her father, Eevie was a twin.

Nahlah remembered her son entering the world. She remembered joy breaking through pain as she saw his tiny set of gills and webbed fingers and toes. She remembered the way he screamed as if angry to have been ejected from the safety of her womb. She remembered the shocked look on Buzz's face as he ran back to her side, still clutching Eevie to his chest.

That was all.

The rest was darkness.

She'd fallen into the kind of sleep one can only have when teetering on the brink of life and death. There she balanced as she waited for the hand that would push her one way or the other.

When she finally woke, her first thought was one of surprise. She'd been certain death would win the battle.

Her second thought was one of panic. Where were her babies? How long had she been asleep?

"Buzz," she called out, realizing she was alone.

She tried to sit up but was still too weak. She lay naked in the heat of the room, a damp piece of cloth pressed to her forehead and a blanket woven from leaves covering her from the waist down.

"Buzz," she called again.

There was a noise in the next room, followed by footsteps.

"Nahlah! Oh, Nahlah, thank goodness. You're awake."

He ran to her side and covered her cheeks with kisses.

She studied him closely. What news did he have for her? She couldn't hear the babies crying. Had they survived?

"The babies?" she asked.

"They're fine." He grinned at her. "They're better than fine. They're amazing."

"Where are they?" Her voice was a whisper, but Buzz had no trouble hearing her. He never had.

"I'll bring them to you."

He left the room, returning moments later, carrying the large basket she'd made for collecting berries. She saw he'd lined it with soft leaves and some of the silver fabric from the parachute. Inside were her babies. Her precious, sleeping babies, both with skin the color of their father. Only one with gills like her own.

He placed the basket next to her on the bed and she reached inside, touching first her son's cheek and then her daughter's. Buzz was right. They were amazing. Two little miracles when she'd been expecting only one.

"How long was I asleep?"

"Three days."

"How did you feed them?"

He knew nothing about babies. Surely he hadn't fed them rainwater. That could have fatal consequences.

"I put them to your breast, and they fed from you." He looked at the floor, seeming embarrassed. "I wasn't sure what I was supposed to do."

"That's exactly what you were supposed to do." She was pleased to know she'd had some input into keeping them alive, despite being present in body only for these first few important days.

Eevie stirred in the basket, scrunching up her tiny face.

Buzz placed his hand gently on her chest and she instantly drifted back to sleep.

Nahlah watched on in amazement. She'd underestimated Buzz. Why had she convinced herself he didn't care? Tears of shame stung her eyes.

"We can call her Valentina if you like," she said.

He shook her head. "She's Eevie now. It wouldn't be right to change it."

Despite her offer being genuine, she was relieved he'd refused.

"Then we should call him Xander," she said, touching their son on the soft skin of his leg.

"No, not Xander." He sounded adamant.

"Why not?" She was surprised.

"Just not Xander. You name him. Please. The whole time you've been asleep I've been waiting for you to give him a name."

"Then let's call him Shadow."

"Shadow?" He laughed. "That's not a name."

"It is now."

"Why Shadow?"

"When you landed here on Neron, a shadow passed over my world. I followed it and it brought me here to you. That shadow turned out to be my sunshine."

She saw a softness pass over his eyes.

"Shadow's a perfect name," he said.

CHAPTER SIX

he following weeks seemed to be lived in fast forward. Nahlah was still so weak, unable to stand for more than a few moments at a time.

Buzz, on the other hand, barely sat still as he rushed between her and their babies, doing his best to ensure they all thrived.

The longing Nahlah felt to see her mother continued to burn, haunting her when she slept, nagging at the recesses of her mind when she was awake.

The babies may have the dark features of their father, but she'd started to see a little of her own family in the slope of Eevie's nose, the shape of Shadow's eyes, the webbing between his fingers and toes. They were her children as much as they belonged to Buzz. Not one like him and one like her, but both a little like each of them.

She saw no sign of her brother though, which pleased her. Some genes were better off not passed on. As always, when she thought of her brother, she immediately drowned him out with memories of her mother. Buzz didn't even know she had a brother, that was how determined she was to pretend he no longer existed. Talking about him would make him real. His name didn't belong in this beautiful forest.

She hugged Eevie to her chest—the child without gills that her own mother would never meet unless she was prepared to come to the surface. That was as likely as her flying to another planet in Buzz's pod, which still lay silently in the field beside their house.

Perhaps she could teach Shadow to use his gills when he was older and take him to her mother. She could show him where she'd grown up, the house she'd lived in deep under the ocean, her school and the parks she'd played in. She'd love to see how her sisters had grown and tell them about the strange life she'd made for herself. But what if she saw *him*? No, Shadow was better off sticking to breathing with his lungs.

Eevie stirred in the basket beside her. She reached down and stroked the smooth skin of her bare chest. The thought of leaving her chased her underwater fantasy from her mind. She could never take Shadow and leave Eevie behind. It wouldn't be right.

She knew that as much as becoming a mother had brought her closer to her own mother—in her thoughts if not in reality—the opposite had occurred for Buzz.

Not with his mother. He'd never known her. It was the memory of his father he seemed to have withdrawn from. She was still surprised he hadn't wanted to name Shadow after him.

She asked him about it in the quiet of the afternoon when the babies were asleep.

"It's hard to explain," he said.

"Why? You used to tell me everything," she pressed.

"You really want to know?"

"That's why I'm asking."

"I looked up to my father. That was one reason I joined

the space program. Mainly, it was my fascination with the universe, but there was a small part of me that desperately wanted his approval. I wanted him to love me in the same way he loved Valentina, even if I didn't admit it to myself at the time."

This was what she'd always suspected and was pleased to hear him say it. "So, what's changed?" Her voice was gentle, as if she could ease his pain with words.

"He saved my life. I'd be dead if it wasn't for him. And when I landed here, my admiration for him grew tenfold. A hundredfold. He was my hero. Then…"

"Then what?"

"Then I became a father myself. Two children born on the same day. A boy and girl. Just like he had. When you were asleep and I held them in my arms, I looked at their little faces and I just knew I couldn't choose one of them over the other. Not now. Not ever."

"Your father didn't choose—" She let her words trail away. His father had chosen Valentina over him. Buzz knew that. There was no point denying it.

"I'm not just talking about the pod. It was everything. She was always the one. He loved me, but I can't explain how he was with her. It was like she was his everything. The only thing that really mattered to him. I'm not even certain he really cared that our mother wasn't around. He didn't need her. He had what he needed. He had Valentina."

"I'm sure he cared. It couldn't have been easy for him raising you both on his own."

"You don't get it. He had two children. Two. Not one. I was his child just as much as she was. I'd never do that to our children. They're both mine—ours. I'll never make one feel inferior to the other."

"I know you wouldn't," she said.

"I used to pretend it didn't bother me. But it does. It really does."

"Of course, it does," she soothed. "And that's okay."

"He left me, Nahlah. He left me."

She reached for him and he laid his head in her lap, tears streaming down his cheeks. In all they'd been through together, she'd never before seen him cry. The wound his father had inflicted had been driven deeply. And he'd kept the pain deep inside, never dealing with it, never letting it go. Until now when it had risen to the surface, leaving him raw and in pain.

She was glad she'd come to the forest to find him, unable to imagine what his life would have been like if she hadn't. And she was just as glad that she'd never left. He was a good man. He didn't deserve to be left again. Someone needed to choose him first.

As the twins grew from babies into toddlers, then children who could walk and talk and swing from trees, it became more and more obvious to Nahlah that someone else had chosen Buzz first.

It was Eevie.

She was smart, she was strong, she was stubborn. And her loyalty lay squarely in the hands of her father. Nahlah knew she loved her too, but it was a different kind of love. Her daughter's love for her father bordered on obsession.

She followed him around by day and slept by his side at night, her little fingers curled tightly around his arm in case he decided to make an escape. She helped him collect wood for the fire, repair holes in the roof and scavenge for roots or grubs for their dinner.

Nahlah often joked that they'd given their babies their

names the wrong way around. It was Eevie who should've been called Shadow.

For a man who'd once thought he'd never see another human being, Buzz had adjusted remarkably well to having barely a single minute of his day to himself.

Occasionally he'd throw his hands in the air and ask Eevie to please give him a moment, but she'd cross her arms and scowl until he relented and took her with him wherever it was he needed to go. She even stood outside the small shack they used as a bathroom and waited for him when privacy was demanded.

As a result of Eevie having staked her claim, Nahlah noticed Shadow drifting closer and closer to her. He helped her weave fabrics from the soft fronds of the ferns that grew deep in the forest. He collected ash from their fire and sat by her side as she mixed it with water and drew pictures on pieces of bark. He climbed with her high in the trees as they hunted rabbits with their slingshots.

But his favorite thing to do in all the forest was to make music. She helped him carve woodwind instruments out of timber and fashion drums from rabbit skins and they'd sit side-by-side, experimenting with noises and sounds, making up words to go with them. Nahlah would marvel at her son and the way music lit not only a torch behind his eyes, but a fire within his soul.

Sometimes Buzz and Eevie would join them and the four of them would play music until their hands ached, their voices were hoarse, and their troubles felt light. Then they'd lie on the ground and listen as Buzz told stories about his own father's love for music, describing how the pod was once able to play the most spectacular music. It seemed almost cruel that Shadow was the one person who would appreciate hearing that the most, yet he never got to. The music in the pod had stopped playing the moment it had touched the ground.

Nahlah didn't know a lot about twins, but she knew enough to realize that the relationship between her twins was an unusual one. They weren't bonded like normal twins were supposed to be, preferring the company of their parents to each other. Although, Shadow seemed to be longing for the company of someone else entirely.

Sometimes she'd catch him staring out at the forest almost as if he was waiting for someone. He'd ask her questions about her life under the water and the people she'd known, listening intently as if looking for some kind of clue. She felt sad for keeping him in the forest. It wasn't how a boy was supposed to grow up. She couldn't blame him if he felt like something wasn't right. It was exactly the way she'd felt when she'd run away.

Every evening after they'd cleared away the meal they'd shared as a family, Buzz would insist on taking Shadow into the pod for some man time, as he called it. They'd climb in and close the hatch as best they could. Eevie would sit on the ground and wail until she ran out of tears. Nahlah would hold her, stroking her hair, wondering if her beautiful daughter would always pine for her father like this. What if something were to happen to him? Would she be able to cope?

This evening ritual was difficult for Nahlah, but she understood its importance. Buzz needed Shadow to know that he loved him, too. As much as he loved Eevie, despite his connection with her. Surely it was only a matter of time before Eevie stopped her tears and turned to look at her mother. If only she'd do that, she'd see a woman who loved her without limits.

She asked Buzz what he and Shadow spoke of in the pod.

"Everything and nothing," he replied.

She asked Shadow and got the same answer.

That made her smile.

This was how the simple life she and Buzz had led before the children, became simple once more. New routines replaced old routines as two became four. Life was busier and happier. It was sadder, too.

Becoming a mother had seemed to result in Nahlah's highs reaching new heights and her lows dragging her lower than ever before. The more she fell in love with her new family, the more she missed her old one. The more she loved her children, the more she missed her mother.

As the years passed and twins grew into adolescence, she found her melancholy growing. Fighting it made her weary.

She withdrew from life, lying in her bed until the sun was high in the sky. Occasionally she was still there when the moon took over its watch for the night. She felt like the energy had been sapped from her bones. She no longer drew pictures, hunted rabbits, participated in the evening meal or played music with Shadow.

"Why are you so tired?" Eevie would ask.

"Please, leave me alone," she'd say, not wanting to tell her the truth. Not even understanding the truth herself.

Buzz would ask her what was wrong, and she'd shrug. So, just as he'd pulled away from her when she had life, he pulled away from her now. He kept out of her way, focusing all his attention on their children. This seemed to be the way with Buzz. The more he feared losing her, the more distance he placed between them. Only this time she didn't mind. This time she wanted to be left alone.

Occasionally she'd feel guilty about what was happening to her. She was stronger than this. This wasn't who she was. But the guilt never lasted long. It took too much energy to hold onto.

Shadow spent hours sitting in the corner of the room

watching her sleep. Often, he played her music, gently tapping on a small drum or plucking the strings of one of his crudely made guitars. She'd given up asking him to go away. He never did. It seemed she'd given him the right name after all. He didn't speak to her, just watched her as if waiting for her to make the first move.

In the end it was he who spoke first.

"It's my birthday soon," he said. "Eevie's, too."

She opened her eyes. His dark eyes were cast down, his mouth pulled into a false smile. He was handsome like his father had been at his age. Broad shoulders, long legs, strong hands. It was a shame he'd never become a father himself.

"Sixteen," she said, hardly able to believe the number. The time had gone so fast.

"Sixteen," he repeated. "The same age you were when I was born."

She nodded, knowing what he said was true, yet feeling that at sixteen she'd been far older than the twins were now. She couldn't imagine Eevie having a baby.

"I'm going to the water," he said.

Her eyes were no longer just open. Those words had launched her back into full consciousness, her focus on the world so sharp it hurt.

"You're not," she said. This was her nightmare coming true. The moment she'd first seen the gills on his tiny chest, she feared this day would come.

"I'm not sure you'll be able to carry this bed to the water to stop me."

"Your father won't let you." Buzz was sure to stop him. There was no way he'd let Shadow go.

"How will he know? You won't tell him. That would require you to actually talk to him."

She winced. "I talk to him."

"Not like you used to." Shadow was right. But how could she tell him that the reason behind this? It wasn't simple.

"What's wrong with you, Mom?"

"Shadow, come here."

She swung her legs out of bed and beckoned him. This moment reminded her of the time she'd threatened Buzz with leaving. The night that changed everything when Buzz finally told her the truth about his feelings. Maybe it was time for her to do the same.

Shadow sat next to her on the bed.

"Don't leave me," she said.

"Why not? You left us a long time ago now."

"No, I didn't! I thought about it, but I never did."

"Well, I wish you did."

"Shadow!' She was shocked. He'd never spoken to her like this and his words stung.

"It might've hurt less if when you left, we didn't still have to look at you every day. For a long time, you've been somewhere else in your head, if not your body."

She fell silent. What he said was true. She thought she'd hidden her yearning for the water and her mother who lived within its depths, but clearly she'd been as transparent as the water itself. The forest was still her home and she knew she'd needed to come here, but more often now she'd begun to wonder if that was for a reason bigger than herself. As if the forest had called her to live beneath its canopy in order for her children to be born.

"I want to see it for myself," said Shadow. "I want to meet people I'm not related to. I want to meet people I *am* related to as well. I can't help but feel like something important is missing from my life. Some*one* important. I want to use my gills and see where you came from. I want to see this world you can't seem to let go of. Do you know what it feels like to never have had a friend?"

"You have Eevie," she whispered.

He raised his eyebrows without needing to respond. They both knew Eevie wasn't his friend. She was his sister on the rare occasions she wasn't busy being Buzz's daughter. Her bond with her father was as strong as it had been the day she was born. Even if she had been born with gills, Nahlah knew she'd never have to have this conversation with her. Eevie would never leave her father's side.

"You can't stop me, Mom."

"You'll get lost. You don't know your way to the water." This wasn't true. She knew he'd find his way if he wanted to desperately enough. She'd been a lot younger than sixteen when she'd made the journey in reverse.

"I do know my way. While you've been busy sleeping, I've been busy exploring. Just be happy I told you. I could've left without saying goodbye, just like you did."

She closed her eyes and drew in a breath.

"Sorry," he said.

"No, it's true. I did do that. And I regret it every day."

"You regret meeting Dad and having us?" His eyes pricked with tears.

"No, Shadow! Not that. I love your father and I'll never regret the life we have together. But I do regret the pain I must've caused my mother. There must have been a better way."

"Then I'll tell her you said sorry." He crossed his arms, still clearly determined to leave.

"I'm sorry I've let you down," she said. "If you stay, I'll be a real mother again. The kind I was when you were a child. We had fun back then, didn't we?"

She hauled herself out of bed and stood to show she was serious.

"It's too late," he said. "I've made up my mind. I'm sorry."

She felt herself losing the argument. There was nothing she could say to make him stay. Nothing that could tie him here to the life they'd built in the forest. He didn't know what he was doing. The world under the water could be a dangerous place if you didn't know how to live within its rules.

"It's not safe for someone like you," she said. "You don't look the same as them. They won't understand."

"Then I'll make them understand."

She drew in a deep breath. "No, you won't. I will."

"You?"

"Yes, me. I'm coming with you."

She could barely believe what she'd just said. But it was the only way to keep him safe. She knew he'd go either with her blessing or without, just like she'd left to follow a shadow into the forest. He was more like her than she'd realized. But she had to keep her child safe in a way she'd never given her own mother the chance.

He looked at her, shock wrapped tightly around his face. Then it slid away, revealing a smile.

"It's about time I went home for a visit," she said.

"Why couldn't you have visited before?" he asked. "Dad wouldn't have stopped you."

"Initially it was because I was afraid that if I went, then I might not want to come back."

"You love the water that much?

She shook her head. "Not the water. My mother. I love my mother that much. Then you and Eevie were born and I couldn't go. Not without Eevie. What if something happened to me? We needed to keep this family together."

This wasn't the full truth, but it was more than she'd admitted to before.

"And now?" asked Shadow.

"Well now, I realize you'll go whether I come with you or not. The family is being pulled apart anyway, so the best thing I can do is keep you safe."

"And see your mother."

"And see my mother. Yes."

She felt a tear roll its way down her cheek. Shadow reached for her hand and squeezed it. The warmth of his skin gave her comfort. For all her faults as a mother, she'd raised a wonderful child.

"To think I nearly left without telling you," he said.

"I'm so glad you didn't. There's only room for one runaway in this family."

"Why did you run away, Mom? I mean really, why? You weren't just chasing shadows were you."

"Perhaps I was running from them."

"What does that mean? Who were you running from?"

She hesitated, wondering if she should tell him the full truth or had enough truths already been spoken? She hadn't told anyone about this, not even Buzz. But if she was going to go to the water with Shadow, he was going to need to know.

"Who were you running from?" he asked again.

"My brother," she said, her voice no more than a whisper.

Now that she'd said it, she felt lighter, in much the same way Buzz must have felt when he finally admitted how hurt he'd been by his father. Secrets had a way of holding you down.

"You had a brother?" Shadow's brow drew together as he took in this information. "You said you only had sisters."

"I didn't want to talk about him. I didn't want his name here with me in the forest."

"Then we won't say his name." Shadow turned her hand over and ran his fingers across the scars on her palm. "Was he mean to you?"

She withdrew her hand, the pain of how she got those scars still sharp in her mind.

"I don't understand," said Shadow. "Why would your own brother hurt you?"

"See! You have no idea what's out there, Shadow. Of course, you don't understand. Here in the forest you've been protected. The world out there isn't like it is in here." The thought of her son going anywhere near her brother frightened her more than she could explain.

"Tell me about your brother then. Make me understand."

He would never understand, but she decided to try. "My brother told lies as easily as he breathed, making the whole world believe he was a hero. My mother and my sisters adored him. I was the only one who knew who he really was."

"Who was he? Did he kill someone?"

She smiled at his naivety. There were so many more ways to be dangerous than by the act of killing. Shadow hadn't even begun to be exposed to all the evils of the world.

"If killing joy is murder, then yes. But I think of him more as a thief."

"What did he steal?"

"My happiness. My belief that the world's a beautiful place."

She hesitated, knowing she was talking in riddles. Shadow wasn't used to being spoken to like this. There was so much he didn't know. She longed for the days when there was as much she didn't know herself.

"You see, my father died while rushing to the hospital when my mother was giving life to me. He had terrible breathing problems. His lungs were extremely weak. Knowing this was my mother's fourth time giving life and it may not take long, he was in a hurry to get to her side. So much that he stressed his lungs beyond what they were capable of and he drowned."

"He drowned? How can someone who lives under the water drown? He had gills, didn't he?" Shadow's hand fluttered to his own gills.

"It's rare, but it happens, just like someone on the surface can choke."

"But what does your father dying have to do with your brother being mean to you?"

"My brother was extremely close to our father and always blamed me for his death. If he hadn't been in such a rush to get to Mom, then he wouldn't have died. Although, he was nice to me in front of everyone else, when we were alone, he'd do things to make sure I knew how much pain I'd caused him."

"Like what?" Buzz reached for her once more.

She squeezed his hand, unsure if he was ready to hear the truth. But he was sixteen now. It was time he learned what kind of world he'd been born into. Especially now that he was so determined to go out and see it. Besides, the way he was holding her hand told her that he already knew her brother was responsible for her scars.

"Like holding my hand on a hot pot until my skin turned to blisters. Slamming my fingers in the door every chance he got. Waking me up by sticking pins in the soles of my feet. Adding small doses of acid to my shampoo so my hair felt like it was on fire." Her left hand fluttered to the patch of bare skin that sat hidden under her braid. "He even held me down on my bed and ate my pet fish. He picked it right up out of its tank and dangled it into his mouth with one hand, while muffling my screams with the other."

"Oh, Mom."

"The things he did to me are unspeakable." It was true.

What she'd just told Shadow was only the beginning. Her brother had been a violent, angry soul.

"Then perhaps we shouldn't speak of them." Shadow let go of her hand and paced the room.

It wasn't clear whether he'd heard enough or wanted to spare her the pain. She was grateful either way. Bringing these memories up had hurt. It was no wonder she'd avoided speaking about them before.

But despite the hatred she harbored for her brother, he had influenced her more than any other person. He was one of the reasons she'd been drawn to the forest. It wasn't just Buzz pulling her toward him, it was her brother driving her away. If her old home hadn't been one filled with pain and fear, she may not have been so desperate to find a new one.

And now it was time to go back. She hated leaving Eevie, but there was nothing she could do about that. She never thought she'd return, but with Shadow by her side, she would cope.

Her beautiful Shadow.

"Thank you for telling me all of that, Mom," said Shadow. "I needed to know that in case we meet… him."

The thought of that punched fear into her gut. "I'm not sure how I'll cope seeing him again. He's another big part of the reason I haven't wanted to return."

"I'll protect you. I'll never let anyone hurt you." Shadow's eyes burned with sincerity and she believed him. He was taller and stronger than anyone else in Aquatica, with thanks to his life on the land. He would look after her just as she'd look after him. They'd make a good team out there. And with any luck, maybe her brother wouldn't be around anymore and she wouldn't have to face him.

"You're a good son," she said. "Shall we tell Dad and Eevie what we've decided?"

"Would you like me to tell them?"

That didn't seem right. Buzz deserved better than that. "I left one family without saying goodbye. I'm not doing that again."

He nodded.

They stood, and Shadow wrapped his arms around her as he used to do when he was a child, only now she was resting her head on his chest instead of the other way around.

"I'm sorry, Mom."

"For what?"

"That your brother did those things to you. That you had to run away. And that once you found your way here, we were what trapped you."

"You didn't trap me. Honestly, you didn't. I love my life here with you."

"I'm also sorry I didn't understand why you were so sad. Instead of sitting by in silence I should have talked to you. Taken the time to understand why you are the person you are."

"Not even I know who I am." She laughed. "That's one of the great mysteries of the universe, I'm afraid."

They walked outside, hand in hand, to find Buzz and Eevie building a fire.

They looked up, surprised to see Nahlah with Shadow. It was still morning.

Buzz dropped the sticks he was holding and rushed to Nahlah, putting his hands on her shoulders. "It's good to see you up."

"We need to talk," she said, wanting this moment over with as soon as possible.

"You're leaving, aren't you?"

"How did you know?" she asked. Had he been eavesdropping? That wasn't like him.

"Because you look happy," he said. "You have the same look in your eyes as the day I first met you."

"What do you mean you're leaving," said Eevie, joining them.

"It's my fault," said Shadow. "It's me who wants to go."

"Go where?" asked Eevie.

"To the water," said Buzz. "They're going to the water."

Eevie's face fell. "I knew you'd do this one day."

Her words weren't for Shadow. They were for her. Had Eevie sensed as a child that one day her mother would leave? Was that why she'd bonded herself so closely to her father? Was this man without gills her only certainty in life?

"I love you, Eevie," Nahlah said, tipping her face up toward her. "You're everything I ever hoped for in a daughter."

"How long are you going for?" she asked.

"I'm not sure. It might be a very long time, or I might be back before you know it."

"Is it because of the way I treated you? Is it because you think I love Dad more than you?" She wrapped her arms around Nahlah's waist and held tight. Buzz and Shadow took a step back, giving them this moment.

"Of course not. Children are allowed to love their parents unequally," said Nahlah. "It's the parents who have to share their love in equal measures. I'm happy you love your father so much."

"Then why are you leaving me? You're choosing Shadow, just like Dad's father chose Valentina."

"I'm not choosing anyone, Eevie." She ran her hand down her daughter's hair, drawing in the scent of her. "I'm just keeping Shadow safe. I'll be back. I promise."

"This is different to my father," said Buzz.

"How can you be so understanding?" said Eevie, her voice raising an octave as she broke away from Nahlah.

"Because I know what it's like to be homesick," he said. "If my home were still there, I'm not sure I'd be able to keep away."

"You mean you understand?" asked Nahlah, looking at Buzz. Really looking at him like she hadn't done for many years.

"I've always understood. Do you remember the last time you tried to leave? Before the twins were born. The night that things...changed between us."

She nodded.

"I knew then when you agreed to stay that it wasn't going to be forever."

"But Buzz, I was never going to leave. I just wanted to hear you ask me to stay." She sighed, relieved to have admitted that at last.

If he was shocked, he didn't show it. "Then perhaps I knew you'd want to go back before you did."

"Why didn't you say anything?" She didn't deserve a man so good. He was giving her so much more than she deserved. He always had.

"I was trying to be grateful for the moments you gave me instead of mourning the ones I knew you were going to take away."

"Oh, Buzz."

"I don't want you to go. Or Shadow. Really, I don't." His face filled with lines, but he kept his voice calm. "But I know that I need to stand by you on this, because by keeping you here I've lost you already."

"You haven't lost me." How could he possibly think that? He'd never lose her.

"Go to the water. See your family. Then come back to me. *Come back to me.*"

She flew into his arms and held him tightly, almost changing her mind and deciding to stay. He was the best friend she'd ever had. The best friend she ever would have.

Her Ardorna. The man she remembered with her heart before she'd ever met him.

He released her, and she saw him reach for his son. Eevie went to her once more.

As they stood there, each holding the child they were to part ways with, they caught each other's eye and held a gaze that would stay in the memory of their hearts forever.

PART IV
SHADOW

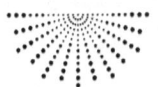

CHAPTER SEVEN

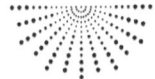

S hadow darted after his mother in the water. How could a person who'd barely gotten out of bed in the last few months swim so fast? He'd never seen her move like this—never seen anyone move like this. Her body was one with the water and she slid though its depths as if she was coated in oil.

He learnt so much about her in those first few moments underwater. The mystery of his mother finally fell into place. *This* was her home. *This* was where she'd grown up. *This* was the reason her heart ached with sadness in ways he could never understand.

He stopped for a moment, hoping she'd turn around and notice he was no longer following.

His gills weren't used to feeding his body with oxygen, making him feel like a toddler learning to walk. He knew what he had to do. He just had to think about every movement as he made it.

Just before his mother was about to disappear from sight, he saw her looking for him. She turned swiftly and came to his side, gesturing to ask if he was okay.

He just needed a rest, that was all. She was too fast for him.

She pointed upward and he shook his head not wanting to leave the water.

When he saw her blurred image kick toward the surface, he had no choice but to follow. He wouldn't survive out here on his own. It wasn't at all like he'd imagined.

He'd grown up knowing about this strange underwater world his mother called Aquatica. His parents had never lied to him about it, just as they'd never lied to him about how his father had come to live on Neron.

It never occurred to him to question either of these stories. His father had come to Neron as the last surviving human from a faraway planet and his mother had spent her childhood living on the floor of the ocean. What was so strange about that?

He'd longed to visit Aquatica ever since he could remember. He loved his life in the forest, but just like he'd told his mother, he could never shake the feeling that someone was missing from his life. He could almost feel himself being pulled in the direction of the ocean. Perhaps he was just lonely. Particularly lately when his mother—who was also his best friend—had retreated within herself.

The only problem with his burning desire to visit the ocean, had been working out how to tell his parents. Although, he suspected his mother had already known long before he'd told her. She'd seen him staring into the forest waiting for… her. Whoever *her* was.

He'd always known his parents would never allow him to leave, so he'd been making plans to run away, slipping into the forest whenever he could, until he found his way to the ocean.

He'd sat on the sand a few times, too afraid to do more than dip his toes into the water. He would immerse himself fully one day, but just as his mother had taken her time adjusting to the forest, he had wanted to do the same.

The ocean was more beautiful than he could have imagined, despite the drawings his mother had sketched for him. It was the colors that took his breath away. The deep green of the water contrasting perfectly with the blue of the sky. The sound of the waves crashing on the shore in a relentless rhythm. The birdlife gliding and circling as they looked for an unsuspecting meal. It was like nothing he'd ever seen before and hard to imagine the strange world his mother had described to him was happening right in front of him. It looked so deserted.

He'd been surprised when he first noticed a plume of black smoke rising into the air from a bare patch of land in the distance. This was the smoke they could sometimes smell from their home and the one that his father had seen when he'd first landed on Neron.

His mother had told them it was coming from the factories that had been set up. Not all of life's supplies could be produced under the water. Crops still needed to be grown upon the land. Ventilation systems were required to pump clean air to the homes. Massive pumps hummed as they converted saltwater to fresh, and something called electricity was also being generated.

Shadow wondered if these things were worth all that black smoke. His family had managed just fine without producing a never-ending stream of pollution like that.

As he'd sat there on the sand imagining the world he couldn't see, he'd try to come up with the right words to tell his parents he was leaving. He didn't want to have to run away.

But then a miracle had happened. His father taken him aside to speak to him about his mother's health. He was worried about her. She was getting worse, not better, and he feared it wouldn't be long until they lost her all together—not to the ocean, but to the heavens above.

Knowing the ocean was the only thing that would save her and that she'd never go on her own accord, his father had begged him to intervene. If he were to pretend it was his own desire to see Aquatica, she'd surely rise from her bed and go with him. She'd never let her child go alone into that strange world. Because if the decision was left up to her, it'd be a decision that was never made.

Shadow hadn't quite known how to handle the conversation. His father was asking him to do something as a favor, not realizing that what he was actually doing was making his dream come true.

"Are you trying to get rid of her?" Shadow had asked.

"Of course not," he'd replied. "I don't want her to leave. I'm just trying to find a way to make her come back."

With a response like that, Shadow realized exactly what a good man his father was. It couldn't have been easy for him to think of saying goodbye to the woman who'd stood by his side for almost two decades. Then again, perhaps that was easier than to watch her fade away before his eyes.

That was true love right there. It was no wonder Shadow harbored such a deep desire to experience this kind of love for himself.

So, he'd confessed his true desires to his father, who'd broken into a smile, relieved not to be asking him to do something he didn't want to do. Shadow would like nothing more than to go with his mother to the water. It was so much less frightening than going alone.

Not that it was completely without fear, he thought, as he broke through the surface and gasped for air, his body transitioning from gills to lungs.

"I was fine, Mom," he complained.

"No, you weren't."

"I just needed a minute."

"That's what I'm giving you."

He knew it would be more than a minute as he followed her from the water to the shore.

"Where are we going?" he asked, as she headed toward the trees.

"To get some equipment," she said, turning toward him. "There's something I think might help you. If it's still there."

He tapped his gills. "I've got all the equipment I need."

"You can see through water, can you?"

"It's clear enough?"

"It's about as clear as your head."

He didn't understand, but followed along anyway, not wanting to be separated.

They picked their way through the ruins of the ancient town that had once housed a village of people. He wouldn't have known they were ruins if his mother hadn't told him. It just looked like an eerie part of the forest to him, with vines and trees sprouting at odd angles, clinging to what he assumed must have once been walls.

"Why did the people leave?" he asked.

"They were scared of the sun."

He looked to the sky. He'd seen his mother's fair skin burn when she wasn't careful, but sunburn was a stranger to the rest of them. The sun was their friend, keeping them warm, bringing them light and sustaining the forest.

"What's there to be scared of?" he asked.

"They thought the sun was killing them."

"Was it?"

"I don't know. Maybe. But it hasn't hurt us, has it? I don't know what was wrong with the sun back then, but we're walking proof that it's no longer as deadly as everyone fears."

"Then why don't they come out of the water?" Now that

would be good. If the world came to him, he'd no longer need to venture out to explore it.

"They've gotten used to life down there. Living here on the land is as foreign to them as living down there seems to you. Plus, it'll take a long time before they're prepared to trust the sun again. Someone would have to prove to them it's safe by actually living up here. Not a job I expect too many people are putting their hands up for."

"You can tell them. We can tell them."

"Let's just get down there first."

They approached a large tree and his mother wrapped her arms around it like it was an old friend.

"This is it," she said.

"It's a tree, Mom."

"Yes, but this is *my* tree."

"You own a tree?" The idea amused him.

He stepped forward and heard a loud creak.

"Careful!' his mother called, before he fell through a large chasm that opened up beneath his feet.

He sailed through the air, his arms flailing, trying to grab hold of something to break his inevitable fall. A loud sound escaped his lips and he wondered if this was it. Time slowed down, and seconds became minutes. Had he made it this far to die before he reached Aquatica? He couldn't. It wasn't possible. He needed to find out what had been calling him from the water. Or rather, who had been calling him.

He landed heavily, knocking the air out of his lungs. He'd fallen out of enough trees in his time to know this fight to breathe wouldn't last long. The important thing was not to panic.

"Shadow!' his mother called.

He saw her face at the opening above him. Her blonde hair was escaping her braid and catching the sun as it streamed in all directions. He imagined if he died and went to the place in the clouds his parents called heaven, that it would be filled with angels who looked exactly like his mother.

Despite only ever having seen two women in his life, he knew his mother was beautiful. Had he sensed it or was beauty something that could be recognized without a point of reference? He'd asked his father, who confirmed it for him. He said she was the most beautiful woman he'd ever seen. And he'd seen a lot of women. Well, a lot more than Shadow had, which made him the expert on such matters.

"Shadow!'

He realized his mother couldn't see him lying in the dark.

He heaved for breath.

"I'm here," he called. "I'm okay."

She slid down the cavity, lowering herself until she was hanging by her fingertips. She let go and landed nimbly on her feet next to him.

A large section of the roof fell with her, missing them by inches and allowing light to flood in.

"Oh, Shadow, thank goodness," she said, placing her hands upon his cheeks.

He fought back a tear. He'd missed being mothered like this. His father had been right to force her from her bed. She was coming back to life with every step they took.

"You should've stayed up there," he said. "No equipment is worth this. How are we going to get out now?"

"Don't worry about that."

She sounded so certain that he decided to believe her. This was her world he was in now.

He sat up and blinked, as his eyes tried to find their focus in the sudden brightness.

They were in some kind of house. Tree roots hung from the ceiling in long trails and dirt covered every surface, but there was no question someone had once called this home.

"What is this place?" he asked. He'd never set foot in a home that wasn't his own and was intrigued.

"An ordinary home. An ancient, ordinary home. Nobody's lived here for hundreds of years. To think this was sitting here the whole time right next to my tree and I had no idea."

"It's like buried treasure," he said, kicking at some kind of box. It spilled open and a strange collection of metal objects clattered to his feet.

"It really is." His mom squatted down to look at what he'd found.

"Why didn't you bring us here before?" he asked, fossicking through the objects. "We could've used a lot of this stuff back home. I'm not sure what for, but we'd have found something to do with it."

"Lots of reasons," she said, avoiding eye contact.

"Such as?" He could feel her slipping away again.

"I explained all this to you before." She put down some kind of hard, plastic object and looked at him.

"I know," he said, remembering their conversation.

She sighed, turning her attention back to the pile of objects at his feet, pulling out a long metal stick with a cup-like object attached to it. She waved it at him, grinning.

"Why would a cup need such a long handle?" he asked.

"It's a ladle. It's for soup."

"What's soup?"

"Food that you drink."

That sounded a little strange.

"What about this one?" He held up another stick with metal loops intersecting at one end.

"It's a beater."

"Sounds a little harsh." He turned it over and imagined the pain such a device could inflict.

"It's for eggs," she added.

That didn't make things any clearer, so he dropped it. The

only eggs he'd seen were tucked away in nests, which was exactly where he'd left them.

"Really Shadow, it's like talking to your father for the first time. He couldn't understand a word I said."

"According to him, you were the one who couldn't understand a word he said."

"Maybe that's why we got along so well."

She was joking, but this wasn't something he felt like laughing at. It implied she didn't like what his father had to say once she could understand him.

"I love your father," she said, as if reading his mind. "And almost everything he says."

Buzz shivered. This place was starting to give him the creeps. "How are we going to get out of here?"

"Easy." His mother took hold of one of the tree roots that dangled down looking much like the branches above ground.

She hauled her tiny frame up the root, reaching ground level in a few seconds.

He waited, ready to catch her if she were to fall. Of course, she didn't.

He took hold of the root and prepared to climb, only to find it break away in his hands. At almost two feet taller than his mother, he was far heavier than her. It wouldn't be as easy for him.

After several failed attempts, he found a root strong enough to take his weight and managed to climb to the top.

He looked around, expecting to see his mother nearby.

"Up here," she called.

He squinted into the sun and saw her sitting in the crook of a branch waving at him.

This was the mother he remembered from his childhood. She was wild, adventurous and brave. Tears stung his eyes, he was so happy to have her back. If only his father could see her. He had to find a way to return to him to tell him he'd been right. His plan had worked.

"Come down," he said, wondering what she was up to.

"Come up," she said, turning her back to him.

She was doing something in the tree, only he couldn't see what.

He sighed and began to climb. At this rate he'd have no energy left to swim to Aquatica.

He reached her to see her clearing away forest litter from a hollow in the trunk of the tree.

"It's still here," she said, grinning as she pulled out a bright purple case, made from hard plastic. It had long straps that dangled as she held it in the air.

"What is that?"

"It's my school bag. I can't believe it's still here."

"What's it doing here?"

"I used to hide it here whenever I came into the forest so I didn't have to carry it."

He slid himself further along the branch so he could see.

She ran her slender fingers across the case, her webbing spreading wide. For a moment he saw her as a girl, her face filled with wonder. How courageous she'd been to leave the safety of her home at such a young age and make a new life in the forest. It'd been hard enough for him to contemplate as a teenager. She'd only been a child.

She opened the case, the waterproof rubber seals peeling as they prized apart. She let out a squeal.

"My pencil case! My water bottle! Oh, look, my goggles. Three pairs!'

In her hand dangled what he assumed were the goggles.

"Purple, orange or blue?" she asked.

"Orange."

She handed him the orange pair and he held them to his

eyes, wondering if this really was all he needed to see clearly under water.

"I think this will really help you," she said. "It's far easier to swim when you can see exactly where you're going."

"Why did you have three pairs of these things?" he asked.

"It's called fashion." She laughed, slipping the blue pair over her head. It was a laugh he didn't recognize as hers, it'd been so long since he'd heard it. "Nobody has just one pair."

"That's fashion?" She looked ridiculous. Did people really wear those things in Aquatica?

It turned out that wearing goggles was the least of his problems when it came to looking ridiculous. Not being able to keep up with his mother soon proved to be far more embarrassing.

Although his next attempt was definitely better than his first. His mother had been right. The googles did make it easier. Somehow not having to concentrate so much on what he was seeing made it easier to think about breathing through his gills.

Breathing underwater was something he'd done since he was a small child floating in the bath his father had made them by digging a hole in the ground and lining it with his parachute. He'd hollowed out a branch that ran from the roof of their house to the water tank. When the tank was full, it would overflow into the bathtub.

Eevie despised the bath, rarely going near it, but not Shadow. He'd spend hours sitting in the water experimenting with what it was like to breathe through his gills. It made him feel at peace. Perhaps he could sense the water was where he belonged. It was where his ancestors had come from. Or perhaps it helped make sense of these strange gills that lined his chest. They had to be there for some reason.

But saltwater felt different to the freshwater from his bath. It was so much more natural. If he could just get the hang of how to move his arms and legs to propel himself a little faster, he'd be fine.

His mother tried to stay next to him, but every now and then she wouldn't be able to hold back, and she'd dart away like a bird released from a cage. The water had woken something in her, just like his father had said it would. But what he hadn't expected was that it had woken something deep within himself as well. And he hadn't even known he'd been asleep.

He tried to copy her movements, only to find himself floundering in the one spot. How was she doing that?

After watching her more closely, he attempted to imitate her movements, managing to move forward in jagged bursts. This was never going to work.

"Who taught you to swim?" he asked on one of their returns to the surface for a rest.

"Nobody."

"Then how did you learn?"

"The same way you learned to walk, I guess. I just did it."

"Then why can't I do it?"

"Of course, you can. Just keep trying. Copy me."

"That's what I'm doing."

Progress was slow, but his determination was strong. Each attempt they made to venture further under the surface was more successful than the last, but still his mother didn't feel confident he could make it to Aquatica.

He hated returning to shore for a rest when all he wanted to do was prove to his mother that he could do it. Or perhaps it was himself he was trying to prove it to. The ocean was calling him. Whatever it was he felt so desperately he was meant to find, was out there.

"Let's just go," he said, his impatience bubbling over when he noticed the sun begin its descent from the peak of the sky.

It was afternoon now and he didn't want to still be out here when it was dark.

"Soon," she said.

"What are you worried about?"

"Have you forgotten already how my father died? I want to be sure you can make it before we reach Aquatica. It'll be too far to turn around once we're down there."

He felt terrible for having reminded her about her father. Of course, she was worried. If her father had lived under the ocean his whole life and he'd drowned, then the danger for someone like him was very real.

"I can do it, Mom. I can. If you could just slow down a little bit until I get the hang of it."

"Okay, but you must tell me if you're struggling."

"I'll tell you."

She looked at him doubtfully.

"I *will*," he said. "Promise."

They set out again at a slow yet steady pace. When he felt tired, he closed his eyes for a moment and imagined how he'd feel to find his one true love. She was down here, he was certain of it. The closer he got to Aquatica, the stronger the feeling grew within him.

He continued to swim, nodding to his mother that he was okay.

His father had sent him here to save her life. Perhaps his own life was the one he was saving. He could feel himself coming alive. The water was reviving him, waking him from what had been a pleasant, yet somewhat confusing dream. Life with his family in the forest had been as difficult as it had been satisfying. They'd had to work hard every day, collecting water, repairing their home, catching their dinner and weaving the beds they slept upon.

When he was younger it never occurred to him that anyone lived any differently. But the more stories he heard from his parents about their childhoods, the more he came to realize how unusual his was.

It wasn't that he disliked the work, it was more the over-whelming feeling of loneliness that gripped him. Despite the effort his father put in to making him feel loved, he was a difficult man to get close to. Eevie could have been his best friend, but she chose not to be. Instead, he'd always had his mother. And the more she'd slipped away recently, the more alone he'd felt.

They swam further than they'd reached before, then further again. He was really getting the hang of breathing underwater and would smile at his mother when she'd turn to check on him, giving her a thumbs up. He could do this. He really could. There was no way he was going to turn back again.

When his mother grabbed him on the arm and pointed to some lights in the distance, he knew he'd made it at last. All that effort and determination had paid off. He was in the place he'd dreamed of. The place of his mother's childhood that he'd yearned for since his earliest days. The place that had filled her with such sadness she'd fled from its depths, yet still it called to her. Beckoning her to return, to be one with the water.

Aquatica. He'd actually made it.

Whatever was about to happen down there, he knew his life would change in a big way. And the thing about change is that once it occurs, it's impossible to go back. Was he ready for it?

He kicked harder, pulling through the water faster with his arms. He was ready. He couldn't wait for his new life to begin.

They swam through a large gate, rusted with time. He recognized it from his mother's stories. This was the gate his ancestors who lived upon the land had used when they'd visited Aquatica like it was some kind of theme park. They spent so much time here their bodies began to evolve. Gills had appeared on their chests and soft folds of skin between their fingers and toes.

The gate was rarely used now. Nobody came up to the surface anymore, except for the workers and even they didn't venture far from the water. It was too difficult in the cumbersome suits they wore to protect their skin from the sun. The expanse of land used for industry was as close to the shore as possible.

His mother pointed to the entrance of what seemed to be the decompression tunnel she'd told him about. This was how the workers got safely to the surface. They sat in chairs that lifted them slowly from the water, their bodies adjusting as they went. He could see them sitting in it now as they headed off for their day's work.

When it was time for him to return to the forest, he'd need to sneak onto this strange contraption as his mother had done as a child.

He looked at her fair skin. She'd been fine without a suit. He glanced down at his own dark skin and contemplated her concerns about him looking different to the others. Would they accept him? Of course, they would. The color of his skin didn't mean anything. He was just the same as these people. Surely they weren't so naïve they'd think he was any different.

He came to an abrupt halt as his brain struggled to comprehend what he was seeing before him.

His mother had described Aquatica to him many times, drawing him pictures as she'd talked, but nothing could've prepared him for what he was looking at.

Rows of houses lined streets, stretching out before him in winding trails. They weren't anything like his timber house in the forest with its leaning walls and densely thatched roof. These houses were every color of the rainbow, all perfectly square and made from some kind of metal.

The sand of the ocean floor had been dyed red, contrasting with the bright green of the artificial trees that lined the streets. Their leaves swayed in the currents of the water and lanterns hung from their branches, sending out colorful rays of light in every direction. Shadow had heard about light made by man, but to see these tiny suns shining from the trees was extraordinary.

It should've been beautiful. He was certain it'd been designed to be beautiful, but it was hideous. He thought of a word his father had taught him once …

Gaudy.

He remembered his father having trouble defining the word, not having any examples in the forest to refer to.

Shadow finally knew what he'd meant.

Aquatica was the exact definition of the word. His eyes were struggling to take it all in.

He had to remind his gills to breathe as he stared at the people swimming through the streets, oblivious to the two intruders watching them. Well, one intruder and one deserter returning home.

It was a strange feeling to look upon a face and find it unfamiliar. The word stranger kept floating through his mind. He'd never seen a stranger before. All these words he'd collected over the years—in both his mother's language and his father's—finally had meaning. Perhaps his mother was right to want to take his introduction to Aquatica slowly. It was overwhelming.

The fair skin of these strangers was like his mother's, but there was so much more that was different. They had short hair, cropped close to their heads. Their clothes were shimmering, lighting their path as they swam.

They were frightening. He hadn't expected them to be frightening.

His mother took his hand, pulling him toward the streets of Aquatica.

He shook his head. He didn't want to go there. It was a mistake. He should've stayed with his father and Eevie.

A group of children pointed and swam toward them. They were young, maybe only five or six years old.

They can't hurt you, he told himself. They're only children.

They approached, tapping each other on the shoulders and pointing at Shadow. There were four of them, all tiny, all petrifying.

Behind their goggles he could see their eyes were blue, like his mother's. Their suits shone light in all directions, and he had to bring a hand to his eyes to shield them.

He gripped his mother, pulling her back toward the way they'd come.

She shooed the children away, flicking her hands in their direction, placing herself between them and Shadow.

They retreated and he sighed with relief, accidentally sucking water into his lungs. He tried to cough it up, only managing to draw in more water.

He felt his pulse rate increase as his body fought for air. He tried to draw water into his gills and instead filled his lungs with yet more seawater.

Panic gripped him. His mother had been right.

He was going to drown.

Time slowed for the second time in the same day. Twice that he'd feared for his life. And twice that he fought against it with every ounce of his strength.

He would *not* drown out here. That may have been the fate of his grandfather, but it was not his. But how could he live without air in either his lungs or his gills?

His mother turned to see him and her eyes widened as if

making room for the fear that spilled into them. An air bubble escaped her lips as she called out his name.

He reached out his hands, wanting to tell her he was sorry. She should have come here alone. Maybe whoever he'd expected to find under the water would have come to him if only he'd waited long enough. He didn't belong here. No human did.

He tried again to draw some water through his gills, but they'd stalled, no water passing in and no water passing out. He was too tense. If only he could relax.

His mouth opened and he took in an involuntary gulp of water, his body convulsing as it cried out for oxygen.

Instead of this being the place he'd come to live, it seemed for sure now that it was the place he'd come to die.

CHAPTER EIGHT

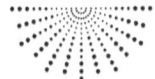

Shadow felt his mother grab him, looping her arm around his waist and dragging him down toward the depths of Aquatica.

As he was about to black out, he felt an unfamiliar pair of hands take hold of him. He turned to see the face of a man, his blue eyes flashing from beneath his goggles. The man hesitated, shock registering on his face as he took in Shadow's appearance.

He dragged him to the nearest home on the edge of the street, pushing him through the large rubber folds of the door.

Shadow fell heavily to the floor, surprised to find himself in an air pocket. He was free of the water, lying on a metal grate in a small room. He coughed, spewing water from his lungs and took several deep breaths, filling them with the oxygen they needed.

The man who'd rescued him burst through the door after him, followed by his mother. There was barely room for all three of them in this tiny room.

"Shadow!' his mother cried. "Are you all right?"

He sat, folding his legs to his chest to create more room and nodded, unable to speak.

"Who are you?" The man pulled his goggles from his face to get a better look at him, crouching down, the blue of his eyes locking with Shadow's dark irises.

Shadow was wondering exactly the same thing about him.

"Who are you?" the man asked again, reaching his hand out to touch him.

Shadow flinched, inching away from him as much as the small room would allow.

"He's my son," said his mother, stepping in front of him and puffing out her chest.

The man looked at his mother. It seemed for a moment that a flash of recognition crossed his face.

"I'm sorry," he said, his demeanor changing. "Where are my manners? How rude of me. It's just that I've never seen anyone like your son before."

He stood, brushing the water from his skin.

This man was paler than his mother, who'd spent so many years in the sun. His skin was almost translucent, with some of his veins visible as they transported blood around his body. It was eerie. Shadow wanted to stare at him just as much as he seemed to want to stare at Shadow.

"This is my home," he said. "Would you like to come in? I can make you a hot cup of tea?"

Shadow stood, still taking deep breaths as his oxygen levels restored. He wasn't sure what tea was, but if it was hot then it sounded wonderful.

"No, thank you," said his mother.

"He just saved my life," said Shadow.

"If you recall correctly, I was in the process of saving your life when this man came and interrupted."

"You were struggling," the man said. "Your son's much

larger than you. You would never have been able to drag him to safety."

It was difficult to understand all of what the man said. Although the language they spoke at home was mostly his mother's, it felt like every fifth word the man used was spoken in nonsense, leaving him enough clues to be able to follow his meaning, but not enough to grasp each nuance.

"Please, Mom," said Shadow. "I'm not ready to go back out there yet."

He wasn't. The idea of going back out into the water frightened him. He needed some time to adjust to this strange world.

"Okay," she relented. "Thank you." She nodded at the man.

"Come in," he said, slipping through the door to his house.

Shadow followed, pleased to leave the claustrophobic airlock. His mother was right behind him.

"My name's Trillion," the man said, handing them both a towel and gesturing for them to sit down at his table.

Shadow barely heard him. His eyes were darting all over the house, unable to decide which item to look at first. Some objects looked familiar, like the chairs or the small bed that sat in the corner, but the vast majority were contraptions so mysterious that he couldn't even begin to imagine what they were used for.

"Sit down." His mother patted the chair beside her.

"He can look around if he likes." Trillion flicked a switch on a cylindrical object that hummed and poured steam from a spout. Was he making fire with that thing?

"What are you doing?" asked Shadow.

"Sorry, I'm not sure I understand what you just said." Trillion looked confused.

"I asked what you're doing?" he said again, using the

words his mother favored, instead of those taught to him by his father.

"Making tea. Relax. It's okay. I'm not going to hurt you."

He smiled and Shadow noticed pink lines tracing their way from the corner of his eyes to his cheeks.

"Haven't you seen a kettle before?" Trillion asked.

Shadow shook his head, taking a seat next to his mother, deciding it was safer there.

"You have a lovely home," his mother said, shifting uncomfortably in her chair.

It was strange to see her making attempts to be sociable with this stranger. At home she behaved however she felt. He'd never seen her like this.

"How long have you lived here?" she asked.

"There's no need for small talk with me," said Trillion. "Why don't you tell me where he's from?"

"I told you. He's my son."

He set the kettle down on the table and Shadow eyed it suspiciously. Trillian took some mugs from a cupboard and poured the tea.

"Do you take sugar?" he asked.

"I didn't take anything," Shadow said, showing his empty palms. How dare this man accuse him of stealing.

"Give him some sugar," his mother said with a tight smile. "It might do him some good."

He realized Trillion had been offering him something called sugar, not accusing him of taking any. He needed to listen to his intuition and trust this man. There was a goodness emanating from him.

Trillion scooped some white crystals into his mug. It looked like some kind of magic powder. Shadow glanced across at his mother to make sure she was good with it. She didn't have the sort of alarmed look on her face she should have if it was poison. He couldn't wait to see what it tasted like. Magic in a cup, he'd bet.

His eyes trailed across this strange room as he took in his surroundings. It was most peculiar. Did everyone in Aquatica live in colorful boxes filled with strange possessions?

He jumped as something on the shelf caught his eye. It looked like a tiny person. A young female.

"Who's that?" he said, pointing.

"That's my daughter," Trillion said, lifting the small girl from the shelf and handing her to Shadow.

"It's called a photo," his mother said. "She's not real. It's just an image of her."

"To be accurate, she's very real," said Trillion. "But thankfully she's not trapped in that frame watching me potter about with my life."

Shadow stretched out a finger to touch her. She looked like her father, yet somehow she was … beautiful. How was it possible to look like this ghost of a man, yet at the same time radiate such beauty? Was it the same set of blue eyes they shared?

She had short, white-blonde hair and skin equally as pale as her father's. Her physique was slim in a delicate looking way, yet the fire in her eyes told him she was anything but delicate. She looked determined, perhaps even a little fierce.

As his finger made contact with the photo, he flinched, half expecting her to back away. But where he expected to touch flesh, he touched paper. Where he expected to feel warmth, he felt coolness. The girl was smiling at him, her face frozen into an expression of false happiness. He could tell she was sad underneath that smile.

He ran his finger over her face, wanting to make the smile real, to bring happiness to the pale blue of her eyes.

"Her name's Ryyder," said Trillion. "She lives with her mother."

"Why's she so sad?" asked Shadow.

Trillion lifted the photo from his hands. "She's not sad, she's just Ryyder."

"She's beautiful," said his mother.

"That's because she takes after me." Trillion winked.

"She does resemble you," his mother replied, smiling politely.

"So, Nahlah," Trillion said. "Are you going to tell me where you've been hiding or are you planning to keep me in suspense all day?"

His mother gasped. "How do you know my name?"

"Everybody knows your name. The girl who vanished into thin air. Or should I say thin water. You had the whole of Aquatica searching for you at one stage, myself included. It's one of our greatest mysteries. *You're* one of our greatest mysteries. You're positively famous."

"What's famous?" asked Shadow.

"It means *everybody* knows who she is," said Trillion, his eyes never leaving Shadow's mother.

Her face was hard to read as she struggled to hold onto a neutral expression.

Shadow was surprised. His mother had told him nobody had noticed when she left. To think the whole of Aquatica had searched for her was impossible to imagine. And she'd thought he was the one who was going to stand out.

"Mind you, you've grown up since you left," continued Trillion. "But I'd have recognized you anywhere. You're lucky it was me who found you."

"Why's that?" she asked, her eyes flaring in defiance. "What makes you so special?"

Shadow didn't understand why she was angry. It seemed to him that Trillion was genuinely trying to help them.

"I'm not special," said Trillion. "But I am your second chance."

"Second chance at what?" she asked.

"To turn around and return to wherever it is you've been hiding. Are you sure coming here was a good idea?"

"It's my home just as much as yours."

Trillion shrugged. "It's nothing to me if you stay here. I just figured if you left then it must've been for a good reason. I'm not certain if I'd ever return if I ever managed to get out of this place."

"What's wrong with this place?" asked Shadow.

"Let's just say, there's a reason I live right on the edge of Aquatica."

"What's happened to it?" asked his mother.

"Nothing. That's the problem. When our ancestors lived upon the land, huge progress was made. We invented electricity, discovered medicines, made cars that sped across the land. But none of that's happened here. Look around you. This place has barely changed since we first arrived. It drives me bonkers."

"Bonkers?" Shadow asked, trying to keep up with what he was saying.

"Crazy," he explained.

Shadow nodded, taking note of this new word.

"You haven't touched your tea," said Trillion.

Shadow lifted the mug to his lips and sipped. It was sweeter than anything he'd tasted before. He took another sip deciding he liked this strange drink. It must be the magic crystals.

"I don't know where you've been, Nahlah," said Trillion. "But I wish you'd taken me with you."

"I didn't know you," she said. "And besides, I didn't even know I was leaving until I was already gone."

"Where were you? There must be others if you say this is your son."

Now this was a question Shadow could answer. He was

145

certain Trillion would love to hear about the forest. "In the—"

"Shadow!' his mother cut him off.

Why wouldn't she want him to know where his father and Eevie were? He wasn't going to hurt them. He fell silent nonetheless.

"I'm sorry," she said to Trillion. "You've been very kind to us, but we don't know you."

"I understand. So, what's your plan?" he asked, not seeming to be ruffled by the evasion of his question. "You're just going to swim on down the main street and tell everyone you're back? You think I ask a lot of questions, you haven't seen anything yet."

"I didn't realize," she said. "I didn't think anyone would remember be."

"Your mother does."

"She's still alive?"

"Oh, yes."

Shadow's heart filled with hope for his mother. He wasn't sure if she had the emotional strength to handle it if her mother was no longer alive.

"You've seen her?" His mother sat forward in her chair.

"Not for a little while, but I used to see her when I lived with my wife. Your mother's a regular of hers."

"Regular of what?"

"My wife's a Truthseeker."

Shadow hadn't heard of a Truthseeker before. He looked at his mother. The surprised look on her face told him she knew exactly what a Truthseeker was.

"My mother would never visit a Truthseeker. You're mistaken," she said.

"I'm not mistaken. You don't expect she's the same person she was when you left her, do you? Your disappearance changed her profoundly."

"What business would she have to talk to a Truthseeker about?"

"You, of course."

"And what did your wife tell her about me?"

"I wouldn't have a clue. That's not my truth to ask. Your brother found that out the hard way."

"My brother?"

Shadow saw his mother's face turn almost as pale as Trillion's.

"Yes, he visits her too, begging for truths that aren't his own. I don't mean to listen in, but I'm afraid my wife has quite a temper and when she tells him that it isn't his truth to ask, I think most of Aquatica can hear her shouting."

"Whose truths does he want?" his mother asked, her voice almost a whisper.

"Yours," said Trillion, laughing.

"What's a Truthseeker?" Shadow asked again.

"Someone who sees things we can't," said his mother. "People visit her to ask questions and she uses her visions to answer them."

Shadow wondered if the feelings he'd been having about missing someone from his life could be considered visions. Probably not. They were more feelings than visions. He wouldn't mind seeing this Truthseeker to ask her what she thought about this.

"Take me to your wife," his mother said to Trillion. "I want to see her."

Trillion smiled. "You seek the truth, do you? That surprises me. You struck me as the sort who runs away from it."

"Not anymore." She locked eyes with him. "I have questions, so many questions. And the problem with questions is that the longer they're left unanswered, the more they burn at you. I have questions burning inside me like a fire."

"I've heard of fire," he said. "Never seen it myself. Mind you, I'd like to."

"Please take me to your wife." She was begging now.

Shadow hadn't realized she had quite so many questions. He'd always thought of her as the one with all the answers.

"Answer some questions of my own first, then I'll take you to her." Trillion seemed unfazed by Shadow's mother's erratic behavior.

"What are your questions?" she asked.

"Nothing I haven't already asked. Where have you been hiding? Who's Shadow's father? How many of you are there? Nothing too difficult to answer."

"Why would any of that matter to you?" asked Shadow, noticing his mother's discomfort with each of these questions. She knew more about this world than he did. Would telling their story put his father and Eevie in danger?

"Curiosity, I suppose," he said. "Burning curiosity, as your mother put it. She's not the only one with fires burning in her soul."

"Your wife's a Truthseeker," she pointed out. "How could anything burn at you?"

"Truthseekers know a lot more about the past than they do the future. I'm not interested in the past. It's the future I want to know about."

"I can't tell you about your future," she said.

"I think you can. You've been hiding somewhere and I'm guessing by the tan color of your skin, it's been somewhere on the land. I never thought I'd live to see the day humans would emerge from the sea and reclaim our right to live on the land but looking at you—and him—now I think I might make it after all."

"I don't know why you're asking me," she said. "You seem to have all the answers yourself."

He shook his head. "I'll take you to my wife, but in return you'll take me to your husband."

"Impossible. I'm not married." She crossed her arms.

"Whatever you want to call him then." He waved his hands in the air. "I'm talking about this boy's father and whoever else is hiding on the land."

"We can find her ourselves, Mom," said Shadow. "Your mother can tell us where to find her. You know how to find your mother, don't you?"

She hung her head in despair. "I have questions I need answered before I see her."

"Then someone else will tell us where to find her."

She nodded.

"I told you, you're famous," said Trillion. "You'll never get to my wife before your mother gets to you. Or your brother..."

Shadow winced, aware that his mother was doing the same.

"I'm not a bad person," Trillion said. "I'm a lost soul just like you. My wife will tell you. You know she can't lie."

That seemed to seal it for his mother. "Take me to your wife," she said. "If she vouches for you, then I'll take you to the forest."

"The forest," he said, his eyes alight.

Shadow was overwhelmed with a sense of trepidation for his father and sister. They hadn't wanted their life to change. They were happy in the forest. That was the thing about change, he supposed. Sometimes you walked toward it and other times it came walking to you.

Trillion came up with a plan that was both brilliant and frustrating.

He told them there was a carnival in a week's time, known as Aquaticus. It was the annual celebration of permanent settlement underwater. All residents of Aquatica would be dressed in outlandish costumes as they paraded through the streets. They'd be wearing wigs and hats and dresses that trailed behind them as they swam. Children would dart around with jetpacks strapped to their backs, while their parents sat in cafés and restaurants drinking an alcoholic drink made from fermented seaweed known as tsuki.

Apparently it was quite a spectacle. It was also the perfect opportunity to travel through the streets unnoticed.

Shadow's mother remembered the celebrations from when she was a girl and her eyes lit up at the thought of being part of it once more.

It did sound interesting.

Shadow had asked why they couldn't simply travel at night, only to be told that there was no night in Aquatica. Without a sun to rule their days, the residents lived the hours they pleased. They slept when they were tired, ate when they were hungry and worked whenever it was required.

Trillion said this was part of the problem with Aquatica. There was no order and without order there was no progress. Hundreds of years of fear had been bred into them by the government who ran campaigns to ensure their citizens remained exactly where they wanted them. Who knew what anarchy would erupt if people reclaimed their right to live upon the land.

When Shadow had asked why the government would do such a thing, Trillion said it was because they didn't want people to see what was happening above the surface. Then he'd drilled Shadow and his mother for more information on how the land was faring with the industry he'd heard about. He was wide-eyed at their descriptions of the black smoke that poured from the clearings.

They had to reassure him the forest was safe for now, a beautiful haven for wildlife—and people if that's what they wanted.

But it seemed the people liked their life under the water. It was all they'd ever known. Restless souls like Trillion were rare. And as restless as he was, even he hadn't been prepared to take the risk of emerging from the water, until now when he had someone to show him the way.

"What will we wear to Aquaticus?" Shadow asked, wondering how they'd make their way through the crowds unnoticed.

"You're not coming," Trillion said. "I said I'd take your mother. I never said anything about taking you."

"He's coming with me," said his mother. "We won't be separated."

Trillion looked surprised. "He'll drown out there. You saw him."

"You can get him a tank," she said.

"What's a tank?" Shadow raised his eyebrows.

"She means an air tank," said Trillion. "They were popular with the kids for a while. They liked the novelty of using their lungs to breathe as they swam through the water. The fad didn't last long. They were too heavy to carry around. But I suppose I can find one somewhere."

"So, I can come with you?"

"You heard your mother. You can't be separated apparently."

She smiled. "Maybe you could find some old-fashioned goggles and one of those rubber suits and dress him up as a deep-sea diver from the ancient times. People will think it's a great costume."

"I don't want them staring at me," said Shadow, remembering how the group of children had looked at him when he'd arrived.

"Trust me, they won't be staring," said Trillion. "That kind of costume sounds tame. It's your mother I'm worried about. I'll have to find her a mask so she's not recognized."

She looked apprehensive but nodded.

"What will we do while we're waiting?" Shadow asked.

"I don't have much room, but you're welcome to stay with me."

He set them up with a mattress on the floor to share, apologizing for its hardness. Shadow didn't know what he was talking about. It was the softest thing he'd ever slept on. He could feel the curves of his body sinking into it when he lay down. He wasn't sure he'd ever be able to sleep on his woven mattress in the forest again.

The thought of going back out in the water made him nervous. This time he could drown for real.

"You'll be fine," his mother whispered to him at night, sensing his fear. "You won't panic. You'll be using your lungs this time."

He wanted to ask her why she needed to see this odd-sounding Truthseeker before she saw her mother? Did it have something to do with her brother and the unspeakable things he did to her?

He didn't understand any of it and instead tried to remind himself that he was supposed to be on this journey for her sake, not his. He needed to follow her lead. He was out of his depth. Two and a half miles out of his depth, to be precise.

He spent his week exploring Trillion's home, with his permission to open any drawer or look in any cupboard. Trillion said he had no secrets, although everything looked like a secret to Shadow. Every object had a mysterious purpose he had to try to figure out.

The house was one large rectangular room with the

airlock entry on one of the narrow ends and a small bathroom at the other.

The first time he stepped into the bathroom he'd run from it in fear.

"Someone's in there," he said.

Trillion went to have a look.

"It's a mirror," he said when he came out.

"Is he your friend?" Shadow hadn't heard of the name *Amirror* before, although he realized there were many names he'd never heard of.

"Who?" asked Trillion.

"The boy in the mirror."

Trillion smiled. "Not yet he isn't, but hopefully one day."

"Why didn't you tell us there was someone else here?" He wondered what else Trillion was hiding from them.

"A mirror's not a person, it's a thing. That's your reflection. You were seeing yourself in there. Go and have another look."

His mother nodded at him and he walked back in with his fists raised, ready to fight.

The boy in the mirror had his fists raised in return.

He took a step back and saw the boy retreat.

"It's okay," his mother said, standing next to him. "Look, it's you."

He saw her standing next to the boy in the mirror and realized it was true. This boy who looked a bit like a male version of Eevie was him. He'd caught glimpses of himself before in puddles or the shining dials in his father's pod. He'd seen himself reflected back in his mother's eyes as she smiled at him, but never had he seen himself like this. The image was so clear.

"You didn't know you were so handsome, did you?" his mother said, resting her head on his arm.

He wasn't sure handsome would be the word he'd use.

His nose was long—longer than the rest of his family's. His eyes were dark like his father's, yet large like his mother's. His teeth were slightly crooked on the bottom row like Eevie's and they shared the same oval shaped face. His hair was long and braided like his mother's, except it was black.

"I look strange," he said.

"You've spent your life looking at three faces that weren't your own. No wonder you think you look strange. But you don't look strange to me. You look very handsome."

"I missed you, Mom," he said, moving his gaze from his reflection to hers. She'd been absent for so long as she'd slept in her bed.

"I'm sorry, Shadow. I've been a terrible mother."

"No, you haven't." He didn't want her to feel bad. She hadn't been a terrible mother. She'd been distant lately. And distracted. But she'd always shown him love. She'd done her best and he knew it. He just wished she did, too. How many people could raise two children in isolation like that?

She patted him on the back and left him to stare at himself.

When he was finally able to tear himself away from his image, he emerged to find her sleeping. Trillion was staring from a large window that had been cut into one of the steel walls. It was the only window in the house and Shadow wondered why it was there. Being on the end of the rows of houses, the window had a view of nothingness. Just dark currents of water. It was like looking at the night's sky, only without the stars.

"Why do you bother with a window?" he asked. "You can't see anything."

"You might see nothing, but I see everything," Trillion replied. "When I look out that window I see possibilities. I also saw you drowning, so count yourself lucky I have it."

That was a reasonable reply, so he pressed him no

further. It was lucky he'd spotted him drowning. He doubted his mother would've been able to save him despite her efforts.

"Your mother says you like music," said Trillion.

Shadow nodded.

Trillion went to get something from a drawer, returning with two small objects that Shadow had seen and not known what they were. He put one inside each of Shadow's ears and went to pick up another small rectangular object.

Shadow looked at him, confused, until something amazing happened.

Music poured into his ears. Not music like his family had played in the forest, but more like the sound of a thousand angels. He heard drums and a guitar and possibly the sound of a pipe, but mostly he had no idea what instruments were making the noises he could hear. His ears strained to hear each note, drinking them in as if they were weaving their way into his soul.

Then the sounds stopped as suddenly as they'd begun.

He looked at Trillion, his eyes wide.

"What happened?" he asked. "Where did it go?"

"Are you okay?" Trillion asked, his face brimming with concern.

Shadow was confused, until he realized he had tears sliding down his cheeks. He put his hands to his face and wiped them away.

"What was that?" he asked. "Can I please hear some more?"

Trillion laughed. "Your mother wasn't wrong. You really do like music."

He handed Shadow the rectangular device and pointed to a few buttons on it, showing him how to use it.

Shadow wasn't sure how long he sat in a chair and listened to the music, but it must have been hours. He couldn't believe he'd lived his whole life without hearing these beautiful sounds.

Eventually he'd gotten up and resumed poking about Trillion's house, earbuds firmly in place.

The house had the appearance of being smaller than it actually was, due to it being crammed with belongings. There were objects of every shape and color imaginable. That was the hardest part to get used to in Aquatica—the color. He was used to a world filled with a palette of greens and browns with the occasional splash of red from a flower or the bright orange glow of their fire. Not here. Aquatica was so bright it made his eyes hurt.

His favorite things to look at were Trillion's books that sat on a row of shelves, their pages filled with squiggles he couldn't understand. Some of them had pictures, which he'd stare at as his world opened up for the first time beyond the safety of the forest.

Yet no photo captivated him like the framed photo of Ryyder and he'd return to it often, picking it up and wondering what it would be like to meet her in person. Would she be there when they visited the Truthseeker? The thought gave him an unfamiliar feeling in his stomach. Like an invisible hand was squeezing it into a ball. He wasn't quite sure if it was a good feeling or a bad one but felt too shy to ask his mother. His instincts told him that these feelings were something to keep private.

If only his father were here, he could ask him about it. It was exactly the sort of thing they might discuss during man time. There was a certain safety that had surrounded his conversations with his father in that pod. He'd said he could ask him anything and quite often he had.

It was nice that his father had made that effort with him, despite the trauma it had caused Eevie. They could see her crying through the transparent walls of the pod. His father would sit with his back to her, determined to focus on his son. He appreciated it. He missed it, too. Maybe one day he'd return to the forest and they could sit in the pod once more and he could ask his father about these strange feelings in his stomach that Ryyder's photo evoked.

He slept well at night on Trillion's mattress, and not just because of the newfound comfort. His days exhausted him. There was so much to see and learn—and hear. He could never have imagined how many different types of music existed. But classical quickly became his favorite.

His mother barely seemed to sleep at all, he could feel the anxiety growing within her with each day that passed. When she did sleep, he'd hear her mumbling to herself in words that made no sense and she'd wake up with sweat beading on her forehead.

Trillion came and went at strange hours, reminding them it was no longer necessary to keep regular sleep patterns.

"I like sleeping at night," Shadow would say. It wasn't a habit he planned to break.

His days felt long without the need to hunt for his dinner, fetch water or start fires using two sticks and the friction of his hands. These people in Aquatica bought food from stores, had fresh water delivered to their homes and used electricity to cook their dinner and light their homes. It seemed such an easy existence.

He soon came to realize that no matter how slowly time passes, it continues to pass.

Aquaticus was upon them.

CHAPTER NINE

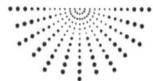

"Does your wife know we're coming?" asked Shadow as he attempted to squeeze his long limbs into the rubber suit Trillion had brought him. How did people wear these things? In the forest they wore very little at all. This suit felt like it was suffocating him, despite the cut-outs on the sides for his gills—cut-outs he wouldn't need, given the air tank Trillion had found him. His arms and legs dangled from the ends of the suit, but once he was zipped in it was surprisingly comfortable.

"Don't worry, my wife's not easily surprised. She probably knew you were coming to Aquatica before I did."

"Why don't you live with her?" asked his mother, as she fastened a mask to her face. It was a butterfly, studded with jewels that seemed to sparkle from a light source of their own. She was wearing her hair loose and it fanned out behind the mask. Upon her back she wore a set of pink gossamer wings in a wire frame.

"You look beautiful," said Trillion, his pale cheeks turning a pink shade. Shadow watched him curiously.

"Your cheeks have gone pink," he said. "Are you all right?"

"Perfectly fine," he said, going a deeper shade of pink.

Was he hot? It didn't feel hot in this room. It was always a little on the cold side.

"Your wife," said his mother. "You were going to tell me why you don't live with her."

"Yes, that's right," said Trillion, trying to regain his composure. "Truthseekers rarely marry. My wife was an exception, but as you can imagine, it wasn't easy being married to someone who knew your every thought before it even entered your head. Not easy for her and not easy for me. Rather than go our separate ways we decided to stay married yet live separately."

His mother nodded, seeming to understand.

"We just wanted different things," he continued. "And neither of us could achieve them while living together. We were driving each other crazy."

"Bonkers," said Shadow, remembering the word for it.

"That's right," said Trillion, smiling.

He glanced at his mother who was deep in thought, most likely thinking of her relationship with his father. She was a lot more like Trillion than he'd first realized. Two restless souls, not happy with the life they had, but unable to figure out what kind of life would bring them peace. Perhaps some souls weren't destined to be filled with joy.

"What about your daughter?" asked Shadow, seeing an opportunity to bring Ryyder into the conversation. "Don't you miss her?"

"Of course, I do." Trillion's eyes dripped with sadness. "I still see her, though. Not as much as I'd like. She's busy with her own life now."

Shadow wondered what that kind of life was like. "What does she do? Is she a Truthseeker as well?"

"I'm not sure."

"How can you not be sure? She's your daughter."

"She's very private about it. She knows things—things you or I couldn't know in a thousand years of trying—but it's not often she'll share them. I really don't know how developed her talents are."

"Your wife must know," his mother said. "Surely she's told you."

"My wife doesn't often talk about other people."

"Not even your daughter?"

He shook his head. "Not even my daughter."

"I can see why she was hard to live with."

Shadow didn't think it would be all that different to living with his own mother.

"What did you say your daughter does?" he asked, keen to keep the conversation about Ryyder going.

"She goes to school, whispers to her friends, swims backward and forward with no purpose. That kind of thing."

"Where does she swim?" he asked.

"Nowhere in particular. Just swims around. I used to ask her when she returned home if she found what it was she was looking for and she'd shake her head, not realizing I was joking. You'd get along well with her, I think."

Shadow nodded. From what he'd heard about her, he thought he would, too. Ever since he'd seen her photo, he couldn't shake the feeling that maybe she was the one he was being drawn to. He could feel it when he looked into her eyes. Like she'd been looking right at him when the photo was taken.

"Anyway, enough about Ryyder," said Trillion, lifting up the heavy-looking cylinder with some breathing apparatus attached. "Let's get you into this tank."

"It won't be heavy when you're in the water," he said, strapping it to Shadow's back.

He hoped not. Trillion wasn't joking when he'd said it weighed a lot.

Shadow glanced at the earbuds he'd left on the table.

"They're not waterproof," said Trillion. "Otherwise I'd let you keep them."

Shadow nodded, unable to hide his disappointment. Although, meeting Ryyder would be even better than music. He wouldn't need the earbuds if he had her.

"How long will it take us to get there?" he asked hoping he could be relieved of this costume sooner rather than later.

"About an hour. Think you can make it?"

He nodded. He'd swim for a hundred hours if it meant meeting Ryyder.

"Let's go," his mother said, already standing by the door. She was even keener than he was.

"Hold your horses," said Trillion. "I need to put on my costume."

"What are horses?" asked Shadow, hoping there weren't too many more things he was expected to hold. It was hard enough with this air tank.

"I'm not sure exactly," said Trillion. "Some kind of animal I think. It's just an old expression."

"He wants us to be patient," said his mother, looking the complete opposite, tapping her foot on the floor.

Trillion disappeared into the bathroom.

"I didn't think he was the dressing up sort," whispered Shadow.

"He'll stand out more if he doesn't dress up."

"I wonder what he'll be. Any ideas?"

"A horse." She giggled and he noticed faint smile lines that had started to appear around her eyes. He wasn't used to seeing her look so happy.

When Trillion emerged, Shadow had to rub his eyes in disbelief. He was wearing a brown suit that clung to his body, covering him from his feet up to his neck. Small slits had been cut into it to accommodate his gills. He'd painted his hands and face brown to match. Upon his head perched a green hat with long fronds trailing to the floor.

"A tree!' said his mother, clutching her sides as she laughed. "You look magnificent."

"I figured the more ridiculous I look the less people will look at you and Shadow. Plus, the paint on my skin will distract people from Shadow's skin. Hopefully they assume he's painted his skin, too."

"We'll be practically invisible next to you," his mother said.

"Shadow just needs two finishing touches," he said, reaching for a bright red cape and throwing it to him. "Put this on."

"But I'm trying to blend in," he protested.

"Just put it on. Trust me. And this." He handed him a pair of large goggles that would be sure to cover most of his face.

Shadow smiled. He liked Trillion and hoped his instincts about him were right. Having known only three people his whole life, he didn't think he was a particularly good judge of character. Although, his mother seemed to trust him, and she'd met plenty of people. Or was she just so desperate to meet the Truthseeker that she was prepared to overlook any apprehension she might have toward this man? Only time would tell.

When they got out to the water, Shadow saw the true spectacle of Trillion's costume. The branches waved out behind him, dancing in the currents and sending out brilliant green sparks of light.

He hovered for a few minutes while Shadow adjusted to the concept of breathing through the tank. It felt strange to be using his lungs underwater. Maybe Trillion would let him keep this tank and he could bring Eevie or his father back down here. But then he'd need to learn to use his gills and he wasn't sure that was such a good idea.

He nodded, trying to smile and realizing it was impossible with a mouthpiece lodged between his teeth.

His mother took him by the hand. He looked at her, realizing why Trillion's face had filled with color when he'd seen her in her costume. She looked beautiful—the kind of beautiful that was obvious to the whole world. Trillion may be married, but that didn't make him blind.

A stab of loyalty to his father shot through him. His mother belonged by his father's side, not this pale man dressed as a tree. He reminded himself of how much Trillion had seemed to love his wife, despite not living together. He wasn't interested in his mother that way. He just couldn't help being affected by her beauty.

They swam. Slowly at first, then when Trillion saw Shadow was keeping up, he picked up the pace.

His tank was lighter in the water, but his goggles bothered him with their size. He could see out of them and they did a good job of covering his face, but they were cumbersome.

The streets were awash with color that hurt to look at. The lights in the trees flashed brighter and faster. Flags hung from doorways and Shadow felt the beat of a drum vibrating deep in his chest. He saw people dressed in wildly colored costumes, the fabric swaying in the water as it shimmered and glowed. Their wigs seemed to be alive as they floated restlessly around their brightly painted faces. Some were dressed as dolphins or stingrays or sharks, but many weren't dressed as anything in particular at all. The aim of these people seemed to be to see how many layers of color they could pile upon their body at once. They were hideously spectacular.

Shadow longed to stop swimming and take a moment to stare. Never in his life did he expect to see such a sight.

Trillion had been right. Nobody paid them any attention.

They moved through the water unseen, invisible despite the bright colors they wore. He was glad for his red cape, billowing behind him, despite the way it dragged in the water. Without it he'd stand out. Nobody else was dressed in black. Even the people dressed as sharks had turned their skin to orange or gold.

He concentrated on his breathing as they moved through the crowd. This was the reason he'd panicked last time. It wasn't his breathing. It was the shock of seeing faces other than ones he'd grown up with. Under their costumes he noticed the variations. Each face was unique. Some ears chose to stick out from their owner's head, others lay flat. Some noses looked like they'd been squashed, and others bent upward as if trying to grow toward the sky. Some eyes sat far apart, and others were close, just as some faces were round and others were oval. He saw one man with a chin that looked almost square.

Once he adjusted to the strangeness of it all, he began to enjoy himself. This place was fascinating. Perhaps these humans of the water had the right idea after all. They certainly looked happy.

They swam over a large open square with people crowded around every side as well as above. There was a group of children performing, darting through hoops at speeds that seemed impossible.

If this was the speed Aquaticans travelled at, then it was no wonder Trillion and his mother thought he was slow.

The crowd built thicker and thicker with revelers, until it became difficult to find space to pass. His mother let go of his hand and they wove their way through in single file. A few times he lost sight of her, only to find her several feet away, her eyes darting around as she searched for him. He spotted two girls with air tanks on their backs, just like his and he felt a sense of relief. He wasn't the only one. He hated to think he was being stared at.

This was paranoia and he knew it. Nobody was staring at him. They were all too busy staring at themselves, running their hands through the shimmering strands of their costumes and trying to catch their reflection in windows or the goggles of their friends.

Then just as slowly as the crowd had built, it dispersed. It reminded him of the summer solstice, the light of each day stretching longer and longer until it could stretch no more and was forced to retreat, shortening the days little by little as the moon took charge of the sky.

Trillion increased the pace and they swam over rows of houses, all identical in shape, unique only in the colors they were painted. Shadow hadn't realized just how many people lived in Aquatica. When his mother had told him there were a million people, he'd been unable to imagine what this number looked like. Only now did he realize how big it really was.

They reached the final row of houses and paused. He was unsure why. He saw Trillion dart into the darkness, the branches of his costume lighting the way. They followed and he soon realized why Trillion had paused. Swimming into this part of the ocean was no different to jumping from the branch of a tree. You needed to steel yourself for impact.

His skin prickled and he saw goose bumps stand to attention on the parts of his arms that weren't covered by his suit. Even the temperature of the air in his tank seemed to drop.

The further they swam, the colder it got. He also noticed the absence of a humming sound that had been caught in his ears for so long he'd ceased to notice it. He knew this hum was what kept the fish away, but surely it couldn't be doing people any good to be living with such a sound. He wished he had his music to drown it out.

They swam on through the dark, through the quiet, through the cold. He tugged at the wings on his mother's back, urging her to lift up her mask. He wanted to see her face. Was she worried about where Trillion was taking them? Surely nobody lived out here. This must be a trap.

His mother pushed her mask up to her forehead, its bright studs shining a gentle glow across her face. She nodded and smiled, clearly unconcerned about where they were heading. He relaxed, letting the stress escape the tightness of his chest.

A fish swam past and he tensed up again. Did this fish have a mother following it? Was it a shark? He'd heard about them and they sounded nasty.

His mother reached out her hand, as if to touch it. The fish ignored her and swam on.

Trillion had stopped in the water ahead of them. Shadow assumed he was waiting for them, but when they approached, he saw he was wrong.

They'd reached a house that was unmistakably the home of the Truthseeker. It was a dark color—a color that had no name, but if Shadow had to call it something, he thought he'd call it murk. It was so gloomy, so creepy, he was certain it must contain evil. No good could reside inside walls the color of murk.

Trillion slipped through the door to the airlock, somehow managing to guide the branches of his costume behind him.

Shadow reached for his mother. He wanted to turn around, swim back through this strangely fascinating world and up to the surface. He wanted to run across the beach and into the forest, straight back into the arms of his father.

His hand trailed through the water without reward. His mother had darted ahead and disappeared through the door without looking back to see if he'd follow. He couldn't let her go inside alone. There was no choice for him but to go with her.

The airlock was dark, much darker than the one at Trillion's house. It was larger though with enough room for the three of them to comfortably stand without being pressed up against each other.

"Well done. You made it," said Trillion, lifting the goggles from his face, revealing large white circles of skin that he'd neglected to paint brown.

If Shadow weren't so nervous, he'd have had to stifle a giggle.

He pulled the breathing apparatus and those annoying goggles from his face and undid the straps that tied the air tank to his body. It was a relief to set it down on the ground. He draped his red cape over it, deciding not to take off his rubber suit. It'd strangely molded to his body. It certainly felt warm. It was freezing in here.

He saw his mother shiver and he put an arm around her. She pushed him away. "Shadow, your suit is freezing."

"Not on the inside. Would you like to wear it?" he asked.

She shook her head.

"It will be warm in the house," said Trillion, reaching for some towels on a high shelf and handing them one each.

Forgetting about the wings on her back, he saw his mother struggle for a moment to wrap the towel around herself. He helped her remove the wings, setting them down next to his air tank. She dropped her butterfly mask and goggles on top.

They squeezed through the folds of the door and found themselves in a dark room so warm he felt like he'd stepped into a cocoon. He smiled, thinking of it as a reverse chrysalis —his mother had shed her butterfly wings and then they entered the cocoon. Did that make her a caterpillar now?

He was about to make a joke to that effect when the lights turned on. He squinted as he tried to adjust to the brightness.

Unlike Trillion's home, this one had been divided into smaller rooms. They were standing in a long corridor that ran down the center of the house. Two doors sat on either side and another at the end. He preferred Trillion's home with its spacious layout. This place made him feel like he couldn't breathe.

"Welcome to my former home," said Trillion, with a sweep of his hand.

"Where's your wife?" asked his mother, getting straight to the point.

Shadow craned his neck as he peered down the hallway. It wasn't Trillion's wife he was interested in seeing. Would Ryyder be here or would she have joined her friends at Aquaticus? He remembered Trillion mentioned she had friends. He'd never had a friend before. It must be a nice feeling to have somebody like you without any family ties forcing them to.

"This way," said Trillion, taking the second door on the left.

A wave of seriousness washed over his mother's face.

"Come on," said Shadow. "It'll be okay."

She looked at him, seeming to take comfort in his words —words he couldn't be certain were true. Would they be okay? He hoped so. In any case, it was too late now. They were here. Trapped like a rabbit in one of their snares, at Trillion's mercy.

The floor was gray and hard under their feet, unlike Trillion's home where the floor had felt like soft rubber. He hadn't walked across anything like this before. His feet were used to walking across the dirt of the forest floor. He missed his home with a pang so deep inside his soul that he gasped.

"Are you okay?" his mother whispered.

He nodded. "I'm fine."

"Hello, wife," they heard Trillion say.

They stepped into the room behind him.

It was a small room, square in shape and lit by dozens of candles that sat upon the floor. Shadow looked closer and saw that just like the rest of Aquatica, the candles were fake, with tiny light globes instead of flames. There were no windows in the room and the only furniture was three plush red chairs; two with their backs to the door and another in the far corner in which the Truthseeker sat.

She was older than Shadow expected, although she must still have been close to Trillion's age. Before coming to Aquatica, the oldest person he'd ever seen was his father, and he was hardly old.

This woman had hair the color of ash, as if it'd fallen from the flames of a fire. Had it once been golden like her husband's? They had the same pale complexion and piercing blue eyes, which made her no different from the rest of Aquatica, but there was an aura about her that set her apart from Trillion or anyone else he'd seen.

She looked wise and kind, yet at the same time sent fear racing through to his core. She wasn't a person to be messed with.

She smiled at them and he saw Ryyder in her face—the same open, gentle expression he'd seen in the photo.

Perhaps she wasn't so scary after all.

"Out," she cried. "Out!'

Shadow stepped backward.

"Not you," she snapped. "Trillion. Out! It's the boy and his mother I need to see, not you."

He wondered how she knew they were mother and son. They didn't look alike.

"Sure, darling," Trillion said grinning sarcastically, the white of his teeth matching the circles around his eyes. He left, closing the door behind him.

"Sit down," the Truthseeker said, looking from Shadow to his mother and smiling, all her anger of moments ago fading into oblivion.

They sat as instructed, frightened of her volcano erupting once more. Perhaps she wasn't as kind as Shadow had first thought.

"I've been waiting for you," she said.

"Did Trillion tell you we were coming?" his mother asked.

"I don't need him to tell me anything."

She laughed and Shadow understood why Trillion hadn't been able to put up with her. How did Ryyder cope?

"Ryyder's not here," she said to Shadow, as if reading his thoughts.

"Will she be home soon?" he asked, trying to cover his disappointment.

"What truth do you seek?" she asked, ignoring his question and fixing her gaze on his mother.

She cleared her throat. "I have one question …"

"Go on," said the Truthseeker.

"Did she know how he treated me?" his mother asked, her face filling with pain.

Shadow was confused. Then he realized it was her mother she spoke of. He should have guessed this is what she wanted to know. Had her mother known how badly she'd been treated by her brother? She needed to understand this before she could meet with her again. She would never put up with him treating Eevie like that.

"That's not your truth to ask," the Truthseeker said, seeming to enjoy his mother's distress.

"Of course, it's my truth. It involves me doesn't it?"

"Let me start from the beginning, Nahlah, my dear."

She knew her name. Trillion must've talked to her, unless when he said everyone knew her this also included his strange wife. His mother didn't seem to notice. Or perhaps she expected this from a Truthseeker.

"I don't want to know about the beginning," she said. "The beginning doesn't matter."

"Don't be stupid." The Truthseeker's eyes narrowed. "The beginning always matters. How can you understand the end if you never understand the beginning? They're linked with bonds that cannot be broken."

"Okay. Tell me about the beginning then."

The Truthseeker smiled, pleased to have gotten her way. Shadow expected she got her way often. All the time, perhaps.

"This boy is your son," she said. "And you call him Shadow. It's an interesting name."

"He was named after his father. The first I saw of him was a shadow. It's no more interesting than that."

"Yes it is."

"How?" asked Shadow.

"Because you're a shadow of your mother's past. You've met before. Many, many times."

"I don't understand. She's my mother. I met her the day I was born."

"In this body, that's true. But our souls live many lives in many bodies."

"And we've met before?" asked his mother, looking as confused as he felt.

"That's what I said. The two of you have a long history, despite not actually being soulmates."

"What's a soulmate?" Shadow asked.

"The soul you're destined to travel through life with.

There's another kind of power that draws the two of you together. It's quite a beautiful thing. Nahlah, you once died trying to protect Shadow, only to strike him down dead in a later life. He rescued you from poverty once and you fell madly in love with him. It nearly killed you watching him marry your sister. It's been quite a journey for you both."

"My mother was in love with me?" asked Shadow, screwing up his face. That sounded so wrong. This woman didn't know what she was talking about. She just made things up for her own entertainment. There was no other explanation.

"Don't get carried away with yourself. She wasn't your mother then. You weren't even living on this planet."

"Where did we live?" asked his mother.

"Planet Earth."

Shadow and his mother looked at each other in alarm.

"Did you tell Trillion about Dad?" he asked his mother.

She shook her head. "Did you?"

"No."

How could the Truthseeker know about the planet his father had come from? Nobody else knew about that. Perhaps she wasn't as great a fraud as he'd been thinking.

"Your father's an interesting soul, too," said the Truthseeker to Shadow. "He's your father in this lifetime, but in his last you were his. It's ironic how he's put so much time into loving you and your sister in equal measures when you did the complete opposite when he was your son."

"This is ridiculous," he said, more out of an automatic reaction to the insulting words spewing from her mouth than through disbelief. If he was his father's father, then that meant he was the one who'd built the pod. That was more than a little hard to believe.

"It's nothing to me whether or not you choose to believe." She looked unperturbed.

"And what about Mom?" He pointed to her. "I supposed you're going to tell us that she was Dad's sister, Valentina."

"Hardly!' She laughed. "Especially given they were alive at the same time. No, your mother's soul has been on Neron for quite some time now."

"Is Eevie Valentina?" his mother asked. "Buzz wanted to call her that."

The Truthseeker shook her head.

"Then how does she fit in?" asked Shadow.

"Not everybody has to fit in," she said.

They both nodded.

"But she does," added the Truthseeker, looking directly at his mother. "Buzz was also your husband a long time ago in a place called India."

"There's a Planet India?" she asked, looking surprised. They'd often wondered if there were more planets with life other than Earth and Neron.

The Truthseeker shook her head. "No, India is a country on Earth."

"I'm not sure what a country is?" she said.

Shadow wasn't sure either.

"Neron is small enough to have all its citizens live in the one place. Earth wasn't like that. Billions of people were spread across the globe. India was just one small part of Planet Earth."

"And Buzz was my husband?"

"That's right. Your name was Tara back then and he was Vikram. He loved you with all his heart. It's the reason you were so drawn to him in this lifetime."

"So, he's my soulmate?"

"No, no, no, I never said that. His soulmate is Eevie. They have a bond you can never break. She was in India as well, at the same time as you, although you never met her. She was his sister."

"If I was his wife, wouldn't I have met his sister?"

"She died when she was still young." There was no emotion in the Truthseeker's voice. It was a fact she was stating, that was all. "And her death almost destroyed Vikram. He would most certainly have died from grief without you."

"How did she die?" asked his mother.

"She had a father who was abusive, just like your brother. A different kind of abuse, but it was abuse all the same. He wasn't a gentle soul."

Tears rolled down his mother's face.

"There's no point crying about it now," said the Truthseeker. "This happened a long time ago, very far away."

"But it damaged Eevie's soul, didn't it?" asked Shadow, his sister's unusual bond to his father becoming clear.

"It did. Her father took a piece of her that's never been able to be replaced. She clings to Buzz now, forever grateful for the way he loves and protects her. It's also one of the reasons she was born to you, Nahlah. She needed a mother who understands her."

"But I've been a terrible mother," she sobbed.

"I don't like self-pity," said the Truthseeker, her voice colder than the ocean outside her door. "You must pull yourself together."

"I'm sorry," she said, wiping her eyes with the back of her hand.

"You're a great mother," said Shadow, reaching for her hand.

She squeezed his hand in return.

"If Buzz's soulmate is Eevie, then who's mine?" she asked, her voice still trembling. "Is it my mother? I dream of her often."

The Truthseeker shook her head. "Your soulmate's a bit preoccupied at the moment. Unless something drastic changes, you won't meet him until the day you die. Anyway, stop obsessing about soulmates. You have other things you should be thinking about."

"Like what?" asked Shadow.

"Like the thing your mother came here to ask me."

"I already asked you if she knew, and you wouldn't tell me." Her brow wrinkled.

"What she knew or didn't know is something for you to ask her yourself. As far as you're concerned, you should be asking why this happened to you." The Truthseeker leaned back in her chair and tapped a finger on her chin.

"Okay. So why did this happen to me?" his mother asked.

"You needed a reason to leave the ocean. You needed to be able to leave your life behind."

"Why did I need to? What child needs to leave their mother?"

"You needed to find Buzz. You were destined to have a son whose own son will one day do something of great importance."

"I'm going to have a son?" asked Shadow. "He'd never once imagined himself as a father.

"You will," said the Truthseeker. "And that son is the chosen one."

"Chosen one? Chosen for what?" This sounded a little like a made-up story.

"Long ago, there was a soul who was chosen to save planet Earth from destruction. He succeeded for a while, but as you know, ultimately he failed. Neron is on the same path. Another chosen one has been selected."

Shadow's mother shuffled in her chair. "You mean there's another asteroid."

The Truthseeker roared laughing. Shadow and his mother glanced at each other, wondering what was funny.

"No! The people here are doing a fine job of killing the planet all on their own, just like Earthlings were so good at it before the asteroid put an early end to their misery. Choosing to live under the ocean was supposed to be a way to save the people, but all it's really doing is speeding up our demise."

These words sent chills racing down Shadow's spine. Could this be possible or was this some kind of elaborate conspiracy Trillion and the Truthseeker had cooked up? They both seemed determined to see people live on the land again.

"Why was it a mistake?" asked Shadow. The people he'd seen so far seemed very happy with their lives.

"Because when you can't see the trees that give you air and the land that grows your food, how are you supposed to care about looking after it? But it's bigger than that ... when you can't look up into the sky and see your planet's place in the universe, how can you learn to appreciate how important it is? It's time the people came back up to the surface and lived once more upon the land. Only then do they have a chance to undo their damage."

"And Shadow's future son is supposed to do that?" asked his mother.

The Truthseeker nodded. "Oh, yes. He is. He'll lead everyone from the water one day. You don't have any idea how powerful his son will be."

"Who will be my son's mother?" asked Shadow, certain it had to be Ryyder.

The Truthseeker's face dropped and for a strange moment Shadow thought she was going to cry, as a layer of vulnerability rose to the surface.

"Your soulmate ... You already know who she is."

He locked eyes with her. Ryyder was his soulmate. The Truthseeker's own daughter. She knew it and she didn't like it. She also knew there was nothing she could do about it.

"What's going on?" asked Shadow's mother.

"It's Ryyder, Mom. Her daughter."

His mother's eyes widened. "I thought you were just fascinated because it was the first photo you ever saw."

"Enough!' said the Truthseeker.

"Your daughter would be lucky to have my son." Shadow's mother stood and glared at her.

"Do not tell my daughter about the baby," she said. "She must not know."

"You just don't want her to be with Shadow," said his mother.

"That's not it," said the Truthseeker. "You, yourself, have given birth to a chosen one before and the pressure that put on you nearly broke your soul. I don't want my daughter to experience that. She'll find out soon enough. I'm asking for her good, not my own."

"But you're prepared to let my son carry the weight of that knowledge?" His mother took a step toward the door. "I think I've heard enough."

"Leaving so soon?" asked the Truthseeker. "Just when your brother was about to arrive, too. That would be a shame for you to miss him."

His mother gasped, and Shadow saw her begin to tremble. She turned to Shadow. "I can't do this. I thought I could, but I can't. It's too much. I need your father. I need Eevie. I need to be far away from here. I can't face him again."

"You can," said the Truthseeker. "When you lived in India, your soul learnt a very important lesson. You learnt forgiveness. If you forgave your sister for what she did to you then, you can forgive your brother now."

"I can't," his mother said.

"You can. And you will. You have a forgiving soul."

His mother shook her head. "I need to leave. I need to go back to the forest. I can't do this."

"But your mother," said Shadow, desperate for her to stay. "You haven't seen her yet."

He wasn't ready to leave. Not without meeting Ryyder. He'd come so far. He couldn't leave now when he was so close.

"I can't. I'm sorry, Shadow. I can't."

"You can, Mom. I'm here. Nobody is going to hurt you."

Silent tears ran down his mother's face and he knew she was leaving no matter what he said. The Truthseeker had failed to answer the one question she'd come here with and now that her brother was on his way, she was in a panic.

"Please, Mom, don't do this."

His chance to meet Ryyder was sliding through his fingertips. And if what the Truthseeker had said was true, if he didn't meet Ryyder, then the future of the planet was in danger.

"You must stay," his mother said, putting her shaking hands to his face. "Stay and meet Ryyder. I won't hold you back from that. It's important. But please don't hold me back from leaving. I'm not ready for this. I'm just not."

Shadow glanced toward the Truthseeker. "If my mother leaves, will I see her again? Will she be okay?"

"That's not your tru—"

"Please!' Shadow shouted, cutting her off.

Her eyes opened wide, but she nodded.

"Let your mother go." Her voice was hoarse, like it was an effort to speak. "But you must stay."

"How long until her brother arrives?"

"She has time," said the Truthseeker. "If she leaves now, they will not meet. Although, I really think she should stay. Forgiveness is in her soul."

He nodded his thanks and followed his mother, who had left the room immediately upon hearing these words. It seemed the Truthseeker didn't know everything after all. His mother's soul certainly didn't seem to be the forgiving sort right now.

He stood with her in the airlock and held her hands. It didn't matter how tightly he gripped them, her trembling wouldn't stop. The idea of seeing her brother again really had been too much.

"You must hurry," he said to her. "Leave before he gets here."

She nodded, letting go of his hands to pick up her goggles and butterfly mask. But instead of putting them on, she placed them beside his air tank and took the goggles from his costume instead.

"I'll swap you," she said.

"No, Mom. Those things are awful."

"I like them," she said, slipping them onto her head and tightening the straps, before lifting them to rest on her forehead. She'd never been a very good liar. Obviously she'd noticed how much they'd bothered him and wanted to give him one last gift. She really was a wonderful mother.

"Thanks," he said, not wanting to take this moment from her.

"I love you." She touched his cheek.

"I know," he said. "You've proved that by coming here with me. And now you're proving it again by letting me stay."

"You'll come back to the forest as soon as you can?"

"Of c-course." He choked on the words, hoping desperately for them to be true.

She turned to leave.

"Hey, Mom," he said.

"Yes?"

"I love you, too."

She smiled the saddest smile he'd ever seen. And with that she was gone, leaving him surrounded by strangers—something that made him feel lonelier than when he'd been isolated in the forest. It wasn't the number of people around you who brought comfort to your life, it was who they were and how they warmed your heart.

But Ryyder was here, he reminded himself. And she definitely warmed his heart. Now all he had to do was wait for her to come home.

CHAPTER TEN

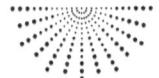

*S*hadow stood in the airlock, unsure of what to do next. Return to the Truthseeker? Look for Trillion? Or stay right where he was and wait for his mother's brother —his uncle— to arrive?

The intensity of the anger that bubbled inside him, forced him back inside. He couldn't trust himself to meet his uncle alone. He might kill him. He might even enjoy killing him after what he'd done to his mother.

"Trillion?" he called.

"In here," Trillion called back.

Shadow followed his voice and took the first door on the right, which turned out to be a kitchen. Pots and pans hung from hooks on the wall and the benches were lined with jars filled with herbs and strange colored powders. A timber table stood in the middle of the room, surrounded by six matching chairs. It looked ancient. He wondered how many meals had been shared at it over the years.

Trillion was seated, drinking a mug of what Shadow now recognized as tea. He was still wearing his tree costume, which looked more than a little unusual in this small kitchen.

The Truthseeker was bustling at the stove with a saucepan in one hand and some bright orange leaves in the other. She looked almost like a normal person.

"Sit down," she said to Shadow over her shoulder. "And stop staring at me like that."

"I'm sorry," he said. "It's just that you look so...so different."

She laughed. "Not the first time I've heard that."

"She's a different person when she's in Truthseeker mode," explained Trillion. "She's much more tolerable when she's just plain old Trudy."

"Trudy," he repeated. It'd never occurred to him that she had a name, although she'd been married and had a daughter, so he supposed that made sense. He didn't think he'd describe her as plain old Trudy though. She was the most fascinating person he'd ever come across. Not that he'd come across very many, but it was a list that was growing.

"Mom's gone," said Shadow, sliding into a chair next to Trillion.

"Gone?" Trillion spluttered his tea and Shadow had to wipe his face. "She was supposed to take me with her."

Trudy huffed at the stove. "I've told you, it's not your time."

"She was in a hurry," said Shadow.

"But we had a deal." Trillion looked furious.

"She wasn't thinking clearly after what she was just told."

"You're always meddling in my life," said Trillion, shaking his head at his wife.

"I've told you a million times that I can't change the things I see," she replied without looking up.

"I need to catch up to her," he said, standing.

"She's long gone," said Shadow. "You've seen how fast she moves in the water. You'll never catch her."

"Then I'll go with you." He sat back down and folded his

arms, looking a little like Eevie when their father would tell her he needed some time alone.

"My uncle is apparently on his way here," said Shadow, avoiding having to agree to take Trillion to the forest.

"And your mother didn't want to see him?"

Shadow shook his head.

Trudy left the stove and sat next to him, resting her hand on his arm.

"He's a different man now. He's very sorry for what he did."

"But how could he do those things?" Shadow shifted in his chair to break the contact. He didn't want this strange woman's hand on him. "She was only a child."

"And so was he," came her reply. "A confused and frightened child, dealing with the loss of his father."

"That doesn't excuse what he did to her. He needs to pay for what he's done."

She shook her head. "No, it doesn't excuse it. But he's spent his life trying to make amends. Believe me when I say, he really has paid for it. Your mother's disappearance really shook him up."

"Enough to turn him into a completely different person?"

"Perhaps. That is possible. People *can* change."

"How do you even know he's on his way?" asked Shadow.

"Because he visits me every week at this time, begging me to tell him if your mother is okay."

"And you've never told him?"

"It's not his truth to ask," she said. "He'll find out when he's meant to."

"How long until he arrives?" asked Trillion.

"A few minutes," she said. "Shadow, I think maybe you should go for a swim."

"But I want to see him." Shadow crossed his arms and planted his feet on the floor.

"You're not ready to see him. This isn't how it's meant to be."

"How would yo—" He stopped himself mid-sentence. Of course, she knew. This woman knew everything.

"Shadow, please. Your uncle never stays long. He'll be gone before you get back. You'll see him one day. But not today. Please trust me on this."

"But where will I go?" Shadow stood, feeling he had no choice but to trust this strange woman who saw things she wasn't meant to.

"Go for a swim," said Trillion. "Maybe you'll run into Ryyder. She's out there somewhere."

Shadow wondered if Trillion knew who Ryyder was to him. It seemed he didn't.

"Quickly now," said Trudy, ushering him from the room.

Shadow allowed himself to be led to the airlock.

"Hurry," hissed Trudy as she pushed him through the door and disappeared from sight.

With no time to strap his air tank to his back, he grabbed his mother's goggles, burst into the water and fought the urge to breathe with his lungs.

He could do this.

The water flowed through his gills. He concentrated, feeling relief as the oxygen reached his blood supply.

He swam away from the Truthseeker's house in the direction of Aquatica, hoping the water would be warmer. A man in a navy-blue suit made out of a stretchy material was swimming toward him. Not trusting himself, Shadow diverted to pass him at a distance.

So that was his uncle. The man who hurt his mother and now claimed he was sorry. Was sorry good enough in a situation like that? Not to Shadow it wasn't.

The man passed, not paying him the slightest bit of attention. His eyes were focused on the Truthseeker's house, the place he came each week to beg for forgiveness.

Shadow felt his heart beat hard and noticed his hands had balled into fists. For a moment, he was worried his gills would stop working, as they had when he'd been frightened by the first children he'd seen. But this time they didn't fail him, continuing to draw in water at a steady rate.

He'd made the right decision, taking Trudy's advice to leave before his uncle arrived. When he confronted him, it was going to be on his terms, with a level head. Nothing productive is ever achieved in anger.

He swam on, taking a diversion to avoid having to pass his uncle once more when he left the Truthseeker's house.

And that was when he saw her.

Ryyder was returning home. There was no question in his mind that it was her.

The freezing water warmed as her energy threaded its way around his heart.

Once again, his heart beat hard in his chest, although this time for an entirely different reason. His gills seemed to slow. Was it possible for gills to hold in a breath? Pushing concern for his breathing aside, he stopped and waited for her to approach, unable to move another inch forward toward her for fear of becoming completely overwhelmed and drowning.

She swam to him, tilting her head with curiosity and pointing toward her house, seeming to ask if that was where he'd come from.

He nodded slowly.

She was exquisite. Her short, blonde hair floated around her head, reflecting the soft light that was filtering from the silver headband she wore. He was surprised to see a set of deep green eyes staring back at him from behind her goggles. He hadn't realized eyes came in this color.

Trillion had said she was the same age as him, yet he didn't think he'd ever seen anyone so different. She had the soft features of a child, with the aura of an older woman. He dragged his eyes from her face and saw she wore a pink dress with a tight bodice with cut-outs for her gills and a skirt that billowed about her legs. She held a silver wand in her hand with a glimmering star perched on the end.

She'd obviously been at Aquaticus, yet this costume she wore suited her perfectly. He found it hard to imagine her wearing anything else.

All thoughts of his uncle evaporated from his mind as Ryyder tucked her wand in her waistband and reached for his hand. He felt the warmth of her fingers as he enclosed them in his own.

She hesitated, then darted upward, still holding his hand. He was pulled along with her, his breathing no longer a concern. He had other things to think about, such as where this captivatingly beautiful girl was leading him.

They continued to head upward, before she sharply changed direction, dragging him down once more. He felt his blood surge with oxygen as she turned to the left, then the right.

She was so graceful. He felt like a giant bear in comparison.

He saw her smile, her face lighting up like the most beautiful sunrise he'd ever seen, and he realized she wasn't taking him anywhere. She was having fun, using the water as a playground. Her movements reminded him of a book about dolphins he'd seen at Trillion's house.

She took hold of his other hand and swam in circles. Soon they were spinning faster, creating a whirlpool between their outstretched arms. He felt himself being pulled toward her.

Her hands slipped from his and he was thrown to one

side, his head spinning with the sensations she was building within him.

The water was dark and quiet. He adjusted his goggles, searching for her.

He didn't find her with his eyes. He found her with his lips. Or rather her lips found him.

She was kissing him, her hands wrapping around the back of his neck as she pulled her body close to him.

His parents had only ever kissed him on the cheek. He hadn't realized this kind of kiss was possible. It'd never occurred to him. He'd never had anyone he wanted to kiss like this, he supposed.

He put his hands on her tiny waist. Her skin was bare on her midriff and he could feel the slippery softness of her body as her gills tingled against his own.

The kiss continued, and he felt strange sensations run through his body. His heart was beating softer yet faster, and his gills were drawing the water in at a quickened pace. Fire shot into his belly and lit him with desire.

He broke the kiss, trying to get hold of himself.

She pulled away and he reached for her once more, pulling her to him and bringing his lips to hers. He didn't want to stop kissing her. Not now. Not ever. He could die right now, and he wouldn't care. Just as long as her lips didn't part from his own.

He felt her fingertips on his cheeks, then his mouth as she broke away. They trailed across his lips and she smiled, taking his hand once more and leading him back through the water.

He followed. He'd follow this girl anywhere. When he'd stared at her photo she'd won his heart. Now she'd won his soul.

They were swimming further away from the house,

deeper into the ocean. It was dark and cold yet being near Ryyder kept him warm.

She stopped and slipped her wand from her waistband, holding it in her outstretched arm. It lit the water around them, bathing the ocean in a soft glow. The water looked deep blue with bright colors reflecting back at them from below. It was like a miniature underwater world with rocks and bushes of all shapes. Some were bright orange or red, some were purple or green. He reached out his hand to touch one only to find it was hard in texture. A small blue fish darted out at him, followed by several others.

Ryyder held her wand higher and he saw fish of all colors swimming around the light, as if drawn to it. It reminded him of a rainbow, so many beautiful colors all in the one place.

A flat, brown rock swam toward him and he saw it had arms and legs sticking out from the sides and a long head at the front. He'd seen one of these in Trillion's books only he couldn't remember its name.

He reached out his hand and touched its hard and slimy shell. It tilted its head, equally as fascinated with him.

He laughed, and it swam away, as if offended.

As he took in his surroundings, he realized that the ocean held far more than the gaudy, artificial world created by humans. Was that why they used such bright colors for their homes? Were they trying to mimic the beauty of the nature they'd driven away with their sonars? If so, they'd failed miserably. Humans could never compete with the clever magnificence of the natural world.

The world that Ryyder was showing him was the first thing he'd seen down here that had even a hope of competing with the beauty of the forest.

He saw her smiling at him and realized that he was

wrong. *She* was the first thing he'd seen that competed with the beauty of the forest.

It was no wonder she and her mother had chosen to live in the depths of the ocean away from Aquatica. Who would want to live in artificial beauty when this lay at your fingertips? Trillion should've moved his home out here.

Ryyder tucked her wand back into her waistband and took his hand, leading him to her house. He didn't want to leave, but once more felt himself compelled to follow her wherever she chose to take him. He just hoped his uncle was no longer there.

They slipped inside the airlock.

"Hello," she said, smiling at him, as she pulled her goggles from her face.

"Hi," he whispered. The full force of her beauty hit him. Her eyes weren't quite green, they had flecks of blue, making them look almost turquoise.

"I'm sorry," she said. "I'm not really sure what came over me out there. You must think—"

"I think you're beautiful," he said, not wanting her to feel like she'd done anything wrong.

"How did you do that to your skin?" she asked. "It looks so real."

He put a hand to his face, confused.

"Oh, the color," he said, realizing she hadn't seen skin as dark as his before. "I didn't do anything to it."

"May I?" she asked, raising her hand to his cheek, in much the same way his mother had done earlier.

He hesitated, confused by her asking. She'd done a lot more than put her hand on his cheek in the water. Having emerged into the airlock, a new sense of shyness had descended upon them. Perhaps he was only feeling this way as she was the first girl he'd spoken to who wasn't his sister or his mother. Did she feel this connection too, or was it all in his mind? She must have. He hadn't dreamed of her kissing him like that.

Her fingers gently stroked his cheek. He noticed her fingertips were wrinkled from the water, just as he'd noticed his had been when he'd been dragged into Trillion's house. Yet, despite the wrinkles, her touch felt smooth. Tingles ran down his spine, landing in his stomach. The pangs he'd had when kissing her returned.

Was this what it felt like to fall in love? When he'd imagined it, he hadn't thought too much about how it would make him feel physically. He'd been too busy imaging all the emotions that would run through his brain. Physically it was almost unpleasant, yet somehow he felt happier and more complete than ever before.

"I feel like I know you," she said. "It's so strange."

The door leading to the interior of the house opened and the Truthseeker's head squeezed through.

"Come inside, Ryyder," she said. "You too, Shadow."

He hesitated.

"He's gone," she added, knowing his concern.

He followed Ryyder through the door and back to the kitchen.

Trillion was seated at the table once more. He'd removed his costume and makeup and was dressed in a black suit that molded to his body. Ryyder kissed him on the cheek as she swung herself into the seat next to him.

"Missed you, Dad. You haven't been here for ages," she said.

She looked across at Shadow and he smiled, self-consciously bringing his hand to his mouth. Maybe he'd dreamed that she'd kissed him. She was acting so casually now. But no, it had been real. He knew it because that kiss had changed his life. Nothing would ever be the same again.

"Ryyder, this is Shadow," said Trillion. "He and his mother have been staying with me for the past week."

"That must've been cozy," she said.

Shadow didn't understand. He'd thought Trillion's home had been spacious. He took the chair across from Ryyder.

"I haven't seen you before," she said. "With that skin I'm sure I'd remember you. Look at your eyes too. They're so dark."

"Don't be rude, Ryyder," Trillion said.

"She's not being rude," said Shadow. "It's true."

"I'm not judging him," she said, crossing her arms. "I happen to like his skin. And his eyes."

The pang in his stomach returned with her compliment.

The Truthseeker came in and picked up a teapot. *Trudy*, Shadow reminded himself.

"I saw him outside," said Shadow. "Did you tell him it was me?"

"I sent him away as quickly as I could," said Trudy. "After I told him your mother was here."

"That wasn't your truth to tell," snapped Shadow, frightened for his mother. His uncle didn't deserve to know anything about his mother. "I thought Trillion said you don't like to speak about other people."

"He needed to know," said Trudy. "It was time."

"What if he went after her?" asked Shadow, standing up.

"Shadow, sit down. She had too far a head start. He won't catch up to her."

"Who are we talking about?" said Ryyder. "Kurt?"

Shadow turned his uncle's name over in his mind. Kurt. He was glad he heard it first from Ryyder's lips. Somehow that took some of the evil out of it.

"Do you know him?" Ryyder asked.

"He's my uncle."

"Whoa! You look nothing alike." Ryyder's eyes were wide.

"Shadow's mother is from here," said Trillion.

"So where are you from?" she asked. "I'm sure I've never seen you."

He hesitated and saw her eyes grow even wider.

"You're from up there, aren't you?" she said, pointing to the ceiling. Her face lit with excitement, just like Trillion's had.

"Yes," he said, knowing she'd work it out pretty quickly anyway.

"Take me with you," she said. "Please, I'd love to go to surface."

"No," snapped Trudy, slamming the teapot on the table so hard the handle fell off. "You're not going with him."

Ryyder sat back in her chair and chewed her lip.

"But Dad's planning to," she said.

"How did you know that?" asked Trillion. "How could you possibly know that?"

"Lucky guess."

"I don't care who's going with him. It still doesn't mean you can go," Trudy said.

"You can't stop me." She stared at her mother, defiance seeping from her pores.

Mother and daughter sat debating each other and themselves in silence.

Come with him? He didn't even realize he was leaving yet. But maybe now that he'd met Ryyder he should consider it. Especially if she wanted to come with him. Although, that was a petrifying thought. He wasn't sure he could spend so much time in her presence without his stomach splitting in two from the pains she gave him. But if there was even a remote possibility that she'd kiss him even just once more in his life, then he was prepared to risk it. Stomach splitting in half or not. He needed to kiss her again, even more than he felt he needed to breathe.

"You're not going," said Trudy again.

"What have you seen?" asked Trillion. "I'm not talking to Trudy now, I'm talking to the Truthseeker. What will happen to her if she goes?"

"I thought you hated the Truthseeker," she said.

"I didn't say that. I just said I preferred you as Trudy."

She closed her eyes and took a deep breath. The light bulb that hung from the ceiling flickered. When she opened them the Truthseeker had returned.

"Ryyder," she said. "You traveled a long way to sit by my side."

"I'm your daughter." Ryyder rolled her eyes, clearly unimpressed by the Truthseeker's appearance. "I traveled from your womb."

"Do you remember the life you had before this one?"

She glanced at her father.

"Do you remember?" her mother repeated.

She nodded. "A little bit."

"Who were you?"

"I had skin like his," she said, nodding at Shadow.

"That's right, only your eyes were blue."

Shadow remembered his father telling him that his sister, Valentina, had looked like a female version of him, only with blue eyes. Could it be possible that Ryyder was in fact Valentina? Was that why he felt so drawn to her?

"Do you remember your father?"

She nodded again. "He's the only thing that's clear."

"Then tell us about him."

Trillion shifted uncomfortably in his chair, not seeming to enjoy the idea of Ryyder speaking of a father who wasn't him.

Ryyder closed her eyes, lifting her hands and rubbing her temples.

"I loved him." Her voice was a little more than a whisper. "But I killed him."

Shadow was taken aback. She couldn't be Valentina then. Valentina hadn't killed her father. Unless that was her guilt talking. Valentina's father had chosen to stay behind with her on their doomed planet rather than leave without her.

He remembered with a jolt what the Truthseeker had told him earlier. He had been his father's father in his past life, which made him Valentina's father, too. *If* Ryyder was Valentina reborn, then he had also been her father. This man she spoke of so fondly that she believed she had killed, was him.

Perhaps he shouldn't have kissed her. *Don't be stupid,* he scolded himself. He wasn't her father now.

"You've figured it out," said the Truthseeker, turning her gaze to him.

He nodded.

"Figured what out?" said Ryyder.

"That Shadow was the father you believe you killed."

"I didn't mean it," she said, her eyes filling with tears.

"You didn't kill me," he said, remembering the story his father had told him so often he'd felt like he was there himself. Perhaps that was because he was. "I chose to stay with you. It wasn't your fault."

It was all ruined now. Every time she'd look at him she'd see her father—the father she believed she'd killed. She'd never kiss him again, not in the way he wanted her to.

"You lied to me," said Ryyder to her mother, her cheeks flushing with anger.

"She can't lie," said Trillion. "It must be true."

"It is true," said Ryyder. "But that's not what I'm talking about. *She* knows what I'm talking about, don't you? Some Truthseeker you turned out to be."

"I spoke to you as your mother, not a Truthseeker," she

said, looking smaller than she had a few moments ago. Trudy had returned, leaving the Truthseeker in her wake.

"I've had enough of this," said Ryyder. "You can't be the Truthseeker one moment and my mother the next. It's no wonder Dad left."

"Ryyder," said Trillion. "Be respectful. What's happened to you?"

"She lied to me," she said, pointing at her mother. "Tell them, Truthseeker. Tell them what you told me about my soulmate."

Trudy looked to the floor, wringing her hands in her lap. "I told her that her soulmate was dead."

"No," Ryyder corrected. "You told me it would be useless to look for him because he no longer existed."

"I was trying to protect you," she said. "You weren't ready to meet him."

"You mean you were trying to keep me prisoner," said Ryyder. "Truthseekers aren't supposed to lie."

"They're also not supposed to be mothers," said Trillion. "Perhaps that's the reason. Her duty as a mother proved to be more powerful than her duty as a Truthseeker."

"Why do you always defend her? Especially after the way she's treated you."

"She means well. She loves you." He stood and put a hand on his wife's shoulder.

"I do," said Trudy. "Forgive me. Please."

"Why did you do it? He doesn't look so scary to me. I knew I was drawn to him for a reason."

"I didn't want to lose you. I saw you living a life on the land and it frightened me. I already lost your father. I couldn't bear to lose , too."

Trillion's face broke with pain.

"I'm not lost," he said, reaching for her hand. "I'm right here."

For a moment they looked like two halves of a whole, this husband and wife who chose to live apart.

Still, something Trudy had said didn't make sense.

"But you knew Ryyder was destined to meet me no matter how much you intervened," said Shadow. She knew so much. It didn't make sense for her to believe she could change the future.

"We can all change the future," she said. "That's why I see the past more clearly than I can see ahead. The past is the one thing we cannot change no matter how hard we try. The future I see is based on my intuition. That isn't set in stone."

"Then why didn't you chase me away as soon as I arrived here?"

"Because I knew when you sat before me at last that I couldn't. It was easier to think I could change the future when I hadn't met it yet. Once I started talking to you I realized how important it is that I let destiny take over. I held you and Ryyder apart for long enough."

She looked at her daughter, whose gaze was fixed on Shadow.

"I've looked for you my whole life," Ryyder said to him. "I circled the water, certain you were here, despite what my mother had told me. Only, I never found you ... until today. Now I know why. I never thought to look above the surface. I thought it was dangerous out there."

"It was," said Trillion. "But I've suspected for a long time now that the danger has passed. Shadow and his mother proved that to me."

"That doesn't mean she should go," said Trudy.

"I thought you'd said you kept us apart long enough?" Shadow pointed out.

"It's hard to explain. The half of me that's Trudy, can't let Ryyder go. The half of me that's the Truthseeker, knows she must. It's like Trillion said… Truthseekers aren't meant to be mothers."

"Why don't you come with us?" Shadow asked. "The four of us can go."

"You're supposed to be on my side," said Ryyder, frowning.

"I am on your side," he said, thinking of the guilt his mother carried for leaving her own mother behind. That wasn't something he wished for her. "Let your mother come."

"She'll never come," said Ryyder, her tone softening.

Trudy shook her head. "She's right. I can't leave here."

"Why not?" he asked.

"People need me here."

"You said yourself that it's time people came back up to the land."

"She said that?" Ryyder seemed amazed.

"She did."

"When I said people, I didn't mean me." There was a definite tone to her voice.

"Then let me go," said Ryyder. "I'm a person."

"I told you before. You're my daughter."

"You know you can't keep me here against my will."

Shadow could see where she got her determined streak. She was more like her mother than she realized.

"I'll be with her," said Trillion. "If I get a say in any of this, I'd like her to come."

"Of course, you get a say," said Trudy. "You're her father."

He looked at her, his brows arched with skepticism.

She sighed and shifted her sad gaze to Ryyder.

"Go," she said, her voice little more than a whisper.

"Do you mean it?" asked Ryyder, leaping from her chair.

"As you pointed out, I can't keep you here against your will."

Ryyder threw her arms around her mother.

"When do we leave?" asked Trillion, getting to his feet. "I don't see any reason to wait."

"You mean, leave now?" asked Shadow. He wasn't sure he wanted to leave so soon. He'd barely seen anything of Aquatica. He did miss the forest, though. And he'd like to make sure his mother was okay. He could always return here again one day soon to see all the things he wanted to see. Perhaps he'd been here long enough for his first visit. Maybe he could convince his mother to come back with him again.

"I don't see the point in waiting," said Trillion. "Now's the best time to get you back without drawing too much attention. The streets will be quiet soon once the festival wraps up."

Shadow nodded. That made sense.

"I'm not going like this," said Ryyder. "Let me prepare."

"I need to check Shadow's air tank," said Trillion.

"No, you don't," said Trudy. "He seems to manage just fine without it."

"How …" Shadow decided not to finish that question, realizing she must've seen him in the water with Ryyder.

"It's so much fun having a Truthseeker for a mother," said Ryyder, shooting him a grin and leaving the room. "Now do you see why I wasn't keen for her to come with us?"

"What are you talking about?" asked Trillion.

"Shadow can explain," said Trudy, leaving the room with Ryyder, no doubt wanting to say her goodbyes while she packed.

"When I went for my swim, I didn't use the tank," he said, hoping that explanation would suffice. "I think I've gotten the hang of it."

"Excellent," said Trillion. "I knew it had to happen eventually."

Shadow smiled, happy not to be questioned further.

"What's it like up there?" Trillion asked. "I wish Trudy could see it."

"You love her, don't you?" asked Shadow, curious about the strange relationship Trillion seemed to have with his wife.

He nodded. "Always have. She won't tell me if I'm her soulmate, but I like to think I am."

"How do you know?"

"Well, even when I want to kill her, I still love her."

Shadow laughed. It wasn't the romantic response he'd expected.

"I knew there was something about you when I met you," said Trillion. "Something more than you just not being from around here. You felt a connection when you looked at Ryyder's photo, didn't you."

He nodded.

"You'll take care of her always, won't you?"

"You have my word on that."

"I'm glad. I never liked the idea of her growing up and falling in love, but I think I could just about cope with the idea if it was with you."

"Who said anything about falling in love?" He was certain he hadn't given his feelings away. Soulmates didn't need to be lovers. From what Trudy had said, your soulmate could be your sister or your mother or even just your friend.

"I don't need my wife or daughter's powers to see how you feel."

"You really think Ryyder has powers?" he asked, deflecting the subject, feeling embarrassed he'd made his feelings so apparent.

"I know she does. How else did she know I was planning on heading to the surface with you?"

"Maybe Trudy told her?"

He shook his head. "No, she knew it, just like she knew

that one day she'd find you. That girl knows things. You'd be wise to pay attention to her."

He thought it'd be impossible not to pay attention to her. She'd haunted him since he'd first seen her photo. No, earlier than that. The idea of her had haunted him his whole life.

He wondered if this was how Eevie felt about their father.

No, that was different. The love was the same—the attachment and feeling of never wanting to be separated—but the love he was feeling was different. There was no denying this love was one of a romantic kind.

Ardorna, he thought, remembering a word his mother had once told him. He'd remembered Ryyder with his heart before he'd ever met her.

CHAPTER ELEVEN

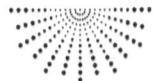

*R*yyder returned to the kitchen with her mother, wearing a black body suit with a midsection cut out for her gills. She had a large brown bag, strapped to her back.

"How long do you think we're going for?" asked Trillion, undoing her bag and taking it from her. It looked heavy.

"I can carry it," she said.

"I know you can, but I'm still taking it." He strapped it to his back and adjusted the straps.

Shadow wondered if he should take it.

"Don't even think about it," she said. "Dad's a better swimmer than you."

He nodded, planning to take it once they reached the surface. Trillion might be a better swimmer, but he'd bet he could beat him to the top of a tree or run circles around him while he walked.

There was a noise coming from the airlock.

"Someone's here," said Trillion. "It could be your mother. Maybe she's come back for you."

"It's not his mother," said Trudy.

A woman walked into the kitchen. She was the oldest woman Shadow had ever seen. Far older than the Truth-seeker. Her hair was gray like Trudy's, her eyes standard Aquatican blue, but her face was covered in deep lines, like she was about to crack into a thousand pieces. She looked oddly familiar. He couldn't figure out why.

"Is it true?" she said, taking hold of Trudy's arm. "Kurt said she was here."

She nodded.

"Why didn't you send someone for me?"

"Sit down."

"I don't want to sit down. I want my daughter. Where's Nahlah?"

Shadow gasped.

The old woman's head spun, and she looked at him, taking in his dark complexion with surprise.

He realized she wasn't as old as he'd first thought. Something had aged her beyond her years. Or someone had, and he was prepared to bet it was his mother.

"Who are you?" she asked.

He opened his mouth to speak, unable to find any words. What did you say to your grandmother when you met her for the first time? What could you say that could make up for all those missing years?

She stepped toward him, as if sensing his significance.

"My name is Shadow," he said. "I'm Nahlah's son."

She placed a bony hand on each of his arms, gripping him tightly as she looked deep into his eyes.

He returned her gaze, seeing his mother's face, only older. His mother had always described her as being young and beautiful. It was hard to reconcile that image from his mind with this woman who stood before him.

Her face crumbled as her fingers dug deeper into his

arms. She saw something in him, perhaps recognizing her daughter in his face, just as he'd seen his mother in hers.

"Shadow," she whispered.

A large tear fell from one of her eyes. He reached out and stroked her cheek with his thumb, taking the tear with him.

Her body shook. He pulled her tiny frame toward him and held her against his chest as loud sobs escaped her. She wrapped her arms around his waist, clutching him with surprising strength.

He looked across at Ryyder to see her smiling, before Trudy put a hand on her back and ushered her and Trillion out of the room. He wished they'd stay. He still didn't know what to say to this woman. But Trudy was right. They needed privacy. He had to find his words.

"Sit down, Grandmother," he said, breaking away. "We have a lot to talk about."

"What happened to your face?" she asked as she took a seat, her eyes still locked on him.

"What happened to yours?" he asked, smiling.

She put a hand to her wrinkled face.

"It was the shock of losing Nahlah," she said.

He nodded, ashamed that he'd asked. He'd already known that.

"I look like my father," he said, realizing he hadn't answered her question. "He has skin like mine. So does my sister."

"You have a sister?" She leaped on this information, her eyes lighting with curiosity.

He nodded. "Her name's Eevie."

His grandmother smiled. "My name's Eevie. Eevangela."

"I know. Mom named her after you. She's told us all about you."

"I don't deserve that," she said, her face falling solemn. "I was a terrible mother."

"That's not what Mom says."

He wondered what it was with mothers, always thinking that they could've done a better job, when their children thought they'd done just fine.

"So, it's true," she said. "She's alive?"

He nodded.

"Where is she?"

"She went home."

"Where's home? I have so many questions. Please Shadow, tell me everything. I've waited a long time for this day."

He wished his mother were still here. It should be her answering these questions. This didn't feel like his story to tell. Which parts should be spoken and which parts should be left aside?

He wasn't sure, so he decided to tell her everything.

He started at the beginning with Nahlah a curious, complicated child looking for peace in a place far away from her brother. He saw the pain these words caused, but he continued. He spoke of the day his father arrived and the way his mother had gone to him. The way they looked after each other, eventually falling in love and pledging to look after each other always. He told her what a good man his father was, how much he loved his mother.

Then he spoke of his own birth and what a difficult time this was for his mother and how much she'd pined for her own mother at this time and in all the years that followed. He saw his grandmother clutch at her chest, and he wondered if he should continue.

He did. It was like he'd turned on a tap and now he was watching the contents spill out.

He spoke of Eevie's bond with her father and the way his mother had done her best to teach them everything she knew, until one day it got too much and she withdrew into herself, sinking into a deeper and deeper sadness until he'd shaken her awake and together they'd come back to Aquatica.

"Why didn't she come to see me?" asked his grandmother.

"She wanted to, but first she wanted to see the Truthseeker."

Her disappointment was obvious.

"She wanted to know if you knew."

"If I knew?" His grandmother seemed confused.

"If you knew what her brother had done to her." He realized that although she'd seemed upset when he'd said his mother had run from her brother, she hadn't seemed surprised.

"Oh, Shadow, of course I didn't know. Not at the time. It wasn't until after she left. One of my other daughters told me." She looked at the floor. "I refused to believe it at first, but it explained so much. All those broken bones and bruises on a child who wasn't the least bit clumsy. I'm afraid I failed both my daughter and my son."

"What happened to him?" He had to know if what Trudy had said was true. Was Kurt really sorry?

"I confronted him," she said. "I needed to understand how he could treat his sister like that. He collapsed on the floor right in front of me and confessed everything. I was horrified. I didn't know what to do. First I lost my husband, then my daughter. And right at that moment, I thought I'd also lost my son."

Shadow nodded. That must have been awful.

"So, I shouted at him. I shouted so loudly that I shouted him right out the door and he ran away, too. I thought he felt bad and had gone after Nahlah, but he was found a few days later, floating near the surface with plastic wrapped tightly around his gills. Almost dead but saved just in time." His grandmother drew in a deep breath and slowly blinked her eyes.

"Someone tried to kill him?" That did sound drastic, but still it was hard to feel sorry for him.

She shook her head. "No, Shadow. He realized far too late that Nahlah wasn't responsible for his father's death. She was only a little girl. He tried to kill himself."

"That's horrible." He'd never before thought about the possibility of anyone taking their own life—just another strange act that set humans apart from other life forms. In the vast amount of time he'd spent in the forest he'd never seen an animal purposely end their life. They fought to survive. It was unimaginable to think of anyone choosing to end their life prematurely. Sometimes it didn't seem a blessing to have been born human.

"Kurt realized that Nahlah wasn't responsible for his father's death. He didn't think he could live with himself after all the things he'd done to her. In many ways he hasn't been able to. He's had a miserable life trying to turn things around. He'd love nothing more than the opportunity to apologize to Nahlah, to try to make up for what he did."

"Mom heard that he was on his way here. That's why she left. She's not ready for his apology right now. He still frightens her far too much."

"I can see that she's been a good mother." His grandmother reached for his hand. "You're a magnificent boy."

"She's a wonderful mother."

"A better mother than me."

"You would've gone to her if you knew how to find her." He wanted her to feel better. It was hard to watch her in so much pain.

"Take me with you. Please, Shadow. Take me to my daughter."

"You want to come?" he asked, wondering if this was a

good idea. Taking two people to the surface already seemed too big a responsibility. What if something happened to them? Could his mother ever forgive him if her own mother was injured under his watch?

She nodded. "Of course, I want to come."

"How long will it take you to get ready?" he asked.

"I'm ready," she said. "I've been ready for almost twenty years."

The streets were quiet. The citizens of Aquatica had exhausted themselves with their celebrations and were now locked away in their homes fast asleep.

Shadow swam at a steady pace, glad not to be slowing the group down this time.

Ryyder was at the front, leading the way to her father's house. From that point Shadow was going to take the lead.

He swam behind her and Trillion for now, with his grandmother by his side. She moved easily in the water, her lithe frame surprisingly strong. Her grief may have robbed her of her youthful beauty, but it'd done little to slow her down.

It felt strange to be traveling in this party of four. When he'd arrived here, he hadn't known any of these people.

His eyes fell on Ryyder. With her back to him, he was free to stare at her. He drank in the way she glided, the strange way she kicked her legs and the graceful strokes of her arms.

Occasionally she'd look back at him and smile, sending electrical impulses to his stomach. What would their relationship be like? Would they really have a child together one day? It seemed so hard to believe. Whatever happened, he didn't plan to tell her about the child. The Truthseeker was right—it was a lot of pressure to put on someone. Ryyder didn't deserve to have that. It was far better to let things unfold naturally, as they already were.

His father had described the way he'd met his mother and it sounded completely different to what he was experiencing with Ryyder. Their relationship had taken years to develop.

It wasn't like that for him. With Ryyder it'd been instant. The first time he'd seen her photo he'd just known. Was that because she was his soulmate?

He thought about the strange thing the Truthseeker had said about his mother not meeting her soulmate until the day she died. *Unless something drastic happened.* What did that mean? It was too hard to figure out. Just another thing to ask Ryyder about one day. He doubted there was any point in asking Trudy. It really wasn't any of his business. *Not his truth to ask*, as she'd probably say.

Trillion's house appeared in the distance.

Ryyder swam to the door and paused. If anyone needed a rest, the plan was to stop here.

Shadow was tempted to go inside and put the earbuds in for just a few minutes to flood his body with music once more. But he resisted the urge. A few minutes wouldn't be enough.

They huddled in a group and nodded at each other. It seemed everyone was keen to continue on.

Shadow looked around to make sure nobody was watching them. He thought he saw a movement behind a nearby house. He blinked and looked a little closer, deciding he'd imagined it. It would be safe to leave unnoticed.

He took the lead and reached to the back of his brain as he tried to remember the way to the decompression tunnel. He just needed to swim directly away from Aquatica in as straight a line as possible and soon they should see the rusted entry gate with the decompression tunnel sitting off to the side.

Nobody headed this way except the surface workers and right now they were all in bed nursing their hangovers. Trillion had told him this was the one holiday Aquatica had each year. Unless there was an emergency, nobody would be heading to the surface today. They just hoped the decompression tunnel would be operating. They could become very ill if they tried to get to the surface without it.

Just when Shadow thought he must have led everyone the wrong way, he saw the gate in the distance. It was as sad and lonely looking, just as it'd been the first time he'd seen it. Perhaps even more so now that his eyes had adjusted to the bright colors of Aquatica.

The tunnel was humming. Empty chairs could be seen through the glass walls as they rose slowly up to the surface.

They swam into the entrance and sealed the door behind them, taking deep gasps of air as they transitioned from gills to lungs.

It was fortunate it was a holiday. Sneaking into the tunnel on his own without raising suspicion would've been hard enough. How would four of them have gotten away with it? He thought of his mother stowing herself away in here as a child. She'd certainly been brave.

"You did it," said Trillion, patting him on the back.

He nodded, pleased to have made it this far, although finding it hard to speak. It was difficult transitioning your airways when you weren't used to it.

"Are you okay?" asked his grandmother.

"Never better," he said, finding his words. He wished everyone would stop fussing over him like this. He was perfectly capable. Couldn't they see that?

"How long will it take to get to the forest?" asked Ryyder.

"It's a long walk. We may need to rest when we get to the surface."

He realized he didn't know if it was day or night outside.

He'd completely lost track. It was no wonder Aquaticans didn't live by the clock. Time had such little importance down here.

"I've always wanted to go on this," said Ryyder, looking at the chairlift.

"It's not an amusement park," said her father.

"Forever the killjoy'. She rolled her eyes

Shadow laughed. He hadn't heard that word before. It sounded strange. He added it to the list of new words he'd had to get used to over the past week.

"We'd better get moving before someone comes," said Ryyder, climbing aboard and strapping herself into a chair.

They followed, beginning their slow ascent to the surface in a single file, Ryyder at the front and Trillion taking up the rear behind his grandmother. Shadow sat behind Ryyder, nervous about her going first. Why did he feel this overpowering need to protect her? She'd survived perfectly well without him for all these years.

He thought back to that kiss for the thousandth time that day. Had she kissed other boys like that? She seemed to have done it before.

It was frustrating how slowly they moved. He tried to be grateful. It was giving them all a chance to rest when otherwise they'd all have preferred to press on at as fast a pace as they were able.

He looked out the glass wall of the tunnel and thought of his father. Sitting here reminded him of what it felt like to sit in the pod with its transparent walls. Traveling to Neron must've been a frightening experience for his father to go through. It'd been scary enough traveling to Aquatica at the age of sixteen with his mother by his side. Not only had his father been younger than that and all by himself, but he hadn't known where he was going or whether he'd be alive to see his destination. And he did all of that having just witnessed the death of his father and sister—the only family he'd ever known.

He thought once more about what the Truthseeker had said about him being his father's father. Did he believe it?

"Xander," he said out loud, testing if the name sparked a reaction. It didn't.

It must be true though. It was a strange thing to make up otherwise. And everything the Truthseeker had told them had explained so much. Not just the way he felt about Ryyder, but the way his parents felt about each other and the attachment Eevie had to her father. Would Ryyder feel anything when she met his father—her brother from a past life? Buzz had said they weren't particularly close, but neither were he and Eevie and he still loved her.

A shiver ran through him. It was cold in the tunnel. He missed the forest with the dappled sunlight breaking through the trees. He missed climbing trees and watching the birds skip from branch to branch as they made their nests. He missed his own nest his parents had made long before he was born. The house they'd built may not be as sturdy or colorful as the ones he'd seen in Aquatica, but there was nowhere else that would ever feel more like home, no matter how much the water had called to him. It didn't need to be filled with fancy possessions and clean water that ran from taps. What it had inside was all that mattered, for it contained his family. Soon it would be filled with guests as they made room for his grandmother, Ryyder and Trillion. Four would become seven.

They'd need to add some rooms to their house. That was if their guests chose to stay. Maybe they'd run back to the water as soon they got the chance. Wasn't that exactly what he was doing?

If that were the case, then he and Ryyder were doomed before they'd even had a chance to get started. He could never live in the ocean. Time would only tell if she could live on the land. He would never pressure her or make her feel trapped. He'd seen what'd happened to his mother. Humans needed to feel like they were free. Trapping them only guaranteed they'd soon be dreaming of escape.

But his father hadn't trapped his mother. He had. And Eevie. It was them she hadn't been able to leave, until her homesickness had grown so large it'd begun to seep from her pores making them all miserable. Would she be cured of that now she'd seen Aquatica again? He didn't think so. It was her mother she missed, not Aquatica and he was bringing her to the forest.

The thought of the reunion that lay ahead made him smile. He couldn't think of any better gift to bring his mother.

He saw Ryyder's chair ahead of him level out at the top of the tunnel. She slid out of the chair. He'd half expected someone to be waiting for them here, trying to stop them, but the exit room was empty.

He climbed out of his chair. For a few precious seconds they were alone. She reached for his hand, brought it to her lips and kissed it, her green eyes shining at him while she did it.

"Ardorna," she whispered.

His heart banged with joy. She *did* see him as her soulmate and not her father from a life gone by.

"Ardorna," he whispered back.

His grandmother's chair reached the top of the tunnel and he went to help her up.

He took her hand as she stood.

"Your father must be very handsome if you look like him," she said.

"I get all my looks from my grandmother," he said.

She giggled, and he saw years fall from her wrinkled face.

Trillion's chair emerged next and the room began to feel small.

"We did it," said Trillion, his face alight with excitement. "Let's get out here."

Shadow stepped toward the exit door to unseal it, but Trillion beat him to it. He wasn't sure why this annoyed him, but it did. This was supposed to be his turn to lead, to show Ryyder that he was independent and capable, not some teenager who needed to have doors opened for him and to be asked if he was all right every five minutes.

Together they walked down another long pipe.

"This must lead directly to the life support systems," said Shadow, concerned.

Surely there must be someone working today. They didn't need any trouble. If anyone saw a group of people walking into the forest there'd be mass confusion. The government would have trouble explaining that one. If the world was so dangerous above the surface, then why were people walking freely toward it?

"We need to find an exit," said Ryyder, immediately understanding his fears.

They scanned the tunnel from left to right.

"Up there," said his grandmother, pointing above their heads.

There was some kind of hatch with a circular handle.

Trillion tried to reach but fell a few inches short. Shadow raised his hands above his head, happy to be able to take hold of the handle. He smirked as he turned it.

The door swung toward him, followed by a torrent of seawater that knocked him to the ground.

An alarm sounded.

"We have to hurry," shouted Trillion.

"How?" asked Shadow, failing to understand how anyone

could swim against the current of water. This wasn't an emergency exit. It was a deathtrap.

Water was rushing down the tunnel, lapping at their ankles.

He saw a wall to their left begin to descend from the top part of the ceiling, cutting them off from the decompression tunnel. Another wall was coming down from the right threatening to cut Ryyder off from the rest of the group.

He scrambled to his feet, but once again Trillion beat him to it, grabbing hold of her and throwing her toward the rest of the group. It should've been him who saved her. He tried not to care. It didn't matter who it was as long as she was saved. They needed to stay together. Whatever happened, they must stay together as a group.

The tunnel was sealed from both ends now. The only way out was through the hatch.

"Give me a boost," said Trillion, trying once more to reach the opening.

"I'll do it," said Shadow.

He took hold of the edges of the opening and tried to lift himself upward, only to be pushed back by the water. It was impossible. His pulse was racing now as panic took hold. They should've continued on to the life support systems and found a way out there.

"It's okay," said his grandmother. "We're okay."

He looked around to find she was calm. Relaxed almost.

Then he realized what she'd realized immediately. There was no point fighting against the water. It would soon fill the tunnel and they could swim out.

He nodded.

The alarm was the only thing that bothered him now. Surely the authorities had been alerted. Would they be arrested? Dragged back to Aquatica against their will? It would be cruel to get this far and not make it back to the forest.

The water was at his chest now and rising quickly. He'd thought he'd said goodbye to his gills for a while. He'd been wrong again.

He pulled his goggles over his eyes, took one last deep breath and waited as the water rose to above his head.

Trillion was the first to swim from the tunnel. He peered down at them, urging them to follow.

Ryyder went next, followed by his grandmother.

Shadow wanted to go last. He'd put them in this danger. If anyone was going to be captured, then it should be him. The rest of them would find their way to their field in the forest if they really tried. After all, his mother had done it when she was only a child. Either that or they could head back home, finding some kind of excuse for being in the tunnel.

But there was no capturing. No banging down the walls by the authorities. No dragging down to a prison cell deep under the water.

Instead, he looked through the door to see a bright light above him. He followed it, breaking through the surface, to find himself bobbing in the water, the sun blinding him.

His three companions were nearby, shielding their eyes. This was their first look at their planet's sun.

"Are you sure it won't hurt us?" asked Ryyder.

"The sun is your friend," he said, raising his hands in the air and letting out a whoop of joy.

Her hands left her face and she stole a peek, blinking rapidly.

It was the morning sun. He had a whole day of this to look forward to. It would've been heartbreaking to arrive at night, although he had to admit the moon could be even more captivating on a clear night.

"Isn't it beautiful?" he breathed.

"It's … bright," she replied.

"Let's keep moving," said Trillion, glancing downward.

"In a moment," said Shadow, not because he needed time, but because he wanted to be the one who decided when to move again.

Ryyder took off after her father.

"He means well," said his grandmother.

"I know. It's okay."

"We'd never have gotten this far without you."

"It's okay. Really, I'm fine."

She nodded. He'd thought he'd kept his frustrations with Trillion buried. She must've been watching him closer than he'd realized. He'd been so dazzled by Ryyder's presence, he'd hardly been paying her any attention. She was his grandmother—the first relative he'd ever met other than his parents or sister. The way she looked at him told him that she loved him. Would he one day love her, too?

"I'm glad you're here," he said.

"Me, too." She smiled, her eyes filling with affection.

It wasn't far to the shore. Soon they found they could stand and dragged themselves through the water with their toes digging footholds in the sand.

They emerged and joined Ryyder and Trillion on the sand, spinning in circles as they took in their surroundings, the vast ocean stretching to the horizon in one direction and the forest looming over them in the other.

Tears were running down Trillion's face.

"I knew it was possible," he said, over and over.

He looked at his grandmother. She had a face so open she barely needed to use words.

"Your world is amazing," she said.

"It's your world, too," he said.

Ryyder was standing off to one side. He went to her and

took her hand in his, bringing it to his lips and kissing it, like she'd done to him in the tunnel.

"Thank you for coming," he said.

"When I said I spent my life looking for you, I don't think I was telling the truth," she said.

His stomach clenched, as his worst fears took hold.

"You d-don't like it?" he asked, his voice breaking with emotion.

She put a hand on his cheek. "I like it very much. I meant that when I was looking for you it wasn't just you that I was meant to find. It was this."

Relief shot through him. She felt the magic of the forest. She knew this was her home. Everything would work out fine.

She looked up and drew a deep breath in through her nose. "I feel like I'm breathing for the first time."

"You are."

"We need to keep going," said Trillion, taking charge once more.

Shadow wasn't sure if he was trying to break this moment he was having with his daughter or if there was real danger approaching.

"Okay," he said, remembering his grandmother's words. Trillion meant well. "How's everyone feeling? It's quite a long walk."

"We can rest in the forest if we need to," said Trillion, taking a water bottle from Ryyder's bag and passing it around.

"Let's go then," said Shadow, picking up the bag and swinging it onto his shoulders.

"I said I can carry that," she protested.

"I know you can, but I'm still carrying it," he said, using Trillion's words from earlier.

She laughed, and he walked away before she could take it

back. He knew he needed to be careful to try not to become too distracted by her presence. There were dangers in the forest. He only needed to remember the story of his father's first day here to realize that. He'd barely survived. Probably wouldn't have without his mother's help. No wonder he'd fallen in love with her, even if she'd called him a boolah.

He must keep everyone safe.

"We need to walk quietly," he said, realizing there was no need for his warning. His three companions were used to traveling in silence. There were no conversations taking place as people swam side-by-side under the ocean.

He walked ahead, feeling at ease in his skin for the first time since he'd left the forest. He understood this world. He knew what sounds were to be enjoyed and which ones to heed as a warning.

They stepped beneath the canopy of the forest. A flock of birds that'd been fossicking for their breakfast scattered, flying into the air with great fanfare.

He smiled, turning to marvel at them, only to find the others clutching each other in fear. They'd never seen a bird before. They didn't know they were harmless. Perhaps he'd frightened them with all his talk of having to be quiet.

"They're just birds," he said. "They're more frightened of you than you are of them."

"Warn us next time," said Trillion. "I thought we were under attack."

"I'm sorry. I didn't think. You have photos of them in your books. I assumed you knew what birds are."

"Don't assume anything. I was patient with you under the water. Please show us the same respect."

"Dad," complained Ryyder. "It's fine. He didn't realize."

"It won't happen again," said Shadow. "Just take your lead from me. If I'm not scared, then there's no reason for you to be."

Trillion nodded and they continued on.

Shadow noticed his companions beginning to slow. Their legs weren't used to walking this far, just as he'd had trouble swimming at first. Walking around your home is a lot different to hiking through a forest. Their lungs weren't as strong as his either. Ryyder was puffing and had turned a pink color. He noticed Trillion had beads of sweat dripping from his forehead. Only his grandmother seemed to be keeping pace. Love and determination were great motivators. Still, he shouldn't push them too hard. They had a long way to go.

"I could use a rest," he lied, knowing they'd never admit to feeling tired. The only way to get them to stop was if they thought he needed to. "Let's stop here."

"No, not here," said Ryyder, putting her hand on his arm, her eyes filling with fear.

"What's wrong?" he asked, turning to face her. Had she sensed something?

"I think someone's been following us." Her eyes were darting around, even though he was sure she'd sensed a presence, rather than seen one.

"There's nobody following us," he said, unsure if that was true, but not wanting her to be afraid. "There are lots of noises in the forest."

A branch broke behind him in the direction they'd been walking.

He spun around to find a large bear watching them. It stood on its hind legs, making it look even larger than it was. It shouldn't have bothered. Even squatting down, this bear would be enormous.

Ryyder screamed and the bear took a step toward them. He heard a collective gasp from Trillion and his grandmother behind him.

"Listen to me right now," said Shadow softly, looking to

the left of the hairy beast, careful not to make eye contact. "You must follow every word I say if we're going to get out of this."

He held his hands up in the air, making himself look bigger.

"Hold your arms like mine," he said, keeping his voice level and calm. He needed to keep talking to show the bear that he was human and not a source of food.

He glanced at his companions to see if they were doing as he said. They were.

"Try not to show him that you're scared. Keep your arms up and take slow steps backward. Slow steps. Don't look directly at the bear, but don't look away. And please do not run. You must not run. Just keep stepping backward. That's the way. We're doing fine. Wave your arms slowly. That's right. We were in his territory. We're showing him we're leaving."

"I think we should run," said Trillion.

"No, we're not going to run. That's the worst thing we can do. My father can tell you about the time he tried to run. My father *will* tell you about it when we make it to him safe and alive."

He continued to step backward as he spoke.

"Are you all okay?" he asked. "Ryyder? Grandmother?"

"We're okay," they replied.

The bear tilted his head, its teeth bared, huge claws waving in the air.

"It's all right," Shadow said. "We're leaving you alone. Leave us alone, too."

He heard a noise behind him. Trillion was running, dragging Ryyder away with him.

"He said not to run," shouted Ryyder.

The bear roared.

"Stay still," he said to his grandmother who remained behind him, her arms waving bravely in the air.

The bear charged at them.

"It's a bluff," Shadow yelled. "Hold your ground."

He put out his arms, shielding her from the bear. If one of them was to be killed, it was going to be him. He'd brought her here. He hadn't paid attention, even when Ryyder had warned him. This was his fault just as much as it'd be Trillion's if he'd led him to the jaws of a shark.

The bear was a mere few paces away now, still charging.

Never had it taken so much strength to stand still. His arms were in the air, his face directed at the bear, his eyes looking to the sky.

He wasn't ready to die. Please let this be a bluff.

The bear stopped, turned and loped away, leaving them standing there.

He turned to his grandmother who remained rooted to the spot, arms still waving. Her eyes had glazed over, and her body was shaking more violently as each second passed.

"We're okay," he said to her, dropping his hands and placing them on her shoulders. "We're okay."

She looked up at him, her focus returning.

He pulled her to his chest and held her, trying to stop her shaking.

"It's okay. We're okay. You were amazing."

"Thank you," she whispered.

He let go of her and saw Ryyder running toward him, her arms outstretched. She leaped into his arms.

"I'm sorry," she said. "I didn't want to run. You could've been killed. I'm so sorry."

"It wasn't your fault," he said, burying his face in the silky strands of her hair and drawing in her scent. He closed his eyes. For a moment there he hadn't thought he'd survive to get the chance to do this. He held her tighter, grateful to be alive.

"I owe you an apology." It was Trillion's voice.

Shadow's eyes snapped open. "You could've killed us. I told you not to run."

"I'm sorry." He looked sheepish, like a child caught sneaking an extra serve of dinner.

"It's okay." He didn't want to make an enemy of Trillion. He was Ryyder's father. Whether he liked it or not this was a man he needed to choose to get along with. And they'd gotten along just find before they set out on this journey. They were both just tense and letting their emotions rule their actions. "I just need to know that next time you'll listen to me."

"Next time?" said Ryyder. "Please don't tell me there'll be a next time."

"We're in a forest. There can always be a next time. There are dangers here, but if we're careful, we'll be fine. Just listen to what I say *please*."

"Maybe we should turn back," said Trillion.

"We're safe," said Shadow. "I've lived here with my family my whole life and none of us have been eaten by bears. You just need to learn the rules here, like I had to under the water."

"There are no bears under the water," said Ryyder.

"No, but there are sharks."

"The shark sonars keep them away. Maybe we need a bear sonar here?"

"Or maybe we just need to live by the rules," he said. "This is their territory we're in. Who are we to say they need to leave? I'll keep you safe, I promise."

She took hold of his hand.

"I trust you," she said.

"Me, too," said his grandmother.

They looked to Trillion.

"Okay. Me, too," he said. "But please, can we just keep moving?"

"Definitely," said Shadow.

Trillion waited for him to take the first step before he followed, listening carefully to his instructions as they walked.

The power had shifted, although now that he had it, he wasn't certain that he wanted it. With power came responsibility and that bear had shown him exactly what that responsibility involved. One wrong move and all their lives were at risk.

CHAPTER TWELVE

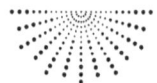

*I*t had only taken Shadow and his mother a matter of hours to make it to Aquatica. It took two days for him to return. His companions slowed him down.

He reminded himself of how patient they'd been with him under the water. They weren't in a hurry, even if his heart felt like it was.

Homesickness burned at him. He missed everything about the field and his family.

Soon, he told himself. Soon he'd be home. At least he had a home to return to. His father would never return home. His mother had, only to be pulled back to the forest.

He wondered what defined a home. Was it the walls of your house or the family who lived inside? Perhaps it was a little of both.

He dreaded the day Ryyder would return to the ocean. That day would have to come. It didn't seem possible that it wouldn't. Everyone he knew pined for their home in one way or another.

His mind was starting to scramble due to lack of sleep. They'd stopped overnight in a small clearing and he'd kept watch, not daring to fall asleep for even a moment. It would've been safer for them to sleep in a tree, but he knew better than to suggest that. They wouldn't get higher than the first branch.

He was tired now. His bones hurt from moving so slowly. His shoulders ached from carrying Ryyder's bag—although he'd never admit that to her. The straps were designed for underwater and dug into his skin from being carried upright. What could she possibly have in there?

She had a water bottle, he'd seen that, but the rest was a mystery. *Secret women's business,* she'd told him.

Although the group moved slowly, they didn't complain. He knew they must be in pain. Their bare feet looked sore and they winced as they stepped on stones. The soles of his feet had been toughened from years of walking on rough ground. He'd heard of shoes, but just like the rest of this group, he'd never owned a pair. They seemed so unnecessary.

"We're almost there," he said. "You've all done so well."

He heard the sighs of relief behind him.

"I can't wait to see your home," said Ryyder.

"Don't expect too much," he said. "It's not as fancy as yours."

He was nervous about her seeing where he lived. He wanted so much for her to like it. He'd never really been bothered about what people liked before.

If only she could love the forest as much as he did, his life would be perfect. With her by his side, he'd have no need to ever go to the ocean again. He might even dare to believe the Truthseeker and dream of one day having a family of his own. Would he make a good father? His own father had set a high standard. And it didn't seem that he'd succeeded too well when he'd given it a shot in his last life. What kind of a man would send their child into space all by themselves?

A desperate one.

He heard a noise ahead. It wasn't the sound of a bird.

He stretched out his arms, pushing his companions back.

He ran on ahead on his own and looked up.

"Shadow!'

He saw Eevie, scrambling down the tree. Her movements were light and quick, her dark skin a blur as she swung herself down to his level.

She landed at his feet. Her hair was loose, its frizzy strands streaming out in all directions.

He thought she looked pretty. It was the first time he ever remembered looking at her and thinking this. He really had missed her.

"Shadow!' she said again, throwing her arms around him.

He returned her embrace somewhat awkwardly.

"I thought you were dead, for sure," she said. "Dad and I couldn't believe Mom came back without you."

"Where's Dad?" he asked, looking around. If Eevie was here, then he had to be close.

"In the house with Mom."

"Then what are you doing out here?" He was confused. Eevie never chose to be separated from their father.

"Just giving them some space," she said, like it was the most normal thing in the world.

"That's new," he said.

"A lot of things around here are new," she said, sighing. "Look, I realized a few things when you were gone. I saw how much Dad missed Mom. If I want them both in my life —together in my life—then I can't keep standing between them. It's time I took a step back."

He was speechless. These weren't words he'd ever expected to hear.

"Come on," she said. "Let's join them. They'll be so happy you've made it back."

"Wait," he said. "I'm not alone." He pointed to a shrub that his three companions were crouching behind.

She looked afraid, so he took hold of her hand and squeezed it.

Their grandmother came almost running from the shrub toward them.

Eevie instinctively stepped behind him.

"Who is that?" she hissed.

He reached for their grandmother, placing his arm around her shoulders.

"Eevie, meet Eevie."

He saw his sister's eyes widen as she realized who it was.

"You're beautiful," said their grandmother, reaching for her.

Eevie stepped back, avoiding her touch.

"Give her time," Shadow said to his grandmother. "You're the first person she's seen outside the family."

"But I am her family."

"You are," said Shadow, squeezing her gently to remove some of the sting of Eevie's greeting.

Ryyder and Trillion stepped out from behind the shrub.

He heard Eevie stifle a cry.

"Don't run," he said, moving to her side. "They've traveled a long way to meet you."

Ryyder put out her hand. Shadow had learned this was a gesture Aquaticans used to greet each other, gripping hands and pumping them up and down. It was odd, and he wondered how it had started.

"I never said I wanted to meet anyone," said Eevie, taking another step back.

"Eevie, please. Don't be rude."

His heart sank. He wanted Ryyder and Eevie to be friends.

"It's okay," Ryyder said to Eevie. "I won't hurt you."

"Who said anything about hurting?" asked Eevie.

"Eevie, please. These are my friends. This is Ryyder and her father, Trillion."

She nodded, still not smiling, but Shadow took it as progress. She just needed time. He remembered how over-whelmed he'd felt when he'd arrived in Aquatica. He'd nearly drowned at the sight of a group of children. Eevie would adjust.

"Can we see Nahlah?" said their grandmother. "Please."

"I'm going to warn her," said Eevie.

Before he could stop her, she took off. He went to make chase but came to a halt realizing the others would never keep up. The last thing he needed was for them to wander off in the forest. He'd gotten them this far, he had to take them all the way.

Besides, perhaps it was a good thing for Eevie to warn their mother. This family didn't seem to do too well with surprises.

"I'm sorry," he said to his grandmother. "That didn't exactly go to plan."

"Life never does." Large tears poured from the corners of her eyes. "Everyone said that Nahlah was dead, but I never gave up. She didn't feel dead in my heart. I just couldn't believe it. And now not only am I about to see her again, but I have you and Eevie."

"What about your other daughters?" asked Ryyder. "You have them as well, don't you?"

"And you have two legs," said his grandmother. "Does that mean you wouldn't miss one if it were to fall off? You'd still have another one."

"I didn't mean that you don't miss Nahlah. I just always thought you should—"

"Ryyder," scolded Trillion. "Stop it."

"No, it's okay," said his grandmother. "She's just saying

what everyone else thinks. That I should have stopped wasting time mourning my missing daughter and spent it loving the ones who were still with me. But it doesn't work like that. I can't love anyone with all of my heart when there's a piece of it missing."

"Then let's go and find that piece," said Shadow, placing his hand gently on her back and guiding her toward the field.

Shadow had expected the reunion between his mother and grandmother would be emotional, but nothing could prepare him for what he witnessed.

As they broke through the trees into the field, he saw his mother running from their home toward them. Her arms were outstretched and even from a distance he could see tears streaking lines down her cheeks.

His grandmother ran, then stopped as if her body couldn't take the strain it found itself under. She fell to her knees, grabbing at the short strands of her hair, her fingers white with tension. Her eyes were wide as she took in the vision of her daughter as a grown woman. For so long she must have pictured her running away and now here she was, running toward her.

Short, gasping sounds escaped her lips. The pain of her joy was acute. He could feel it emanating from her pores and seeping through into his soul.

His mother stumbled as she took the final steps to close the gap between them. She steadied herself, took a deep breath and knelt before her mother.

The two women stared at each other, their bodies still, silence hanging in the air.

"Nahlah," said his grandmother. "My Nahlah."

She reached for her daughter, her shaking hands taking

hold of her face as love flowed between them. It was the love only a mother can feel for her child.

They pulled each other close until their foreheads touched, and they breathed in each other's essence.

"I'm sorry I left you." He watched his mother wrap her arms around his grandmother and rest her head on her shoulder.

"You never left me." She stroked her daughter's hair in the way she must've done when she was a child. "You were with me the whole time."

Shadow looked at Ryyder. She'd reached for her father, linking her arm through his and together they stood watching the reunion between mother and daughter. It was impossible not to be moved.

Ryyder noticed him watching her and gave him a sad smile. He wanted to know what she was thinking. Was she missing her own mother? Was she wishing she had this kind of bond with her? Maybe she did have this kind of bond.

He really didn't know very much about her at all. He knew her with his heart, but how much did he know her with his head? He didn't know what food she liked to eat, what her favorite color was, what kind of jokes made her laugh. How much did these things really matter? What was it that was really important? The things you liked or the things you felt? Despite only knowing her for such a short time, he honestly believed he knew what she felt in her heart. Surely that was all that mattered.

"Shadow," said his mother, reaching for him with one hand, still holding her mother with the other.

He crouched down and was pulled into the arms of both women. Together they formed a circle of three.

The love of these two women flowed through him and he knew as much as they loved each other, they loved him, too. He was their flesh, their blood, the spirit that lit their souls.

In that moment he understood their bodies weren't the only thread that held them together. They were connected through their souls. What the Truthseeker had said had been right. They'd known each other in a time long before now. He wasn't sure exactly how his grandmother fitted into this, but he was sure she did. He'd met her before. He knew it.

"Shadow," called Ryyder, breaking the moment.

He looked across to see her staring into the forest, her eyes wide.

"There's someone there," she said.

He jumped to his feet and ran toward where she was staring. He'd ignored her warning last time and the consequences had almost been deadly. He wouldn't make that same mistake.

"Wait here," he called, as he went back into the forest, away from the group.

A man stepped out from behind a tree. He held his bare palms in front of him to show he held no weapons.

Shadow recognized him immediately.

"Kurt," he said, coldly. "You followed us."

It was no wonder Ryyder had been on edge. It wasn't just the bear she'd sensed following them. There had been a beast of an entirely different sort creeping behind them in the forest.

"Nephew," said Kurt. "Please. I've waited my whole life to see your mother. I need her to know how sorry I am."

"Will that make you feel better?" snarled Shadow. "Because it's not what she wants."

"How do you know that? She's frightened of me. Surely if she could see how much I've changed, she could let go of some of that fear. Wouldn't that help her? I've hurt her enough. I don't want her to hurt anymore."

Shadow looked deep into his uncle's eyes, as he judged his sincerity.

"I can't take away what I did," Kurt said. "But I'd really love the chance to make it up to Nahlah. If she'll let me. If you'll let me."

"You keep away from her," shouted Shadow. "I want you to turn around right now and head straight back to the ocean where you belong. Never come back. Never! My mother doesn't want to see you."

Kurt was looking over Shadow's shoulder, not seeming to hear a word he'd just said.

Shadow turned around to see his mother standing behind him. She was holding her mother's hand, the contact seeming to bring her a strength she hadn't had before.

"It's okay, Shadow," she said. "He can talk to me."

"Nahlah," Kurt said, taking steps toward her, then dropping to his knees. "Forgive me. Please. What I did was inexcusable. I blamed you for our father's death when it was nobody's fault. He would have hated what I did to you. *I* hate what I did to you. I'm sorry. I'm so sorry."

Shadow almost felt sorry for him. *Almost.* He turned his eyes to his mother to see if she felt the same.

"I forgive you." His mother's voice was little more than a whisper.

Shadow gasped. He hadn't expected this. What the Truth-seeker had said must be true. His mother had a most forgiving soul.

Kurt rose to his feet and reached out his arms. Shadow tensed and took a step toward his mother.

"Not yet, Kurt," she said, shaking her head. "Please. You must give me time to trust you."

"Of course," he said, tears streaming down his face. "Thank you, Nahlah. Thank you. You've already given me more than I deserve."

"Let's find Dad," said Shadow, keen to give his mother some space from Kurt and see what his father's take on all of this was. If he was okay with his mother forgiving Kurt, then maybe he could try to come to terms with it, too. It was hard to know what to think about it all right now.

He led them back toward the field where Ryyder and Trillion were waiting and saw Eevie and his father approaching from their house. It was strange to see so many people in their field at once. It'd been home for the four of them for so long, yet somehow he'd always known that one day this would change.

Today was that day.

Tomorrow would be another one.

Change floated in the air like a spring breeze. He just hoped the change was good.

PART V
RYYDER

CHAPTER THIRTEEN

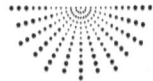

*R*yyder had always carried a feeling deep inside her that she couldn't explain. She'd tried to name it many times, coming up with words for it, but would end up dismissing each one as she tried to think of the next.

Anxiety. Restlessness. Apprehension. Angst. Unease. Trepidation. Fear. Despair. Anguish …

As the list of words grew longer, so did the feeling inside her. It was eating at her, nibbling away at her nerves, sucking the marrow from her bones. It made her tired, which in turn kept her moving. If she gave into the feeling, her life would be over.

She had to keep on moving. Searching. Looking for the answer to what was disturbing her.

As the daughter of a Truthseeker, she shouldn't have had this feeling. Her mother should've been able to tell her what it was that made her like this. Yet, she never could. Was that because she didn't know or because she didn't want to tell her? After all, her mother wasn't just a Truthseeker, she was also a woman with her own private fears and desires.

There were so many things that didn't make sense to

Ryyder that she became certain they were connected to this feeling she had.

For a start, she felt like someone was missing. Or more accurately, that she was the one who was missing. There was a group of people out there she was sure she was connected to. Who were they? Where were they?

Her mother had told her that her soulmate didn't exist in this lifetime, but she'd always found this hard to believe. She'd swim laps of Aquatica looking for him, listening to the quiet of the ocean, hoping to find a clue, to feel a pull in a certain direction. But the only direction she ever felt a pull toward was up to the surface. And everyone knew there was nothing up there. Or rather, no one up there. Unless it was the trees she was connected to.

There must be something up there for her. If only she had the courage to look.

So instead, she continued to look within the borders of the world she'd grown up in, hoping there was a clue she'd missed, yet knowing that was impossible.

These problems only added to what she'd always considered to be her main problem—as much as there were things she didn't know or understand, there were other things she did.

The things she knew presented a much bigger problem than the things she didn't, because many of these things she should never have been able to know.

How did she know her father had planned to go with Shadow to the surface? She just knew it. Nobody had to tell her.

How did she know Shadow was the clue she'd been searching for her whole life? She just knew that, too. She'd felt him in the water before she'd seen him. She'd had to leave her friends at Aquaticus and head home early. It was like a rope was pulling at her, the same rope that had been pulling her toward her father's house all week, only she'd ignored it.

She hated going to her father's house. Hated that he had a house at all and therefore refused to go inside. He hadn't needed to move out. He loved her mother. Anybody with eyes could see that. They could've worked out their differences.

If she visited him at his house, this would be seen as her giving him her approval, and she did anything but approve. Let him see how much she hated it. Maybe then he'd come home.

She'd thought her intuition was telling her she needed to see her father, not suspecting for a moment that it was his house she was being pulled toward, not him. When she'd felt the energy shift to her own home, she assumed he was visiting, which of course he was. She hadn't realized he had someone with him.

But when she'd seen Shadow in the water near her home, her heart had beat so hard she thought for a moment she might pass out. The energy pouring from his soul had moved her and she'd felt giddy. When she'd taken him by the hand and kissed him, it had felt so natural when it was in fact possibly the most unusual thing she'd ever done.

She'd never kissed a boy before, unless you counted Regg and really that was more him kissing her than the other way around. A few other boys from her school had tried to kiss her, too. Girls as well, but she'd never felt like returning their affections. Regg's lips had felt like rubber and she'd pulled back in disgust.

But not Shadow's. His lips had felt like they were made from magic. She'd kiss him every minute of every day for the rest of her life if she had the choice. To think she'd kissed him like that without even knowing his name.

He was her Ardorna. She knew it. Her heart knew it. She didn't need to know his name. She knew him instead.

She also didn't need her mother to tell her that he was her soulmate. It was obvious. Secrets like that weren't easily hidden. It was surprising her mother had tried to make it a secret at all. Disappointing, too. She shouldn't have lied to her like that. She'd found her soulmate early on in life, didn't she wish the same for her daughter?

That was another thing she knew but wasn't sure how. Her parents were soulmates. They'd known each other over many lifetimes. They were meant to be together, belonging in the same house, not on opposite sides of the ocean.

She knew in her past lives that she'd been with her soulmate. Her favorite memory was when he was a boy with hair the color of fire and she'd been a girl who'd known things, just like she did now. In that lifetime her skin had been dark and his fair. Now it was the other way around, yet still she'd recognized him the moment he'd come near. The color of their skin didn't matter. The color of their hearts was the same.

In their most recent life together they'd been father and daughter on a faraway planet. They'd died on the same day and their souls sent to Neron, destined to find each other once more. She had a strong feeling they were destined to do a lot more than just find each other, but the intentions of the universe were being unraveled to her slowly. It would become clear to her in time.

It was a burden to know all these things and not know how she knew them. She wasn't a Truthseeker, even if she could walk that path if she chose. She didn't want to be a Truthseeker. She was different to her mother. She'd seen what being a Truthseeker had done to her and she didn't want that for herself.

Being a Truthseeker came with a large dose of pain. It

drove more people from your side than it brought to it. Even your husband—your soulmate—couldn't stand to live in the same house as you. You delivered truths to people that would fill them with joy, then tell them other things that would blacken their soul. You weren't like anyone else and life wasn't easy.

Often Truthseekers would retreat from the world, living out their days as a recluse, surrounded by nothing but their visions and dreams. She wouldn't be like that. She didn't choose it, as much as it seemed to be choosing her.

She wanted a life—a normal life—lived out with the man she loved. She knew that man was Shadow.

She looked around in the dark, the moonlight sending rays of light through the gaps in the walls of Shadow's house.

Was she the only one awake?

She listened to the sound of her father sleeping on the other side of the room. They were in the living room, which was also the kitchen. There was only one other room in the house—the sleeping room. That was where Shadow was.

This was their first night in the forest. It felt strange. There were noises here not present in the ocean. Animals were calling to each other, wind rustled the leaves of the trees and the walls of the house creaked and groaned. How did anyone manage to sleep with this racket? Although, it didn't seem to be bothering her father. But he'd always been a deep sleeper.

She wished she could check if Shadow was awake, but his parents and sister were with him. It was a little strange that they all slept in the same room, but she supposed if you had to build your own bedroom from scratch there was less incentive to do so. Shadow had said the thought had never crossed his mind. He was surprised that people in Aquatica chose to sleep in separate rooms.

Kurt and Eevangela were asleep inside the strange pod

that Shadow's father had arrived in. She wouldn't have minded sleeping in there herself. It was one of the most fascinating things she'd ever seen. But Shadow's mother hadn't wanted Kurt to sleep anywhere near her. It seemed trust was far harder to earn than forgiveness. Whatever had happened when they were children must've been bad.

So, they'd slept in family groups, which seemed the best solution for now.

"You've never wanted privacy?" she'd asked Shadow, when she first saw their sleeping room.

"What for?" he asked.

"What about your parents? Surely they need privacy from time to time."

"What for?" he asked again.

He was so naïve about a lot of things. Was he even ready for a relationship?

She thought back to the way he'd kissed her under the ocean. Yes, he was ready. More than ready.

She startled to see a large shadow hovering in the doorway.

It wasn't just a shadow, it was Shadow.

He crept over to her bed.

She sat up and slid her hand into his.

"I want to show you something," he whispered, pulling on her arm and leading her outside into the night.

They walked several paces away from the house.

"Up there," he said, pointing to the sky.

He needn't have pointed. The sky was like a magnet for her eyes. She'd thought the sun was beautiful. Well, not so much the sun, it was hard to look at that directly, but the blue of the sky and the white of the clouds.

But this was extraordinary.

The sky was black, darker than the depths of the ocean. It was lit by thousands of stars, shining at her, winking and glimmering, each one spectacular on their own but together they were like some kind of sparkling miracle. When they'd gone to bed earlier in the night, the moon had been high in the sky with a few stars standing guard, but now a whole army of stars was out in force.

"We're a small planet in a big universe," said Shadow.

Even though she knew they weren't the only planet and she'd lived lives far from Neron, seeing the universe like this was something altogether different. Humans really were missing out by closing themselves off under the water. How could they appreciate the beauty of their planet and the universe without witnessing its magnificence like this?

"What are you feeling?" Shadow asked.

"Like I've spent my life locked in a cupboard."

It was the only way she could describe it. Under the ocean it was easy to believe they were the only humans in the universe. But not up here. Up here it was impossible to deny the sheer scale of the universe.

"It's so big," she said.

He laughed. "You're only seeing a very tiny part of it. It stretches further than our eyes or imaginations are able."

She looked to the darkest corners of the sky. What lay behind that darkness?

"It's hard to believe my father was born somewhere out there," he said.

"I know."

"And that we once lived out there, if what your mother said is true."

"It's true."

She shivered, and he put his arm around her shoulders. She felt the warmth from his body and melted into his chest.

As beautiful as the sky was, it couldn't compete with Shadow. It was a shame the rest of the population didn't look like him. The darkness of his skin was so alluring. It made him look foreign and dangerous. By complete contrast the darkness of his eyes made him look kind and gentle. His hair was tied back in a long braid, held by some kind of thread.

She reached for the thread and pulled at it, letting it fall to the ground.

"What are you doing?" he laughed.

She didn't answer. Instead she reached up and combed her fingers through the soft strands of his hair until it fell free past his shoulders and down his back. The sight of him like that took her breath away. She hadn't thought it was possible for him to look any more appealing. She realized she'd been wrong.

He looked to the ground, self-consciously.

Her eyes trailed to his lips, remembering what it was like to kiss them. What would it be like to kiss them in the open air, without the sting of the saltwater surrounding them?

"Shadow," she whispered.

"Ryyder."

She liked it when he said her name. It made her feel like she was a part of him.

"Say it again."

"Ryyder." His voice was almost a moan, his eyes dripped with need.

The knowledge that she was the one making him feel like this fueled her own desire.

He bent toward her, his hands gripping her firmly on the back as he pulled her close. He kissed her. More assertively than he had the time before. It was like he was trying to possess her, to take her into his soul. Except she was already there.

It should've frightened her, but it didn't. His passion lit fires deep inside her and soon she was alight with longing. Her fingers threaded through his hair and she let out a moan of her own.

She wanted more of him. She wanted all of him.

The feelings that had plagued her since birth—all the despair and anguish—disappeared. She had what she needed right in front of her. The person who not only made her feel whole but had led her to a foreign world that felt like home, filled with people she was certain she'd met before.

Her world would never be the same now that she'd met Shadow. It was no wonder her mother hadn't wanted them to meet. She'd never be able to return to the ocean now. *This* was her home. *He* was her home.

New words began filling her mind as the old ones were banished. Joy. Relief. Vindication. Elation. Rapture. Peace …

For all the lifetimes she'd lived before, she felt like only now had she just been born.

Sneaking out into the darkness became a nightly ritual for Ryyder and Shadow. The days were difficult, not so much because of life in the forest, but because of the need to keep their hands off each other.

They found themselves avoiding each other. It was easier to be nowhere near each other, than to be close by and not be able to run their hands across the now-familiar shape of each other's bodies as they pressed their lips together like they depended on it for air.

There were other challenges during the day. She wasn't used to having to do everything for her own survival. Nahlah taught her to hunt rabbits and birds and Eevie showed her which plants could be eaten and which were best left alone. Buzz explained the water collection system he'd designed and once she helped him repair a tear in the silver lining of the dam using a sticky substance he cut from the trunk of a tree.

She loved the time the group spent together in the evenings, often playing music on cleverly made instruments. Shadow's face would light up in a way that warmed the center of her soul.

The days were long and tiring. Her body ached each night as she fell onto her hard, scratchy bed made from dried leaves, collected from the forest floor. Yet despite being so tired, sleep evaded her. Instead she'd lie there and wait, knowing Shadow would come for her.

Together they'd tiptoe outside and there she'd find energy that would escape her during the day. Eventually they'd sneak back inside and try to sleep for at least a couple of hours.

Once they fell asleep on the soft grass, her head tucked in the crook of his arm. Eevie had found them and shook them awake, giving them just enough time to crawl back into their beds before they were discovered.

They weren't certain why they felt the need to keep their relationship so private. It wasn't as if everyone else didn't know how they felt. It just didn't feel right to flaunt it. It was best if they cloaked the depth of their feelings in the secrecy of the night.

Shadow's parents had each other, but her father was missing her mother dearly. Shadow's grandmother had been alone for a long time and Kurt had said once that he'd foregone searching for love as he hadn't felt he deserved it. Eevie had never known what it was like to be in love—and with the way she latched onto her father, it was doubtful she ever would. Anyway, she couldn't exactly go to the ocean to find a boyfriend. She didn't have any gills. She'd shown her chest to Ryyder once. It looked so eerie with its smooth skin. Maybe they'd have to convince a boy to come out of the ocean to meet Eevie one day.

The other advantage of sneaking into the night was that it

made their love feel forbidden, which was so much more exciting than the regular kind of love.

She wondered how much longer her father and Shadow's grandmother would stay. It had been weeks now. Kurt had headed back after a few days promising to visit again, but everyone else had stayed. It was a relief when Kurt left, not because of the tension between him and Nahlah, but because of the animosity between Kurt and the two men who loved Nahlah most—Shadow and Buzz. They hadn't found it easy to accept him. Perhaps that played in Kurt's decision to leave. The mood had been uncomfortable at best.

Ryyder knew before she'd even arrived here that she would stay permanently but had never expected her father or Eevangela to stay so long.

It'd been confusing at first with two Eevie's around, so the older one of the two had offered to be called by her full name. Just one more concession she'd made in life in order to find her way into the hearts of her newfound family.

She was a mysterious woman. It was impossible to guess what she was thinking. The only thing that was clear was how much she loved her family. She seemed particularly fond of Buzz, too.

Usually if Ryyder closed her eyes and concentrated, she could see the lives a person had lived before. This didn't happen with Eevangela. She had some kind of invisible shield up. She'd have to ask her mother how to lift the shield. If she ever saw her mother again.

"You seem very tired," said Nahlah, as they sat weaving what would become a new and hopefully softer layer to add to Ryyder's bed. "Maybe when this is finished you'll be able to sleep better."

Ryyder smiled briefly and looked back down at her work, hoping not to be pressed further on this topic. Nahlah was Shadow's mother. It was awkward to discuss their secret nightly encounters together. Yet, she felt so comfortable with Nahlah. They had history.

"We were sisters once," said Ryyder, immediately regretting her words. Nahlah would think she was crazy.

"Your mother told me," said Nahlah. "In a place called India. Do you have your mother's gift?"

She shook her head. "No."

"Are you sure about that?"

She studied the frond she was about to thread more closely.

"I'm sure," she lied.

"You love my son, don't you?" asked Nahlah, letting it go.

"I hope that's okay with you."

"I'm happy that Shadow's found you. I just …"

She put her weaving down. "What? You just what?"

Nahlah sighed, freeing her own hands so she could grasp Ryyder's.

"Be careful," she said.

"Of what? I don't understand."

"I don't know what you and Shadow do together, but I do know you spend more time under the stars than under our roof. I just hope you know what you're doing."

She nodded, feeling heat rise in her cheeks. It seemed their secret romance wasn't so secret after all.

"When I first came here, I thought it was paradise," she continued. "Everything was so different to life in Aquatica. And just like you, I fell in love. It was a love that trapped me here."

"But Buzz isn't your soulmate," she protested. "That's why you felt trapped. It's different for me and Shadow."

She regretted her words as soon as she'd said them. It wasn't a respectful way to speak.

"Having a baby out here is one of the hardest things you could ever choose to do."

"I'm not having a baby."

"Not yet, but I'm sure you will." There seemed to be more that Nahlah wanted to say but was holding back.

Ryyder wanted to protest, but fell silent, knowing Nahlah's words were true. She would have a baby out here one day. It was like the baby was already aware of this as it floated out there somewhere waiting to be born.

Eevangela approached and sat down next to Nahlah, picking up a frond and beginning to weave. Ryyder was pleased at her arrival. Their conversation wouldn't be able to continue.

She watched the two women sitting with her, their bond stronger than any mattress they were able to weave.

Her mother had told her once that souls liked to reincarnate in groups, extending beyond their soulmates.

The group of people she found herself with at the moment held true to this. She'd met them before. She remained certain she'd met Eevangela, too. Why was the universe holding this information back from her?

She studied Eevangela's fingers as she wove, wondering what story her soul had to tell.

"Eevangela," she said.

"Yes?" She put her weaving down and looked at her. It was one of the first times they'd made direct eye contact.

She held her gaze, begging the universe to place her, knowing it was important but not knowing why.

Two faint threads of light appeared from the center of Eevangela's belly. One went directly to Ryyder and the other wound away from her and out the door of the house.

"Excuse me," said Ryyder, getting up and following the light. As she walked, the thread of light that was attached to her stretched longer, keeping her connected to Eevangela.

She traced the second thread of light as it continued out the door and around the corner of the house. It was only a wisp now, the daylight diluting it, until it was almost invisible.

She went around the house.

Buzz was there, on the roof of the bathroom, making a repair, the thread flowing up to him and connecting to his core.

Eevangela was joined to both her and Buzz by two threads of light. This didn't make sense. Eevangela was Nahlah's mother, not Buzz's mother. And she was no relation to her. Why would a light be joining their souls?

She wondered if this was how her mother had to piece together truths when people came to see her. It felt more like a jigsaw than her usual visions.

"Everything all right, Ryyder?" Buzz called down.

She nodded, rubbing at her temples as a headache took hold.

He slid from the roof, landing at her feet.

"Let's get you some water," he said, leading her to the tank and passing her a cup he'd hollowed from the branch of a tree.

She scooped up the cool liquid and took a large gulp. It was nice, but it did nothing for her headache. The threads of light were what caused her head to ache, not her thirst.

"Can I ask you about your mother?" she said, feeling this was the right question to ask.

He looked surprised. "You can, but there's not too much I can tell you."

"I know your father raised you, but you must've had a mother. Everyone has a mother."

"She left when I was a baby," he said.

Colors swirled in her mind, faster and brighter until she fell to the ground.

"Ryyder," she could hear Buzz calling. "Ryyder."

The colors became images she didn't understand. She was

in a pod. It looked like the pod that sat in the field next to the house, only smaller. It was warm inside and dark. She felt safe. A small hand crossed her face and she realized it was her own. She was a baby.

A crack of light appeared. It grew wider and brighter until a face appeared. Her tiny eyes blinked. The face smiled at her. It was her father—Shadow from a time gone by. There was a woman next to him, holding another baby in his arms.

She looked more closely at the baby. It was Buzz. Not from another life, but this life. He was a tiny, beautiful baby.

She looked up at the woman, desperate to see her mother, only to find it was a nurse.

"You're a brave man to attempt parenthood on your own," the nurse said to her father.

"I had no other choice," he said.

"You were lucky to find a woman prepared to sell you her eggs."

"She could hardly complain," he said. "She died almost fifty years ago."

"Really?" said the nurse. "I didn't think they allowed that anymore."

"They made an exception for me. Compensation for my forced retirement. Someone out there felt sorry for me."

"I see." The nurse furrowed her brow and baby Buzz began to cry. She jiggled him in her arms. "I'm not your mama."

As she spoke these words, an image of Eevangela floated into her mind. Her mother who died fifty years before she'd been born as Valentina. She had no doubt it was her.

She opened her eyes, the visions falling away as her consciousness took hold. The threads of light made sense. Eevangela was Buzz's mother. Her own, too, when she'd been his sister. Only she didn't leave them as Buzz had always believed. She didn't even know they were born. By the time the eggs extracted from her were fertilized, she was already living her next life here on Neron.

It was yet another reason why Nahlah and Buzz had been drawn to each other. They were connected through Eevangela, Nahlah's mother from this life and Buzz's mother from her last.

"Thank goodness," Buzz was saying as he hovered over her. "You scared me."

"I know who your mother is," she said.

"What are you talking about?"

"Eevangela's your mother."

"Eevangela is Nahlah's mother. Here, drink some more water. You're not making any sense."

She sipped on the water. It made perfect sense to her, but she knew better than to push the point now. She'd need the right time to give him news like that.

She smiled up at the man who'd believed his whole life that his mother had abandoned him. It was a cruel trick to play on someone. She wondered why his father had done it. She could ask Shadow, but he remembered nothing of that lifetime. He wouldn't know why he'd told such a lie.

She'd need to think about it when her brain was a little clearer. Right now, there was far too much to take in.

"Ryyder!' Shadow was running toward her now. "What happened?"

He crouched down next to her, placing a hand on each of her cheeks and tilting her face toward him.

"She fainted," said Buzz. "She's okay now. She's talking. Not making much sense, but she's talking."

"Are you okay?" he asked her, his dark eyes filled with concern.

"I'm fine," she said. "Really I am."

She tried to sit up, but he gently urged her back down.

"Take your time getting up. Just lie there for a bit."

More faces appeared before her and soon everyone was there, asking questions and speculating on the state of her health.

Eevangela and Buzz were standing to one side, Nahlah and Eevie to the other. Shadow and her father were crouched down, one holding each of her hands.

"What happened?" asked Trillion.

"I'm fine, Dad. I just felt a bit light-headed."

He squeezed her hand, not convinced.

"Is this a family meeting?" she asked, looking at all the faces staring at her.

"She's not sleeping enough," said Nahlah, ignoring her question.

A hush rippled through the group.

"I'm sleeping enough," she said, propping herself up on her elbows. If she admitted how desperately tired she was, then she'd be made to sleep more. This translated directly into spending less time in the moonlight with Shadow. She couldn't let that happen.

"No, you're not," said Shadow, placing a hand on her back and helping her to sit up.

She shot him a look. Was he tired of their nightly encounters? Why would he say that?

"Your health's at stake," he said. "You have to take care of yourself. This is all my fault. It's time we made some changes around here."

Her stomach contracted. Was he sending her home? He couldn't. She wouldn't leave. This was her home now.

"Since we're all here, let's talk," he said to the group.

"Good idea," said Buzz.

"Our house is too small," said Shadow.

Ryyder gasped. He was asking them to leave. This couldn't be possible.

"You're asking us to leave?" Her father squinted his blue eyes in the sun.

"What?" said Shadow. "No! I was asking you to stay."

"You just said the house was too small," he said, furrowing his brow.

"That's right. I think it's time we all pitched in and built some new rooms. Starting with one for Ryyder … and me … if she'll have me."

Joy lit her heart. He wanted her to stay and build a life with him.

She opened her mouth to say yes when Nahlah interrupted.

"Don't pressure her, Shadow."

"I'm not pressuring her," he complained.

"Nahlah's right," said her father. "It must be her decision. Ryyder hasn't decided if she wants to stay yet."

"I'm not telling her what to do," said Shadow. "I would never do that."

"That's true," said Ryyder, taking Shadow by the hand and pulling herself to her feet so she could face the group properly. "Everything you're all saying is true. I have decided if I'm staying. I decided the moment I left the ocean. I'm not going anywhere."

"Your mother will be out of her mind by now missing you." Her father was wringing his hands in front of him, not seeming to understand the depths of her feelings for Shadow.

"She misses me. Yes. I miss her, too. But Dad, I'm happy here. For the first time in my life I'm really, *really,* happy. I love Shadow. And Nahlah and Buzz and Eevie. Eevangela, too." She nodded at the older lady, feeling a bond now that she'd placed her in their group. "I belong here."

"So, you won't be returning home?" her father asked.

"I am home."

He nodded. "I feel the same. You know I do. But I'm afraid I must return home, Ryyder. At least for a while. I miss your mother. I was hoping you'd come with me."

"But Trillion," said Shadow. "You once told me that if you ever managed to leave Aquatica that you'd never return."

"People say a lot of things when they don't know what they're talking about. I had no idea how hard it would be to be away from my wife. I love it here, but ... I've realized I love Trudy even more. And I'm not talking about returning permanently."

"You can visit," said Ryyder. "And I can visit you. Nobody says we have to choose land over ocean. We can travel between both."

Her father nodded and gave her a smile that filled her heart with pain.

"Buzz," said Nahlah, taking her husband's hand. "I think the time's come."

He nodded.

"What time?" asked Eevie, before Ryyder had a chance to ask the question herself.

"To move our home to the ocean's edge," she said.

Ryyder's heart leaped at hearing this, healing all the pain of only moments before. Traveling to Aquatica was a long and tiring journey, but if they lived closer to it, then she could see her parents almost as often as she liked. The idea seemed almost too good to be true.

"Your father and I have been talking about this for years," Nahlah said to Eevie. "It's the only solution. We can't hide here by ourselves anymore. We need to be near other people. We need to be able to visit our families and for them to visit us. One day you'll want a family of your own, Eevie. There's nobody out here for you. We've been selfish keeping you here."

"I can't go under the ocean," said Eevie, crossing her arms.

"No," said Buzz. "But maybe if people can see us on the land, some will come to visit. Some might even choose to stay, like Ryyder."

Ryyder smiled at him. Her brother from her past life. She was so glad she'd found him again.

She felt Shadow's hand on her back. It slid down her spine and slipped to her hand. He squeezed it and didn't let go. It didn't matter now if anyone saw them. They were in love and were planning a life together. She could climb to the highest tree and shout it out loud and it wouldn't matter. Everyone already knew.

"What do you think, Mom?" Nahlah asked Eevangela, who'd been so quiet Ryyder almost forgot she was there.

"I think you've just caught heaven in one of your snares and dragged it down to Neron." She reached for Nahlah and touched her arm. "Now I'll be able to see all of my children. I'll no longer have to choose."

"But I love our home," said Eevie, still defiant.

She was the one person in the group who'd never been anywhere else, and the thought clearly frightened her. Shadow had said he'd felt the same when he'd first set out for Aquatica and that was something he'd wanted to do. Ryyder couldn't blame Eevie being scared.

"We can still come back here to visit," said Buzz, wrapping an arm around his daughter. "Come on, Eevie. You know better than this. Home isn't this pile of branches we've tied together to keep off the rain. Home is your family. We'll still be together."

She sniffed, nodding through her tears.

"Then you could change your mind and come home with me, Ryyder," said her father. "You can visit Shadow in his new home."

"No, Dad," she said, squeezing Shadow's hand tighter. "I'm

staying on the land. I will visit you though. I promise. Just as I expect to see you back here."

It was sweet that he was making so many attempts to bring her back to her mother, but he needed to accept her decision. She couldn't go with him. If she'd thought her life had been painful before, searching and not knowing what for, then now it'd be torture. She'd found what she'd been looking for. It was impossible to turn back.

"Then it's decided," said Eevie, with sadness in her eyes. "Just like that. We're moving to the seashore."

"Think of it as an adventure," said Buzz, putting his arm around her.

"But there are no houses out there." Her voice was starting to sound like a whine.

"There was no house here when I landed either," he said.

"There are houses," said Shadow. "They're just buried. You won't believe it when you see it. Come on, Eevie. It'll be great."

"I like our life," she said. "I don't want anything to change."

"But sweetheart," said Nahlah stepping toward her and running a hand down her hair. "Look around you. It already has."

CHAPTER FOURTEEN

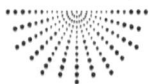

*R*yyder thought a lot about Nahlah's words of change. The decision Shadow and his mother had made to leave the forest and dive under the ocean, had changed life for everyone.

Their sheltered little family of four had expanded to take her in, with room in their hearts for her father. And Eevangela of course. And one day maybe Kurt. They'd also profoundly changed the life of her own mother, who they'd left alone in her house with nothing but the truth to keep her company.

No doubt the lives of others would also be affected as they moved closer to the ocean and showed them the possibility of a life lived upon the land. The workers would see them first. They'd tell their families, who'd tell their friends. Soon everyone would have heard about the people who lived safely under the rays of the sun.

Change would sweep through Aquatica like an underwater tsunami.

She wondered what they'd think of Eevie and Buzz with their smooth chests and dark skin. Shadow, too. She'd loved his skin at first sight, but would others? Would they be as taken with it? It was doubtful. Aquaticans weren't known for their acceptance of differences. Under the ocean, people looked the same, dressed the same and lived the same. Well, not exactly the same, but close enough.

It wasn't like that on the land. Living under the blue of the sky was a different kind of life. She understood better now the books that lined her father's shelves. They were filled with photos of life in ancient times before they'd lived underwater.

Humans had first lived solely upon the land without any gills to help them breathe. But they were selfish, unintelligent humans who turned their sun against them by treating their environment with such little respect that it repaid them by burning their skin with disease. Instead of finding ways to heal the land, they escaped to the safety of the ocean, their bodies conspiring with them by growing gills to aid their escape.

As a result, the land had been left to heal. It was ironic that what saved the land was the lack of respect humans had for it. So little did they care for it that they walked away—exactly what the land needed to regenerate. And now that Aquatica had expanded, they'd gone back to destroying the land. Taking what they needed, without caring about the result.

She hadn't ever thought much about what damage had been done to the ocean, but it must be enormous. Humans hadn't gotten any smarter. They just shifted their destruction from one place to another until they ran out of places to destroy.

Humans needed to be better than that. It was time for them to emerge and live life upon the land, only this time they needed to live with respect. Shadow's family was the perfect example of that. They didn't create rubbish that needed to be buried—everything they used was recycled and returned to the land. They didn't waste water or even use electricity. They loved and respected the animals around them, catching only what they needed for survival and using every scrap for some useful purpose. Nothing was wasted. Nothing taken for granted. As such they didn't just live in the forest, they became a part of it.

That was how humans needed to live. She just hoped they were smart enough. Their bodies had evolved to keep up with the times, but had their brains?

Buzz had told her stories about the planet he'd grown up on. The humans there had been no different, treating the planet as if it was there to serve them. They'd paid the ultimate price for it. The planet was no more. Perhaps if the Earth had been a healthier and more harmonious planet, the people could have found a way to divert that asteroid. She couldn't bear to see the same thing happen to Neron. It was her home.

"Do you have a moment?"

She looked down from the tree she was sitting in. Buzz was standing at the base with an odd expression on his face.

"Sure," she said, reaching for a branch to climb down.

"Stay there," he said. "I'll come to you."

He scaled the tree with ease, taking less than half the time it'd taken her to get up there. Shadow had promised her she'd get better at it. She hoped so.

Several days had passed since their decision to move to the seashore. Slowly they'd been gathering the possessions they'd need and planning their journey. It wouldn't be long now. Soon they'd be ready to leave. Her father and Eevangela had decided to help with the move, returning to the ocean only when they were settled.

Buzz swung himself onto the branch she sat on. It

buckled slightly under his weight and she gripped the trunk nervously.

"It'll hold us," he said, laughing.

She relaxed. He knew even more than Shadow did about these things, after living in the forest for two decades. If he wasn't worried, then nor should she be.

The strange expression he'd had on his face earlier returned.

"What's the matter?" she asked.

"What did you see when you fainted?" he asked.

"Nothing," she said, not wanting to take part in this conversation. His initial reaction to what she'd said to him about his mother had thrown her.

"You said Eevangela was my mother," he reminded her. "But that's impossible. When I was born, she was already alive and well living here on Neron."

"Then why are you asking me about it?"

"Because Nahlah told me about your mother, the Truthseeker. She thinks you share her gift."

"My gift is different," she said, feeling annoyed. Why was everyone so desperate to turn her into a Truthseeker?

"It's still a gift. Please tell me what you saw. Why would you say that?"

"Has Nahlah explained to you about how we live different lives—the same soul rebirthing into new bodies?"

He nodded.

She wasn't sure if she should continue. He didn't look like he was convinced. Her story was useless to him if he didn't believe in this one simple fact.

"Your father lied to you," she said. "Your mother didn't leave you. He used her eggs that were harvested from her years before your birth. By the time you were born she'd been dead for many years on Earth, her soul having been reborn here as Eevangela."

"So Nahlah and I are sisters?" he asked, looking even more worried.

"No."

"But we share a mother."

"Your mothers share a soul, not a body. That doesn't make you siblings. You're genetically different."

He let out a breath, seeming relieved as he took all of this in.

"You know that I share a soul with Valentina, don't you?" she asked.

"Yes, Nahlah told me that, too." He touched her gently on the arm. "You know, Valentina always believed she'd be born again. That was her thing."

"What do you mean *her thing*?"

"She used to have dreams that she believed were of her past life."

Ryyder nodded. It seemed she hadn't been all that different when she'd been Valentina to the person she was now.

"Did you believe her?"

He shook his head. "Forgive me, but it's just so hard to believe. How can we all be connected like this?"

"Groups of souls like to find each other as they journey through their lives."

"What was Valentina's favorite color?"

She sighed. He wasn't taking her seriously.

"I don't know," she said. "Nor do I know her favorite animal, what her nickname was as a child or what foods she was allergic to."

"Then how can you be her? How can I believe this?"

"You don't have to believe it. I can't answer any of your questions about her as I can't remember her life."

"Then how do you know that you were her?"

She tried to think of the right words to use so he'd understand. "I've had some dreams, just like Valentina used to. Small snatches of time in her life."

She paused. It would be too much to share these with Buzz now. They had years ahead of them to have conversations like this.

"Tell me about the dreams."

She laughed. "We'd be here all day. I've dreamed of everything from living beside a pile of rubbish to being queen of the desert."

"Queen of the desert?" His eyes widened. "Valentina used to have that dream. How did you know that?"

"I didn't know that."

"It's true then," he said, more to himself than to her. "It's true."

She put a hand on his arm, and he looked into her eyes, no doubt searching for his sister within her face.

"Have you had any dreams about what happened to her after I left?" he asked.

She shook her head. "I'm sorry, no."

"Can you bring on a vision? Nahlah said your mother knew everything about her."

"I'm not my mother." Her tone was harsh. There he was again trying to turn her into a Truthseeker.

"I'm sorry," he said. "I didn't mean to upset you."

"I'm not upset," she said, softening. "It's just that I don't even understand how this works. I'm sure in time I'll be able to answer all your questions. You do realize though that the fact I was born means Valentina … must have died."

It felt like a harsh truth to dish out, but one he needed to grasp. She couldn't have him holding onto any hope for Valentina when there wasn't any.

"I know," he said. "I know she's dead. My father, too. Nahlah said he was reborn as Shadow. Is that true?"

She nodded.

"I like that you've found each other again. Dad and Valentina were always so close."

Ryyder smiled, wishing she could remember more.

"Do you think Shadow knows why my father lied to me about my mother?" Buzz's brow wrinkled.

"He won't know because he won't remember. Don't be angry with him. He had his reasons for not telling you the truth."

These reasons had become clear in a recent vision in surprising detail, but she bit her tongue. She hadn't wanted to get into this with him just yet. She'd already given him far too much information to take in on one day. There was a reason her mother's clients came to see her many times before getting the full versions of their truth. She doled it out in just the right measures they could handle.

"What reasons? Please, Ryyder. You must tell me. This has plagued me my whole life."

She took a deep breath, deciding she may as well serve up the whole dish. She wasn't a Truthseeker and had no idea how to do any of this properly.

"When your father was forced into retirement, he decided to pursue the only other ambition he'd had in his life—he wanted to be a father. The problem was he had no wife. His boss at the space station felt sorry for him and arranged the purchase of some eggs on the black market. Your father would never have taken them if he'd known it was illegal. His boss forgot to tell him that bit. And everything would've been fine if he hadn't said something about it to the nurse who was there when your pods were opened. She told the authorities who tried to take you away."

Buzz's mouth dropped open.

"Your father was devastated. Luckily his boss intervened and somehow he was allowed to keep you both on the condition he stuck to the story of your mother running away at your birth. He was so afraid if he told you the truth you'd blurt it out as innocently as he had, and you'd be taken away for good. He couldn't let that happen."

"So, she didn't run away?"

"She never even knew you existed, but the way I understand it, your father loved you enough to make up for it."

"He loved Valentina more than me." There was something rehearsed in his voice, like this was something he'd said so many times that the emotion had fallen away from the words.

"That's not true. He loved you the same. He just felt closer to Valentina."

"And that's why Shadow feels so close to you."

She nodded. "Our souls are connected, just like yours is connected to Eevie's."

"Nahlah said Eevie had a terrible life on Earth. That she was once my sister and our father hurt her."

"Try not to think too much about that. It's not good to dwell on lives gone by."

He snorted with laughter. "That seems to be all anybody talks about lately."

"Our past lives help us understand our present," she said. "That's all. But the present is what's most important. Don't lose sight of that. You have a wife and two children who love you. And your family circle's growing every day with more people who love you. Me included."

"I really am glad Shadow found you," he said. "I worried for my son. He's a lot like me. I didn't want him to spend his life alone."

"He'll never be alone," she said.

"Thank you," he said. "Not just for that, but for speaking with me now. I could see you didn't want to."

"Life's all about doing things we don't want to," she laughed. "And plenty of things we want to do, too."

"I'm glad you added that last bit," he said. "You had me worried for a moment."

"This conversation made me think, that's all. I've never wanted to be like my mother. Her life is so difficult. But seeing the difference that knowing the truth just made to you, I'm wondering if maybe I need to try a little harder and accept my gift, as you call it."

"I'm glad," he said.

One day perhaps she would be a Truthseeker, only her version of it. She could never live like her mother. But it did feel good to help people. For the first time she understood why her mother had chosen to take up her calling in life.

"Maybe my gift is a blessing, rather than a curse."

The tree branch they sat upon gave a large groan.

"I think this branch may be the one that's cursed," he said. "Let's get down from here before it falls."

"I thought you said we were safe." She climbed to a lower branch.

"I don't know everything," he said, following her.

She missed a branch and slid the last few feet, ungraciously landing on her behind.

"Ouch."

"You mean you didn't see that coming," laughed Buzz, putting out his hand to help her up.

"If only it worked like that."

Shadow appeared before them.

"If only what worked like that?" he asked.

"Life," she said, wrapping her arms around his waist. "If I'd seen you coming, I would've left the ocean ages ago."

"You came when you were ready," he said, kissing her on the top of her head.

Buzz gave them a smile and walked away in the direction of the field.

"Have you got a moment?" Shadow asked.

"Your father asked me the same question earlier. He also said you were very alike. Clearly, he wasn't joking."

"So, have you got a moment, or did you use them all up on him?" He grinned at her.

"Of course, I have. What's the matter?"

"Come with me."

He took her by the hand and led her further out into the forest.

She felt safe, walking by his side. He'd look after her, in exactly the same way they'd taken care of each other for thousands of years.

They came to a large tree.

"Up here," he said.

"Not another tree," she complained. "I fell out of the last one."

"You won't fall out of this one," he said, pointing to some footholds he'd made in the trunk.

"Fancy," she said, looking up into the branches.

She saw some kind of platform high above her and started her climb.

"I'm right behind you," called Shadow. "Best view in Neron."

"Don't be wicked," she called back.

She reached the platform and hoisted herself onto it, puffing from the climb. Her lungs weren't used to being worked this hard.

"Oh, Shadow," she said, as her eyes tried to take in all she was seeing.

The platform had been positioned in the tree so as to take in a view of the forest. She was seeing the trees from above instead of below. They looked like some kind of field that stretched for miles. Her beautiful new home. In the distance she could see the blue of the ocean—her first home, Aquatica.

Shadow had strung forest flowers from the branches all

around the platform and they hung there like colorful ribbons. It reminded her a little of the coral reef she'd taken him to when they first met.

She felt his arms slip around her from behind, as he rested his chin on her shoulder.

"I love you, Shadow," she said.

"Stop stealing my lines." He turned her around, so she was facing him.

"Sorry. What lines?"

"I built this for you because I wanted to tell you how much I love you. To *show* you how much I love you. Here we see the forest. My home. Yours now, too, if you'd like. We also see the ocean, the place where you grew up and where we first met. I realized that the whole time I've known you, we've thought of these places as two separate worlds when really, they're not. The forest and the ocean are part of the one and same planet. We don't come from different worlds. Our worlds are the same."

She held him a little tighter as she absorbed the beauty of his words. Everything he said was right. The world was about perspective. They could see it as two separate places, or they could see it for what it was. Two important parts of the one planet. Their planet.

He picked a flower from a branch and tucked it behind her ear.

"Ryyder, out here we don't have marriage or weddings or official pieces of paper. All we have are our hearts. I used to think my heart belonged in the forest, but I was wrong. My heart belongs to you. I give you my heart today. I give you my heart tomorrow. I give you my heart forever. Will you accept it and give me your heart in return?"

"You've always had my heart," she said, her voice breaking. "You always will. Today. Tomorrow. Forever."

He bent to kiss her. Of all the kisses they'd shared, this

one stood apart as different. This kiss wasn't just a kiss. It was a promise. A promise of love and a promise of a life together. She didn't need the ocean. She didn't even need the forest. All she needed was Shadow.

They heard cheering from the forest floor. They broke their kiss and bent their heads over the platform to see her new family pulling on long vines that trailed up the tree. She looked up to see baskets of flowers spilling over and raining down upon them. Petals tickled her nose and stuck to her hair.

"I love you," she said to Shadow, through the flowers and the kisses he was covering her face with.

"I love you, too," he said.

"I love Shadow!" she called out to the forest.

"I love Ryyder!" he called in return.

A flock of parrots heard their call and flew into the sky in a rainbow of color.

The cheers from their family continued. She saw her father among the group, his face lit with joy. She felt so lucky to have this wonderful father, a mother who loved her, a new family she'd felt she missed all her life and most of all, Shadow.

The boy she'd known with her heart before she'd seen him with her eyes.

Her Ardorna.

EPILOGUE

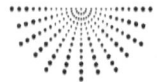

*S*oulweaver Shen watched this group of beloved souls from the Loom, as they tipped their baskets of flowers and shouted words of love into the sky.

He stood beside another Soulweaver—the being who held the fate of Neron's souls in her hands.

"You've placed them well," Shen said to her.

"I wasn't certain they'd find each other," she replied.

He smiled. He'd known they would. He'd been watching this group of souls for hundreds of years. One of them was his soulmate and despite his position in the Loom, he missed her.

Although, he wasn't certain what his position was anymore. He'd ruled over Planet Earth until its final moments, caring for the influx of souls, as they'd rushed toward him in numbers never seen before.

He'd taken his time with each of them, relocating them to new homes on planets across the universe. It hadn't been an easy task. With each soul he placed, he was one step closer to completing the work he loved so passionately.

The most difficult were the souls he'd lived with in his

human form. He'd decided to send them to Neron. Shadow and Ryyder had lived there once before, many lifetimes ago. It made sense to return them there. Besides, Nahlah, Buzz and Eevangela were already there. It wouldn't be fair to separate this group of souls.

When the final soul was placed, the Author had appeared at his side, choosing the form he'd taken when he first appeared to Shen. Dark hair and skin, much like the final souls to roam the Earth.

"I've failed you," Shen had said to him.

"You're the best Soulweaver I've ever had." The Author poured love from his core directly to Shen's.

"My planet is gone. That's not success." He hung his head, not wanting to meet the Author's eye.

"Your planet had reached its capacity and the end of its lifespan. It was time to shift the souls to other planets. That's no failure of yours. I'm happy with your work."

"What will happen to me now?" Shen asked, feeling weary for the first time since being appointed a Soulweaver.

"I have other planets I can spark into life. These planets will need Soulweavers."

"Of course. It's my honor to serve you." The thought of this dimmed the light in his soul. He didn't want to weave for another planet, far away from the one that held the souls who made up the pieces of his heart.

"You don't serve me, Shen," said the Author. "You know that. This universe is ours. It belongs to all of us."

"Yes, Author."

"You don't want to weave for another planet, do you?"

"No, Author."

"What is it you want?"

"You know what I want," he said, knowing there was no use in speaking his thoughts. The Author knew his desires before he did. He may have been tied to planet Earth for all these years, but Neron was where he belonged now.

"I need to hear you say it."

"I want to breathe the same air as Nahlah once more."

The Author nodded. "Are you asking me to take her life, so that you can see her again?"

"No! Don't take her life. Please, Author. She's still young and has a family who depend on her. She's only just started living in this lifetime."

"But she mourns your absence. She yearns for her soulmate."

"I can wait for her. I've waited this long."

"Shen, you were the one I chose to be Earth's Soulweaver. I chose you carefully. You were always going to return to Nahlah. It's your destiny. If I were to tear your souls apart, it would leave a crack in the universe that not even I'd know how to repair. And that's why I'm choosing you again."

"Again?"

"You will not need to wait to be with Nahlah. She can live in peace with her intended, Buzz, and continue to raise their family. A family that will include a very special grandchild. I'm sending you to Neron as Shadow and Ryyder's future child."

"I am the chosen one again?" asked Shen.

"You were always my chosen one," said the Author. "You must bring the people from the water. It's time they returned to the land."

"Yes, Author." He was relieved. This seemed like an easy task compared to what he'd just achieved on Earth.

"Then let us get on with this," said the Author, placing a hand on his back and leading him across the Loom to the female Soulweaver that he stood beside now. She wore a pale blue cape that clothed her in soft light and kindness and had long dark hair that cascaded down her back.

"This is Shyla, Neron's new Soulweaver," the Author said. "The Soulweaver before her who wove for Neron tried to save the planet by evolving humans to live underwater. I let him try this but realize now that it can't be sustained. I didn't design humans to live like that. Trust in Soulweaver Shyla. Her soul is pure."

Shyla smiled at Shen and he stepped toward her warmth.

With these words, the Author left Shen with the soul not only responsible for the souls of all he loved, but now his own.

Soulweaver Shyla wrapped his weary soul in her cloak of light and together they'd travelled down to the forest to watch the group of souls he pined for.

"Are you certain this is what you want?" she asked. "You want to be returned to them?"

"Yes. Just please give me a few more moments," he said, looking at Nahlah who was laughing at Ryyder and Shadow professing their love as they shouted it to the sky from the top of a tree. Buzz took Nahlah's hand and they shared a look that said *I love you* without using any words.

He was happy she'd found love. Even happier she'd found joy with the souls who surrounded her.

When he was born to Ryyder and Shadow, she'd have a baby to love—a grandchild who was destined to be her best friend and the person who showed her that her life had taken her to exactly the place she needed to be.

His life had been the most incredible journey. It was hard to believe it had only just begun. The universe would stretch on forever, making these moments in time seem like specks of dust floating in the cosmos. He'd live thousands more lives. Billions perhaps. On and on, time would continue to pass.

"I'm coming," he called to Nahlah.

She tilted her head to the sky, unaware he was watching her, as he had been in every one of her lives.

All she knew was now.

The future was intangible, taking turns that were impossible to predict. The past was the opposite—set firmly in place, unable to be altered no matter how great the desire.

What mattered most was now. *This very moment.* Because that's the only moment out of all life's moments we have any power over.

"I'm ready," he said to the Soulweaver.

THE END
Ready to discover another series by Heidi Catherine?
Check out The Kingdoms of Evernow!
http://mybook.to/hcwhisperers

THE KINGDOMS OF EVERNOW

BOOK 1 THE WHISPERERS OF EVERNOW

Five kingdoms. Five senses. One secret that will change them all.

Manipulated by a vicious King, Jeremiah is stripped of his identity and forced into a life of silent submission as a Whisperer. Allowed only to speak at the command of the King, one thousand Whisperers must line up in rows and chant their sadistic ruler's darkest desires. As each evil wish comes true, the King's power over his impoverished kingdom grows.

When Jeremiah's fears for the family he left behind are confirmed, he turns in desperation to the most unlikely person for help—the King's eldest daughter. But is Princess Rose as kind as she is beautiful, or will she lure him into a trap?

To save those dearest to him, Jeremiah has no choice but to put his trust in Rose, whose own life is threatened as her father prepares to clear the path to the throne for his newborn son. Together, they embark on a bold plan to overthrow the King and set the Whisperers free.

As love blossoms in this most unlikely place, Jeremiah and Rose must discover how to use the power of the spoken word to conquer more than just the kingdom. They will need to conquer their hearts.

The first full-length book in the spellbinding The Kingdoms of Evernow series, this is a must-read by award-winning author, Heidi Catherine.

Grab your copy now!

http://mybook.to/hcwhisperers

ALSO BY HEIDI CATHERINE

The Kingdoms of Evernow
Five kingdoms. Five senses.
One secret that will change them all.
The Kingdoms of Evernow (Prequel)
The Whisperers of Evernow
The Alchemists of Evernow
The Empress of Evernow
The Guardians of Evernow
The Angels of Evernow

The Soulweaver series
Two girls. Two lives. One soul.
The Soulweaver
The Truthseeker
The Shadowmaker

The Sovereign Code
Humans saved bees from extinction...
and created the deadliest threat we've seen yet
Harvest Day
Hive Mind
Queen Hunt
Venom Rising
Sting Wars

Elemental Games

Elemental powers. Deadly games. No escape.

Elemental Games

Elemental Uprising

Elemental Wars

Elemental Solution

The Thaw Chronicles

Four tests. Seven days. Nine teens.

Only the chosen shall breed.

Burning (Prequel)

Rising

Breaking

Falling

Reckoning

Extant

Exist

Exile

Expose

Tournaments of Thaw

Conquer the Thaw

The Oasis Trials

The Oasis Deception

The Last Oasis

WANT TO STAY IN TOUCH?

Heidi loves to connect with readers, so please say hello on social media, leave a review on Amazon or Goodreads, or visit her at www.heidicatherine.com

facebook.com/HeidiCatherineAuthor
instagram.com/HeidiCatherine
tiktok.com/@heidicatherineauthor
amazon.com/author/heidicatherine

ABOUT THE AUTHOR

Heidi writes fantasy and dystopian novels, which gives her a chance to escape into worlds vastly different to her own life in the burbs. While she quite enjoys killing her characters (especially the awful ones), she promises she's far better behaved in real life. Other than writing and reading, Heidi's current obsessions include watching far too much reality TV with the excuse that it's research for her books.

www.ingramcontent.com/pod-product-compliance
Lightning Source LLC
Chambersburg PA
CBHW031606240626
47153CB00002B/646